Means of Escape

Spencer Dunmore: born in London, educated in Yorkshire during World War II, left Britain for Canada in the mid-50s. He lives at present in Burlington, Ontario, where he is an advertising executive during the day, an author in the evenings and a private pilot at the weekends.

Spencer Dunmore

Means of Escape

Pan Books
in association with Peter Davies

First published 1978 by Peter Davies Ltd
This edition published 1980 by Pan Books Ltd,
Cavaye Place, London SW10 9PG
in association with Peter Davies Ltd
© Spencer Dunmore 1978
ISBN 0 330 26014 6
Printed in Great Britain by
Richard Clay (The Chaucer Press) Ltd, Bungay, Suffolk

for my daughter,
Janet

━━━ DECEMBER 1944 ━━━

1

He was spinning, whirling like a top. His limbs flopped about as if they didn't possess a bone between them. He couldn't control them. He didn't know how.

Pull it! For Christ's sake, pull it!

Someone yelling at him, telling him what to do – someone a yard or two away, someone watching all this happen.

The air was so cold, so mercilessly, agonizingly bloody cold; it felt as if it was congealing about him, forming a weird sort of solidity. But still he plummeted, still he tumbled, helpless, every sense reeling. It would soon be over. The plunge. Everything. A fragment of an instant of pain. A sound, perhaps. A crack, a thud. After that, nothing. Zero. Blankness for all eternity.

Go on!

But he knew it was hopeless, pointless. The mechanism was broken. Waste of effort even groping for it. Besides, he wasn't sure where his fingers were any more.

Try, though! Keep trying!

That insistent, urgent voice again.

You haven't got all bleeding night, mate!

He touched the ring. Felt it. His frozen fingers closed on it. Gripped it. But it came loose. Broken. Snapped off.

That was it, then. All over. The end. Everything had just been settled, finally, permanently. No need to wonder or worry about anything ever again. Farewell, cruel world.

He caught a glimpse of a light or a flame. It revolved about him, describing a perfect circle in the blackness.

Just as it completed its revolution, there was a thunderclap, a great snapping, cracking explosion of sound. Something grabbed him. Simultaneously squashed and stretched him. He had hit the ground. Smashed to bits. Pulverized.

No, he wasn't. He was alive. And he had stopped falling. It

took a moment to sort that fact out. His brain still seemed to be turning somersaults, but his body was the right way up, floating in space, swinging from side to side like a pendulum. Three cheers for the Parachute Section, their capable hands and big tits.

His heart started working again.

'Strewth,' he said. Aloud.

His voice sounded thin, as if it was being filtered through something. His breath condensed in a silvery cloud that was whipped away by the wind the instant it was formed. The wind battered him on his right side, stinging with its chill. He moved to fasten the straps of his helmet under the chin. The movement caused him to swivel in the harness; for a mind-numbing instant he thought he was falling out of the ruddy thing, God only knows how many thousands of feet up in the air. Terrified, he grabbed the straps above his head and clung to them with the desperation of a drowning sailor on a lifeline.

He was alive. No question about that. Heart thumping and pumping; breath puffing out of him. Proof enough. Now he knew what they meant when they talked about being snatched back from the jaws of death. Oh, but it was cold, ruddy bloody cold. Perhaps, he thought, I've been saved just to be turned into a great block of ice dangling at the end of my parachute . . .

He looked about him, and below. There was nothing to be seen. Not a light, not a sign of anything. Where was the aircraft? The rest of the crew? Where, for that matter, was the ground? Only blackness seemed to lie below. The whole world was presumably still down there, but it was invisible.

The cold was a million needles. Clever little buggers, they had ingeniously fastened themselves to the inside of his flying suit. The slightest, tiniest movement caused them to thrust their freezing selves into him, injecting him with their chill.

It was then that he got panicky about his feet. He couldn't feel them. He couldn't see them. They weren't there. They had been torn off when he jumped! Below him were ugly, ghastly stumps, dangling horrible bits of bone and ligament wobbling in the wind. The cold must have frozen the mess, cauterizing the wound, a sort of horror-story local anaesthetic . . .

Now he would never play tennis.

He shook his head, wondering about himself. Why worry about playing tennis? He had never played tennis in his life; he didn't know how. On his street in Kilburn no one played tennis.

Christ, was he going to be another Bader?

Ice was forming on his sleeves and on the metal fittings of his parachute harness. Brittle, glass-like stuff. He wriggled. Some of the ice cracked and fell away. Above him, the wind rustled the parachute canopy. It sounded like a sail flapping on some rich sod's yacht on the Crouch.

He listened. Was that an aircraft engine? Ours? Theirs? He sighed, producing another silvery cloud. It really didn't matter any more whether it was ours or theirs. Those days were behind him for ever; blokes without feet didn't have to worry about such things . . .

Suddenly, shockingly, the trees hit him.

They came hurtling out of the night. One instant he was slipping gently through a bottle of Waterman's Blue-Black, the next he was struggling in a nightmare of thrusting branches, cracking splintering swords of wood that jabbed and cut and tore at him. The strange thing was, he seemed to be stationary; it was the trees that were moving, reaching up, trying to skewer and slash him.

He fought them. Blindly he kicked and flailed. He was still kicking and flailing when he realized something.

He had arrived. He was dangling, trussed up in his harness like a netted mackerel. He gulped down air; freezing stuff, it hurt as it went down but he had to have more of it. Something was stinging his cheek. He groped and found a broken branch pressed hard against it. He heard his father's voice:

'Do you want to lose an eye? Is that what you want to do? Is it? Because that's what you're going to do if you play around like that. It's obvious, plain as the nose on your face . . .'

Dad did go on and on.

He was down. He had survived, in spite of everything. No, he hadn't, not by a long chalk. He still had to get out of this tree. And he didn't know how high he was. He couldn't see a thing below; above, the naked, angular branches were just visible against the dull grey of the sky. The wind was an insistent hand that kept pushing him, urging him to jump.

'Sod you,' he told the wind. He wouldn't be hurried.

He felt about him. At last he found a branch that seemed strong enough. He leant on it; it squeaked and groaned but held.

One half of him wanted to stay up in the tree where it was relatively safe. Wait till daylight, said that half. You'll freeze to death if you do, said the other half. Go on, mate. Have a go.

Yes, he would have a go. Firm grip on the branch with one hand; quick turn and bang on the harness release with the other.

The instant his weight transferred itself from the harness to the branch, the branch snapped. It sounded like a pistol going off. Helpless, he pitched forward. This time the trees stayed put and he was the moving object. A stouter branch caught him in the stomach. He tumbled out of the tree. Holding a branch that he had caught on the way, he was revolving in space again.

But only for a moment.

He hit solid ground.

The impact punched the air out of his lungs. He gasped and croaked and wondered if he would have to go through dying all over again.

But at last his lungs replenished themselves. He clutched his aching chest and exhaled more silvery clouds.

His eyes became adjusted to the dark. A forest. A dense one. The ground was dusted with snow.

Cautiously, he pulled himself up to his feet.

His *feet*.

His *unshod* feet!

Crikey, no wonder he couldn't feel the bloody things! He was in his socks! He must have lost his flying boots when he jumped; they probably flew off the moment he pulled the ripcord. You couldn't blame his poor sodding feet for being icicles. Not a bit of feeling in them. He might have been holding on to two pieces of frozen cod! Move! Run! Get the circulation going or you'll lose them! They'll turn black and fall off!

So he started to run, lifting his feet high off the ground, like some ballet dancer gone mad. He went prancing between the great looming trees, leaping, jumping, trying to get some feeling back in his extremities.

That was how he tripped over the man.

He caught one foot on him and went sprawling in the biting-freezing snow, half winding himself again.

A yelp of pain.

An automatic apology. In English.

A voice said 'Who the hell are you?' Also in English.

Christ Almighty!

'Sorry, sir. I didn't see you.'

The man propped himself on to one elbow. His name was Woods-Bassett; he was a Squadron Leader, the skipper.

'You're the engineer, aren't you?'

'That's right, sir. Pollard. Ron Pollard.'

'Of course. Pollard.'

The skipper was still wearing his parachute; the lines were entangled in the trees above him like long, skinny snakes.

'Are you all right?' Pollard asked him.

'Perfectly all right.'

But it wasn't convincing. The skipper lay in an odd, twisted way; he seemed to have made no attempt to take off his harness. Pollard helped him out of it. The pilot did a good job of hiding the pain, but not quite good enough. His mouth tightened and his fingers balled into fists when Pollard helped him to move.

'Does that hurt, sir?'

'Hurt? No, of course not.'

Typical. Hurt but wouldn't admit it. Hero to the bitter, bloody end. Never submit to human weakness, especially in front of a mere sergeant.

'Why were you running? Someone after you?'

'No sir. Lost my boots.'

'Ah, did you now.'

Sheer bloody incompetence, losing one's boots.

'I was running to try and get the circulation going.'

Woods-Bassett nodded, the pain still evident on his hand-some, film star features. A perfect Brylcreem type, the

Squadron Leader, with a more than passing resemblance to Robert Taylor. DSO and DFC. Small wonder the WAAFs were all potty about him. According to rumour, some of them had his picture in their lockers, others regularly gave him their all, more than willingly.

Lucky sod. But not so lucky now.

Pollard said, 'Have you seen any other members of the crew, sir?'

Woods-Bassett shook his head. 'The Jerries will be looking for us,' he said. 'You can be sure of that.'

'Yes sir.' It was, Pollard supposed, nice to be sure of something. Until a few hours ago, he had never exchanged a word with Woods-Bassett; now the Squadron Leader's was the only recognizable face in God only knows how many miles. He felt small and frightened.

The wind blew the powdery snow into their faces. Pollard's feet were becoming numb again. He resumed his running on the spot.

Woods-Bassett was peering at his silk escape-kit map, trying in vain to make out the lines in the darkness. He stuffed the map in his pocket.

'We were a couple of minutes past the target,' he declared. 'We were still heading south when we were hit. My guess is that we're somewhere north-east of Cologne. And that means that we're not such a tremendous distance from the Belgian or Dutch borders. Which means the Allied armies, sergeant. So that's where we'll go. I shouldn't think it's more than seventy or eighty miles. Not too bad. We'll manage it. Piece of cake.'

Pollard stared. Eighty miles! In snow and socks! The silly sod was out of his mind!

'Walking, sir?'

'Yes,' said Woods-Bassett. 'Unless you happen to have a car or a couple of bicycles handy.'

Pollard pulled his arms together across his chest. He'd have given ten years of his life to have produced a Mercedes touring car. Or a bicycle made for two. He felt in his pockets. What the hell had happened to his Woodbines? God, he felt more like a smoke now than anyone had ever felt in all the history of mankind.

'You don't happen to have a cigarette, do you, sir? I seem to have lost mine.'

'I don't smoke,' Woods-Bassett declared. 'Never have.'

Pollard sighed. He might have known.

Woods-Bassett began to pull himself off the ground. 'I don't intend to sit here and wait to be captured.'

'Right, sir.'

'We'll have to march at night and rest during the day.'

March? The poor bugger was having trouble getting to his feet; how could he hope to march? But he shook his head when Pollard offered to help. No, he had to do it by himself. His legs wobbled when they took his weight. Pollard watched, aghast. The bloke was barmy, thinking about traipsing all those miles through the snow. Anyone in his right mind could see that. But perhaps Woods-Bassett wasn't in his right mind. Perhaps he had never been in his right mind. Perhaps that was why he had become a hero, with an array of gongs and three tours to his credit.

'What did you do with your parachute?'

'Left it in the tree, sir.'

'Then they shouldn't have too much trouble finding it, should they?'

The bastard could be as frosty as the weather.

'I tried to get it down,' Pollard said untruthfully. 'But it was too high up. I must have fallen about twenty feet when I got out of my harness. I couldn't get back up there. I tried, sir.'

Woods-Bassett grunted, probably not believing a word of it. The two of them spent the next ten minutes disengaging his parachute from the branches. Pollard cut a couple of large patches out of the canopy and wrapped them around his feet. They were poor substitutes for fur-lined flying boots, but considerably better than nothing. The remainder of the canopy was torn in two; they wrapped the halves around their bodies beneath their flying jackets. Afterwards they looked stout and rather ungainly.

Woods-Bassett peered about him. 'I wonder how close the Jerries are.'

Pollard thought of snarling Alsatians, straining at their chains, slavering in their eagerness to sink their fangs into

English flesh. Would there be time to surrender before the beasts were upon them? He gulped, shivering. A sturdy young man of slightly less than average height, Ronald Pollard was twenty. He had dark, rather unruly hair, a determined chin and a broad, humorous mouth. His nose had been broken in a schoolyard scrap; it was set inexpertly and now possessed a distinct bump in the middle. Curiously, it suited him, imparting a faintly disreputable quality to a face that might otherwise have been quite dull.

Woods-Bassett said, 'No point in hanging around here any longer.'

Pollard was of the opinion that Squadron Leader Woods-Bassett looked like death warmed up.

'Want a hand, sir?'

'No. Perfectly all right. Come on, we've dawdled about here quite long enough.'

The inference seemed to be that the delay was Pollard's fault. Pollard sniffed. Lower ranks were there to be blamed; it was the natural order of things. He wondered how long it would be until he started getting merry hell for permitting the Jerry night fighter to shoot them down. God, it still seemed to be happening. Still clutching the window handle. Still peering, trying to pierce the night sky until eyes were aching and imagination was playing tricks with every shadow. He had seen shapes flitting by; he had seen the spitting flames of flak; he had seen the agonized torment of a Lanc going down on fire, shedding a burning wing, turning over and over, revolving like some blazing boomerang.

But he hadn't seen the night fighter. He hadn't even heard the shooting. The Jerry must have been one of those Ju 88s or Me 110s with the '*schräge Musik*' guns positioned to fire upward instead of forward. They would fly beneath the British bombers where none of the gunners could see them. Then they'd blaze away, usually into the wings to set the engines and fuel tanks on fire. Pollard had been sitting on the jump seat beside Woods-Bassett, thankful that the bombs had been dropped and that the aircraft was clear of the target and beginning the turn for home. Then, suddenly but soundlessly, the two port engines burst into flames that were battered by the wind into fiery jets, until they looked like great, airborne Bunsen burners. It was what he had sweated about for months, the sight that had been a regular feature of his nightmares. But when it happened he wasn't frightened. He didn't have time. Instinct took over. All that mattered was doing important things, like jabbing at the feathering and fire extinguisher buttons and clipping his chute pack on to his harness and scrambling down into the nose compartment where the freezing air was already screaming in through the open hatch. But even as he did these things, he vaguely expected someone to come and tell him everything was under control. After all, he was flying with Woods-Bassett, wasn't he? The Squadron Leader had done a hundred ops, hadn't he? Never a scratch, right?

A couple of seconds later he was in the air, spinning.

* * *

The ground was treacherous. In places the wind had created deep pockets of snow; they plunged up to their ankles in the stuff. Further on they found themselves on hard, solid ground with just a powdering of snow on top. But then they skidded on ice, tumbling, sprawling in the darkness. When Pollard fell it was unpleasant but not serious. When Woods-Bassett went down it became a major crisis. Getting him back on his feet was exhausting, and each time he fell he became weaker. After a couple of hours the pilot was groggy with fatigue, swaying as he plodded on. Pollard suggested resting up for a while. But Woods-Bassett wouldn't hear of it. No, they had to get as much distance as possible between the crash site and themselves.

'We can do a few miles every night. What's reasonable? Ten miles? Then we should do it in about a week. Not too bad at all.'

Not too good at all, thought Pollard.

They found Meade.

Broken, crushed, a ghastly caricature of the burly navigator whose strident Canadian voice had barked over the intercom, he lay in a tiny clearing. His parachute was still neatly packed, still clipped to his harness.

'Meady . . . for Christ's sake.'

Woods-Bassett was shaking his head, as if trying to deny the sight.

Pollard tried not to look at the squashed, staring face, but it seemed to draw him. The one visible eye was very blue. And utterly lifeless.

He must have hit the kite when he jumped. The tailplane or the wing, probably. Pity. Bad luck, hard cheese and all that. But it was a quick way to go. No pain. No lingering. No nothing. Just a quick tap on the noggin by a tailplane travelling at a couple of hundred miles an hour . . .

Woods-Bassett clicked his tongue as if he was mildly chiding Meade for getting killed. 'Bloody shame . . . hell of a fine navigator . . . awful waste . . . did an entire tour with me.'

'Pity,' Pollard murmured.

'What a thoroughly good type he was. He came from Montreal.'

Pollard wondered if Meade had any cigarettes on him.

The Squadron Leader said, 'We must bury him.'

'Bury him?' Pollard sighed. Where did the stupid sod think the spades were hidden?

'We'll bury him in the snow,' said Woods-Bassett. 'We're not going to leave him here, like this. He deserves better.'

Pollard sniffed, wondering how concerned Woods-Bassett and Meade would have been if they had stumbled upon *his* body. Chances were, they'd have given the remains a couple of shakes of the head; and they'd have said, 'Tough titty' and 'Wasn't his name Prollerd or Plarder or something?' and moved on.

'We haven't got time to bury him, sir. And we haven't got any spades.'

'What?' Woods-Bassett wiped his brow. 'Perhaps you're right. But we can put some snow over him.'

They straightened Meade's limbs. It was easy; every bone in the poor bastard's body must have been pulverized. His sleeves felt as if they were filled with jelly. Pollard crossed the Canadian's hands over his chest. Surreptitiously he patted the dead man's pockets. Sod it! No fags!

Woods-Bassett took one of Meade's identity discs and dropped it in his pocket.

'Cheerio, old chap,' he said. 'Awfully sorry to leave you like this, but there really isn't much I can do about it, is there?'

'I want his boots,' Pollard said.

'What?'

'I haven't got any boots,' Pollard said. 'He has. And they're not going to do him any good, are they?'

Woods-Bassett didn't answer. He turned away and began to walk in his stiff, awkward manner. He seemed to have forgotten about burying Meade.

As Pollard slipped on Meade's boots, he wondered at his own adaptability. In the normal course of events he'd have been appalled at the thought of taking a dead man's boots and putting them on. But, he reflected, squeamishness doesn't last long when the temperature plummets. He revelled in the warmth of Meade's boots.

'Ta,' he said to Meade as he set off in pursuit of his leader.

2

He slept fitfully, dreaming fragments of dreams about Kilburn and the Hampstead Heath Fair and the *schräge Musik* guns on a twin-engined Messerschmitt and an Austin Seven colliding with a Daimler on the Hendon Way and the smashing redhead at the Gaumont State and a dead man without boots.

He awoke. He felt as if the cold had shrivelled him, made him brittle. He would undoubtedly break if he tried to move too suddenly. His bones would snap like icicles. He held his jaw but couldn't feel it; his fingers seemed to be grasping something inanimate, something that had no connection with him.

Frostbite! What sort of love life are you going to have if the bottom half of your face falls off? He could see himself: hideous reminder of the war, allowed out only on Armistice Day.

He rubbed at his jaw until he felt the blood moving. But had he saved it? The ominous blackening process might have started before he began rubbing. He had no mirror. He couldn't check the colour of his jaw. Anxiously, he worked it, biting at nothing. The bitter air made his teeth ache.

His watch said a quarter past nine. But it had stopped. He didn't blame it. Slowly, painfully, he got to his feet. It was still light, but there was no sun; the sky was grey; it looked like the bottom of an enormous battleship. Snow was falling, heavy wet flakes that glided down and spread themselves in a lazy, proprietary way when they landed. The wind had died, thank God.

Woods-Bassett groaned in his sleep. He grimaced as he moved. His eyes opened.

Pollard asked him how he was feeling.

'Wizard.'

Stoutly said, but Grade A bullshit.

14

Christ, it was cold. Pollard jumped up and down, wondering if his blood had already congealed in his veins, forming a solid network of bright red pipes inside him, like something out of the engine room of the *Titanic*.

They ate some snow, a couple of dry biscuits and two squares of Cadbury's Dairy Milk chocolate – emergency rations carted aboard the kite a few minutes before takeoff, God knows how long ago, in another life.

'Half a bar left,' Woods-Bassett announced. 'When it's all gone we'll have to see what we can scrounge. We'll save the benzedrine tablets,' he added, 'until we really need them.'

Pollard's stomach growled. He looked around. The country seemed unpromising for scrounging purposes. Somewhere, he supposed, there must be villages and farm houses. But where? All he had seen of Germany so far was trees and snow.

Woods-Bassett's watch still worked. It said three o'clock.

'We'll wait until dark then we'll push on.'

Poor sod, he looked as if he would never move again. His face was drawn, his eyes much too bright. But he talked about the next 'leg' like a teacher telling the class about tomorrow's hike. All very stiff upper lip. And all very daft, in Pollard's opinion. Facts had to be faced. Woods-Bassett was simply being stubborn, unrealistic. He was in a bad way; it obviously hurt him like hell every time he moved. Why wouldn't he admit it? If their positions had been reversed Pollard would have talked about nothing else. It had long been his credo that a bloke had to look after his body because it's the only one he'll ever have. In Pollard's opinion the intelligent course of action was to surrender to the first available German and ask for medical aid and a warm meal. Not that surrendering was without danger. There were lots of horror stories about the things bombed-out Jerries had done to downed Allied airmen. *Terrorflieger* the Germans called them. Aerial sackers and pillagers. But that was in the cities. Out here, it was hard to imagine that anyone had suffered much from the RAF or the Yanks. Pollard was willing to take the chance. But not Woods-Bassett. He was the original 'press on' type.

They waited for darkness.

'Damned shame about Meady,' the Squadron Leader muttered. 'I hope the other lads got down safely.'

'Yes, sir,' Pollard said automatically. Actually he hadn't given a thought to the other lads. He didn't know them and he had enough problems of his own without taking on theirs.

'Londoner, are you?'

'Yes, sir.'

'Thought so.

'Kilburn.'

'Ah yes. Edgware Road.'

'That's right, sir.'

Kilburn should have been flattered that he'd heard of it.

Pollard shook his head; he was being unkind. The poor bastard was hurt, wasn't he? He hadn't meant any harm, had he? Pollard asked him where his home was.

'Not too far from town,' he said. 'Quite nearish, in fact. On the river. Place called Cookham. Do you know it?'

'I've heard of it,' Pollard lied.

'Pleasant spot. Lady Astor used to live there. We're only half a mile or so from her place.'

'Interesting,' Pollard said, trying to remember who Lady Astor was.

'Married, are you?'

'No sir.'

'Well, plenty of time for that.'

He rambled on, about someone called Marjorie and what an absolute brick she was and how she hadn't raised the slightest objection to his going back for a third tour. 'Not many women like that . . . a fellow can count himself extraordinarily lucky to find someone of that . . . *calibre*.'

He sounded as if he was talking about a gun. Pollard sighed. It was obvious that the skipper was running a fever. God only knows what might be wrong inside him. Was he bleeding internally; would his body fill up with blood until it poured out of his eyes and ears and nose and mouth? In his condition was there anything worse for him than sitting outside, getting covered with snow in a temperature minus something horrible?

The last glimmer of daylight faded. It seemed to snap

Woods-Bassett out of his daze. Press-on-regardless, never-say-bloody-well-die, he tottered to his feet. His lips were blue, his face chalky. Deep breath.

'Well, let's get cracking shall we? Can't dawdle about here; long way to go.'

Rah, rah, rah. You're off your rocker, Pollard told him, forcefully but silently.

At first they made good progress. Woods-Bassett set a brisk pace, striding stiffly through the snow as if the officers' mess was just around the next corner. But he quickly tired. He began to grunt on every step. It was maddeningly monotonous. Pollard felt like wringing his neck. Only when he stumbled and fell did the pilot stop grunting. And then it was one hell of a job to get him back on his feet. And exhausting. But he refused to stop and rest. 'Have to push on. Long way to go. No time to waste.'

He kept confusing Pollard with a gunner named Dryden. He burbled endlessly about the occasion on which Dryden made a public nuisance of himself in a hotel called The Saracen's Head in Lincoln. He told Pollard that he should have been locked up for what he did and it was only because the Station Commander applied some pressure that he remained at liberty. Pollard didn't bother to tell him that he wasn't Dryden, that he was a nobody named Ron Pollard, a spare bod who had done only one op and whose crew got themselves killed and who was waiting to be re-crewed when he was picked to fly because the Squadron Leader decided that he should participate in this particular show. The Squadron Leader needed a flight engineer; his FE was down with the German measles, of all things. Pollard kept remembering how lighthearted he was about the trip. It was as safe as houses flying with the Squadron Leader: he always came back.

Meade had completed his tour; he had been due to return to Canada in a few days. In the crew room he had talked loudly of how he intended to spend his first week on Canadian soil: in the Royal York Hotel in Toronto – with three women: one white, one black, one yellow. 'I'll get anything else I need through Room Service,' he added. 'I won't come out of that goddam room for seven whole days!'

The rear gunner, a wiry little Geordie, said, 'And when you do come out, lad, it'll be on a stretcher!'

'Right,' said Meade. 'Still at it.'

Woods-Bassett staggered on, wobbling and sagging like a beaten boxer who hasn't got the sense to lie down and admit that he's had it.

The forest gave way to open country. It felt colder away from the protection of the trees. Dimly they saw a village, snug and cosy, curtained by falling snow.

Pollard suggested a closer look at the place, hoping to be arrested by the local constabulary. Woods-Bassett shook his head.

They crossed a stream. It was frozen solid at the bank but a slender thread of water bubbled merrily down the middle. There were voices – vaguely military. A patrol perhaps. Woods-Bassett kept going, still grunting, apparently unaware of them. Pollard followed him, expecting to walk straight into the Jerry equivalent of Salisbury Plain. But they encountered no one. The voices faded into the night.

They ate the last of the chocolate. Glimmerings of dawn could be seen over the hills. Pollard regarded it without enthusiasm. Another day. Another stinking, stupid day. He flopped down against a tree, delighting for a moment in the inaction of his limbs; but quickly, efficiently, the cold began to penetrate, stealing through his kapok-lined flying suit, probing at his flesh. Woods-Bassett was already asleep.

'We've had it, mate,' Pollard told him. 'Admit it. We've got to get you to a doctor or you'll bloody well *die*.'

It was odd, listening to himself. His voice sounded tinny, as if his tonsils were icing up.

He contemplated leaving Woods-Bassett and going to find someone to surrender to. It was the sensible thing to do. But he didn't do it. He asked himself why. Scared stiff, was he, of Woods-Bassett? Terrified of being accused of disobeying a direct order? No, he assured himself, it wasn't that. What he was really scared about was going off, wandering for miles and miles, then being unable to find the skipper again. He liked that explanation better.

He collected branches and the withered, shrunken remains

of shrubs and tucked them around the pilot. When he had finished he started to laugh in a feeble, hopeless sort of way. It looked as if he was making Woods-Bassett ready for an Indian cremation, a sacrifice for the Gods of Bomber Command.

He huddled in the shell of a dead tree and felt sorry for himself. Life was a bugger, it really was. He thought about his room in Kilburn and how he used to complain about it. (He should have had the second bedroom on the first floor but the lodger had it, Mr Roseberry.) A cramped little place in the attic, it was dominated by a sloping ceiling that made the end wall only about four feet high. All the heat of the house would rise and collect in that little room. In the summer it was stifling (a delicious thought now!). The room possessed only one window, a miserly, square thing that seemed unable to interest outside air coming in or inside air going out. He used to complain about the air: it was stale, he said; his health was sure to suffer if he continued to breathe it. There was a balsa model Hurricane hanging by a cotton thread from the ceiling. It turned endlessly, collecting dust on its carefully sand-papered wings and celluloid cockpit canopy. Was it still turning? Would he ever get back to Kilburn? Or would he end his days, frozen solid, in this foreign place? Homesickness was a sharp pain that lanced through him like a needle. He felt tears spring to his eyes. He was actually crying for himself! Some bloody warrior he turned out to be!

* * *

The snow had stopped but now the wind had picked up strength again. It whistled around the two forlorn figures, icy and utterly merciless. You could burrow down in your little hole like a bloody hedgehog but the wind would find you and punish you for being so stupid as to stay out of doors.

Where were the Jerries? Pollard cursed them. Dozy buggers, no wonder they were losing the war if they couldn't even find a couple of RAF hikers on the road to Belgium. Huddled in his tree, he wished with all his heart that they would come and arrest him and take him away to a nice warm POW camp. It would be infinitely preferable to this, and it wouldn't be for long; everyone said the war would be over in a few months or even weeks; in fact, according to the experts it might even be done with by Christmas. Christmas. His stomach growled. He could recall every mouthful of that last Christmas dinner. He had left some potatoes and sprouts. Couldn't finish them; hadn't got room for them. Never again, he swore, would he ever leave food on his plate.

Scout's honour.

Was it at OTU, with Hatch and the rest of the crew, that he had eaten that last Christmas dinner? *His* crew: tight little group, comrades to the end, sergeants all. And fiercely proud of it. For a few short months he had been closer to those blokes than any other people in the whole world. They worked, played and relaxed as a group, a team. But now, just a couple of weeks later, he couldn't recapture their faces. He could see them at a distance but when he attempted to get in close to any one of them, the details blurred. Was it because of some weird form of guilt on his part? No, definitely no; there wasn't the tiniest fragment of a reason for him to feel guilty. Could he help getting laryngitis? Could he therefore be blamed for lying in bed in Sick Quarters reading *Picture Post* while the Lancs took off, one after the other? The din of their engines made the water glass shiver and rattle on the bedside table. Comfortable and warm, Pollard had thought what a noisy lot they were. A thudding, cracking bang in the distance had startled him. The windows shook. Later he found out that the bang was Hatch and the boys. An engine failed, he was told, a moment after they lifted off. Hatch couldn't correct in time; the kite cartwheeled through a butcher's house, then blew up. Pollard wondered about the engineer who had substituted for him. Were his last thoughts of the rotten sod who had caught laryngitis and had missed the trip? Did he curse Pollard as he died? God knows. In any event, it must have been quick; they were carrying an eight thousand pound 'cookie' plus incendiaries and Lord knows how many thousands of gallons of hundred-octane and rounds of ammunition. It all went up in one gigantic boom. Someone told him that Hatch's head was found two miles away. Pollard didn't believe it. Blokes were always thinking up jolly little yarns like that when there was a bad crash. And you never seemed to be able to talk to the bloke who actually found – or even *saw* – the head. It was always someone who had talked to someone, etcetera.

By now his parents would have received the telegram from the Air Ministry, telling them how much they all regretted to have to tell them that their son had gone missing.

I'm all right.

He concentrated, trying to will the message across the miles, over the Channel, all the way to Kilburn. Number fourteen Armitage Street, he thought, as if he was sending a mental telegram.

I'm all right.

But for how bloody long?

*   *   *

It was time to move again. But Woods-Bassett was having difficulty standing up, let alone marching. Pollard offered to help. The pilot shook his head. No, he was perfectly well, thank you very much. They trudged a few hundred yards. Then Woods-Bassett fell down. Pollard tried to get him to his feet but he kept toppling over, as if his sense of balance had failed. At last, panting and exhausted, they were ready to set off once more. This time Woods-Bassett maintained a hold on Pollard's shoulder. His boots pushed a painful path through the slush; it seemed to be too much of an effort for him to lift them. They ploughed on in silence, listening to the wind and to the sound of their own breathing and the noise of their stumbling footsteps. Pollard lost track of the hours; his head ached with hunger and cold. Woods-Bassett's hand became heavier with every passing minute. Soon it was like a lead weight. The going became progressively harder. But they kept shuffling on against the biting wind, over fields, across roads, once skulking in bushes while a convoy of *Wehrmacht* trucks went thundering by, their headlights masked to mere pin-holes. Near a village they almost stumbled over two figures lying beside a tree. Two more members of the crew whose parachutes didn't open? No, these figures were alive. Very much alive. And enjoying themselves. Pollard stared, disbelieving. Boy, girl, and several blankets.

Shagging.

Where there's a bloody will . . .

He thought of stealing their blankets, or their cigarettes, or both. But he was in no condition to engage in fisticuffs with two strapping youngsters.

An hour later they came across the house.

3

Afterwards Pollard realized that he would never have found the house if it hadn't been for those two indefatigable lovers. To avoid them he retreated a few yards, then made a wide curve to the left. He picked up a line of bushes into a ploughed field. It was frozen solid; the two airmen stumbled and fell in the furrows. Groggy, Pollard thought the two of them must have looked like a couple of drunks, flopping and falling about. He was so exhausted and cold and hungry that his mind played tricks with him. This was all that life had ever been. Everything else – Kilburn, Mum, Dad, the job at the United Dairy, the RAF – was all imagination. Only this mad hike was real.

'We can't go on,' he told Woods-Bassett.

The words didn't emerge properly; his mouth was numb. But it didn't matter. Woods-Bassett appeared not to hear. His eyes were glazed; sweat dotted his forehead in spite of the cold. Pollard walked on a few yards, then stopped. Woods-Bassett thudded into him, his head rolling forward as if it was on a hinge; slowly, painfully, he straightened himself up. He looked as if he was going to salute.

Pollard had stopped in his tracks because he was considering going back to the lovers and surrendering to them. But would he be able to find them? And would he be able to convince them that he wasn't a Peeping Tom? It was crazy; everything was crazy; in a moment he would be crazy himself.

Helplessly he wondered what would happen when his sanity finally snapped. Would he go berserk? Would he fall down, frothing at the mouth?

At last they came to the end of the ploughed field. They were in another forest. It was even denser than the first. Pollard couldn't see anything. All he could do was grope his way forward, with Woods-Bassett clutching at his shoulder. They kept bumping into trees, bringing down showers of snow from the branches. The place was so damned dark, it was frightening; it was as if they were stumbling their way into a giant trap of some sort. But they kept going, for hours it seemed, blindly, stupidly. Pollard's senses became confused. He kept seeing people ahead of him: boys in running shorts and policemen, erks and German soldiers; but he only saw them in the corner of his eye; when he turned to look at them directly, they vanished.

Then he saw the house.

It materialized out of the trees, like some beautiful mirage. He stared at it, afraid to blink in case it vanished too. But it was real, snug in a small clearing, surrounded by the forest. He gave no thought to who might live in the house. It didn't matter. The place represented warmth and the possibility of some food, perhaps even a bed. Nothing else in the world was of the least importance.

'Time to rest,' he told Woods-Bassett.

The pilot went tottering on; Pollard caught his arm.

'It's almost light,' he said, untruthfully. 'We must kip down.'

'Good show, good show,' Woods-Bassett mumbled through cracked lips.

Pollard made him as comfortable as possible with the parachute canopy and assorted branches and bracken. His eyes closed. In a minute he was breathing heavily and huskily.

'We can't go on,' Pollard informed him. 'If I don't get you into the warm and have a doctor look at you, you'll die. That's right, *die*. You're in a bad way, mate. But you'll be all right now.'

It seemed necessary to say it, even though the skipper didn't hear a word. Self-preservation, Pollard thought. Actions have to be explainable. It is the cardinal rule. He could declare, quite truthfully, that he had told Woods-Bassett of his intentions, therefore he couldn't say that he had acted without his knowledge. '. . . I didn't know you were asleep, sir, honest. You sort of nodded when I had finished, as if you agreed with the proposed course of action . . .'

He dozed a little. Odd snippets of dreams: a plump German

girl under every tree in the forest, every one of them stark naked, exposing enticing breasts and thighs, but every one of them frozen solid.

When he awoke the sun was shining. The clouds had vanished. It was a symbol, of sorts. There was hope.

Now he could see the house properly. It was a neat, two-storey affair made of wood and painted white, except for the doors and shutters which were green. A pleasant looking spot, nothing military about it.

And no sign of life.

He watched the house for an hour or more, casing it like a burglar. All he succeeded in doing was to delay the moment of truth, the getting to his feet and the walking over to that green front door. It wasn't far, not more than a hundred yards. Yet it was the difference between freedom and captivity. He shook his head wondering about the peculiarities of the mind: you long for something, then when it's finally at hand you start to wonder if it's what you really want after all.

Still no sign of life from the house.

Woods-Bassett started shivering in his sleep. That tipped the scales. Pollard gave him a nudge.

'Rise and shine, sir.'

Obediently, the pilot stirred, struggling out of his sleep, trying to get himself to his feet. He was semi-conscious; his arms hung limply at his sides and his eyes were half closed. The poor sod didn't even realize that it was daytime.

'Not much further to go now, sir.'

'Good show.'

'This way.'

They stumbled out of the trees, into clear ground. The snow was thick and frozen; it crunched beneath their boots. The air was perfectly still.

Pollard swallowed nervously as he approached the house. The windows were shuttered, but was someone watching from behind one of them? Was that someone already telephoning the police or the Gestapo? Or was that someone levelling a huge elephant gun, ready and eager to blow the enemy intruders to bits?

As he drew closer Pollard could see that the shutters and the front needed painting. Was there a shortage of paint in Germany?

Woods-Bassett chose that moment to come to his senses.

'Where are we? Holland? Belgium? Are we across the border?'

'Nearly there, sir.'

'Good. I told you we would get there, didn't I?'

'Yes you did, sir.'

'You're positive this is the way?'

'Definitely, sir.'

'Good man . . . er.'

'Pollard, sir.'

'Of course. Pollard. Sorry. Better let me talk to the authorities.'

'Right you are, sir.'

They arrived. There was a small bench beside the front door, a dainty thing that looked as if it had been made for a child. Woods-Bassett immediately slumped on it, his head rolling back against the wall of the house. His eyelids drooped.

The door knocker was brass, but it was in sad need of a polish. Perhaps, Pollard thought inconsequentially, Brasso's in short supply too. Deep breath. Silently Pollard told Woods-Bassett that it was for his own good. Then he took the knocker and rapped. Once. And waited. Twice. And waited. He could hear the sound bouncing about inside the place. He knocked again. He kept anticipating thudding footsteps followed by the unlocking of the door. Then what? Terror? Anger? Both? What was he going to say? 'Good morning, we're from the RAF and we're here to surrender'? The only German word he could think of was *kaputt*. He supposed that if he said that often enough the idea would eventually get across.

No answer.

He knocked again. Harder, louder.

Nothing. Hope began to glow. A bit of luck! The place was empty!

'I'm going to have a dekko round the back of the place,' he told Woods-Bassett.

A weak nod in reply.

Snow had drifted against the side of the house in smooth, sweeping hillocks. There were no footsteps to be seen, no indication that anyone had recently come in or gone out.

All quiet at the back, too.

He listened. Somewhere deep within the forest an animal scurried through the undergrowth. Silly little twerp: should be hibernating.

Silence, but for the sound of his own breathing.

He knocked on the back door. Again he heard the noise of it echoing inside the place. And again the banging produced no response.

He stood back, hands on hips, contemplating the business of breaking in. Heave a stone through a window? Smash the lock on the door? It looked substantial. He fiddled with it. He was still fiddling when he realized that it was unlocked.

He shook his head in disbelief. 'You are a jammy bugger,' he said aloud.

He gave the door a push. It held for a moment, caught by the frozen snow around its edges; then, with an audible crack, it opened.

He was in a sort of scullery, a neat little room, very orderly, very bright with red and yellow walls. Whoever built the place had a taste for colour.

Through an arched doorway he could see a kitchen.

He closed the door behind him. Heat – delicious, delectable heat – enveloped him. Hedy Lamarr's soft hands couldn't have felt better than the warmth that slid effortlessly around his face, along every finger, up his sleeves, inside his collar. It caressed him; he was in ecstasy. He tingled from head to toe. Eyes shut tight with the pleasure of it, he turned, as if to get himself equally done on all sides.

He shouted, 'Anyone at home?'

No reply.

Good God, he'd almost forgotten about poor old Woods-Bassett! He hurried through the kitchen – a brief glimpse of neat white table and chairs and glittering chrome appliances – and into the living room. It was pretty, like something out of 'Heidi' or one of those American ski-lodge pictures.

Woods-Bassett hadn't moved. He seemed only partially aware of Pollard's presence.

'Open house, sir. We've got the place to ourselves.'

'Good show.' An automatic croak.

Pollard guided the Squadron Leader inside, kicking the front door shut behind him. There was a good-sized settee against one wall. Woods-Bassett sank onto it, mumbling something about mod cons. Pollard unzipped the pilot's jacket and loosened his collar. Before he had finished the man was sleeping.

Now there was the all-important matter of food. Back in the kitchen Pollard found some bread, grey stuff – *ersatz* presumably. There was a refrigerator in one corner, a huge white and chromium contraption that looked as if it belonged in a laboratory rather than a kitchen. No matter. It contained slices of cold meat and a jug of milk. In a moment Pollard was happily gobbling a sandwich and washing it down with fresh milk. It was delicious, a magnificent feast, every bite a joy.

He chuckled to himself. If the boys could see him now! He could hear them: 'There he was, large as life and twice as ugly, calm as you please, having a snack in some *Frau's* kitchen while half the German army was outside in the cold combing the countryside for him!'

He felt like Robert Donat in *The Thirty-nine Steps*.

As he ate, he glanced about the kitchen. It was all very neat and colourful; almost too neat, it put one in mind of a display room in a furniture shop – FOUR GUINEAS A MONTH AND THIS ULTRA-MODERN KITCHEN CAN BE YOURS. He was intrigued by the taps; they had levers instead of the knobs possessed by every other kitchen tap he had ever seen. A cluster of four paintings adorned one wall: studies of animals in a forest, very colourful (like everything else in the place) but a bit slapdash, in Pollard's opinion. He liked pictures that told you precisely what they represented, pictures that didn't mess you about and make you wonder.

He went back into the living room. It had a large stone fireplace that looked as if it hadn't been used for years. A group of framed family photographs stood on the mantelpiece. The usual thing: young people, middle-aged people, old people: all smiling at the camera and trying not to squint in the sun. One young man was in uniform. German uniform. The enemy. Pollard swallowed. It was an odd feeling, standing in that German room. *He* was the enemy, an intruder, an invader, in a manner of speaking. He shivered. God knows, the young man in uniform might have been killed on the beaches of Normandy; the old lady might be buried beneath the rubble of some house in Hamburg. Best not to think about it. One wall consisted of bookshelves, row upon row of them, packed with volumes large and small. Some of the books looked ancient, like those you see behind closed cabinet doors in stately homes. A dozen or more pictures were scattered about the walls. The house was like an art gallery. In Kilburn people hung a maximum of one picture per wall. Here, the idea seemed to be to occupy every available square inch. A bit much, was his feeling.

The alpine style furniture that filled the front room was ornate and colourful, not at all like the staid and sensible stuff that everyone bought on the never-never at home. He tested a sofa, nodded his approval. Not bad at all.

It was a large room with a high ceiling. At one end a staircase led to a landing that overlooked the room like the bridge on a ship. Beyond the stairs there was a well appointed bathroom and a studio with an enormous window. Easels and canvasses were piled in one corner. The mystery of the art gallery was solved. This was an artist's house. But where was he?

Pollard went into the bathroom to have a wash. A shock awaited him in the mirror. He hardly recognized himself. Grubby, bristly, wild-haired, he looked like some tramp who'd spent the night on a goods train from Glasgow. You, he informed his reflection, are a disgrace to your uniform. He found some soap. It had a peculiarly gritty feel to it but it did an adequate job. The accumulated grime of goodness knows how many days went spiralling down the drain. He felt better. Later on he would see if he could find a razor, but first he had to rest. The warmth of the house was working on him. He kept yawning; he could scarcely keep his eyes open. He dragged himself back into the living room and flopped down in an easy chair opposite Woods-Bassett.

Blissful, total relaxation. He yawned again, expansively, luxuriously. What a turn-up for the books: after nearly being killed in that bloody aeroplane and just as nearly frozen in the forest, here they were, tucked in as snug as proverbial bugs. He smiled to himself as he thought of the BBC interview:

'And is it true, Sergeant Pollard, that you and Squadron Leader Woods-Bassett spent the rest of the war in that house, deep in the German forest?'

'Yes, rather. We made ourselves comfortable, had a good rest after our long hike. We were very tired, of course.'

'Of course. But didn't you expect the owners to return?'

'Most definitely. But they never did.'

'And the next thing you knew the war was over.'

'Right. One morning we woke up and looked out of the window and there were the Coldstream Guards marching past!'

'An exciting moment, Sergeant Pollard.'

'Yes indeed; the sort of thing that makes one proud to be an Englishman.'

He could see that BBC chap – glasses and watery eyes and a wobbly little chin – and he could hear his mother murmuring things about his being a rare one and knowing which side his bread was buttered . . .

Bread!

The thought hit him like a wet towel.

That bloody bread was *fresh!*

Which meant that it had been made only a matter of hours before! Which meant that someone was recently here! And that probably meant that the someone would shortly reappear! He sat up.

And there she was.

4

She stood at the foot of the stairs, a slim, capable looking woman. She possessed good features, but they were pale; she wore no makeup. Her light brown hair was pulled straight back from her forehead and tied at the back in a school-teacherish way. She wore a plain house dress. And she held an enormous pistol. She needed both hands for the thing. It was a Luger or something of the type. Ugly and dangerous. And heavy enough, it seemed, to tip her over.

Pollard gulped. 'Hullo,' he croaked. He had to clear his throat. 'Look, I'm very sorry we've barged into your house like this. We thought the place was empty, you see. I tried the door . . .'

He stopped. She was frowning, not understanding.

'You are American? English?' Thick accent.

'English,' he told her. 'RAF. We were shot down . . . miles and miles away. We've been walking for days, or rather, nights.'

He stopped. She couldn't care less how long he'd been walking. Why should she? All that mattered to her was the fact that two disreputable looking members of the enemy's armed forces had suddenly materialized in her front room.

'I did knock,' he said. 'Front door and back door. I used the door knocker on the front door but just my fist on the back door. I made quite a lot of noise, I thought . . .' Belt up, he told himself. You're going too bloody fast for her and she doesn't give a damn how hard you knocked on the doors.

She pointed the pistol at Woods-Bassett.

'He is . . . *krank*?'

'Pardon?'

'Ill, I mean. He is ill?' She spoke slowly and carefully, having to think about every other word.

'Yes, he is ill,' he told her, wishing he had found a razor

and had had a shave. 'You see, that's why we came in. The poor bloke isn't well at all. I was afraid that if we stayed outside any longer he'd kick the bucket.'

'What?'

'Kick the bucket . . . I mean die. That's what "kick the bucket" means. It's a silly sort of expression when you think of it, isn't it . . .' He stopped and took a breath. 'He needs a doctor.'

'A doctor?' She gazed at Woods-Bassett, frowning, her lips tightly pursed as if she was restraining a flood of words.

'He's really not well at all. Nasty fever and goodness knows what else.'

'*So.*'

'Yes.'

The interchange seemed to be leading nowhere. The woman continued to stand there, pointing the Luger at him.

She said, 'You have guns?'

'Us?' Pollard shook his head vigorously. 'Not us. Never carry the things.' He patted his pockets as if frisking himself.

'There are more of you.'

She stated a fact rather than asked a question.

He shook his head again. 'No, no more of us. Just two. Me and my friend here.' He indicated Woods-Bassett – and observed that his hand was shaking; it occurred to him that every part of him was beginning to shake. 'There were others,' he explained, telling himself not to bother explaining it all but going on anyway. 'There were seven altogether. That's how many there are in a Lancaster crew, you see. Seven. But when we jumped we got scattered all over the place. I was lucky. I bumped into Mr Woods-Bassett. That's Mr Woods-Bassett, the sick bloke. He was the skipper, the pilot, you see. I was the engineer. One of your night fighters got us,' he added. 'Didn't see him . . . just came in under us . . .'

She wasn't interested in the night fighter. 'Where?'

'Where?'

'Where did your aeroplane come down?'

'Sorry, I don't know.'

She frowned. 'You do not know?'

'No, I do not.' Odd, how he aped her. He supposed it was

the presence of the gun. 'When I jumped I lost sight of it.' He realized that he was saying it almost apologetically, as if it was her aircraft and he had lost it. Why the hell did she care?

'But was it far away?'

'It was bloody far away,' he told her, feeling the sweat breaking out on his forehead. 'We've been walking for God knows how long.'

She gazed at him. He guessed that she was a few years senior to him: twenty-six or seven. She possessed a very trim figure. Her eyes were blue and unusually large. Altogether she looked too feminine to be connected to that enormous item of artillery. He wished she wouldn't point the thing at him; she might fire it accidentally. Then she'd be sorry. Or would she? Why was the room beginning to wobble?

She nodded in Woods-Bassett's direction. 'What is the matter with him?'

Pollard was beginning to wonder what was the matter with himself. He felt as if he was going to dissolve. But there was a question to answer first: 'He cracked himself up a bit when we baled out, or when he landed. Our little stroll didn't help matters.'

'Stroll? What do you mean?'

He was going too fast again. But he couldn't help it. 'We walked for two days, or three days, perhaps four; I can't remember. Or rather, nights. We walked at night, you see. And rested up during the days. Nippy as hell.' He cleared his throat again. And babbled on: 'Cold. That's what "nippy" means. It was very cold. And I thought he would die if I didn't get him to a warm place . . .'

His legs became rubbery. His stomach gurgled. Sweat rolled down his back in great globules.

'I'm sorry,' he said. 'I don't feel very well. I think I'd better go outside.'

'No!'

'But –'

'No!' She gesticulated with that huge gun. 'Do not move!'

He closed his eyes. At once the room started to play at being a roundabout. He felt as if he was on the outside of it and he was about to be flipped off by the centrifugal force. His insides were frothing. He opened his eyes. The door to the kitchen was only ten feet away; beyond that, a dozen feet or so, was the scullery, then the back door.

'Sorry,' he said.

And ran.

The journey to the back door took only a matter of seconds. Four or five, perhaps, no more. Why, then, did it consume fifteen minutes, at the very least? Something strange happened to the time span. Perhaps it was the immediate prospect of a bullet in the back. He could *feel* her, levelling that gun at his back, holding it in both slim-fingered hands as she got his body in the rear notch and then lined it up with the sight at the end of the barrel. No matter. A bullet smashing through his spine seemed at that moment to rank in importance far below the need to get outside. He hit the corner of the stove, glanced off it and thudded painfully into a large grey tub in the scullery. Staggering, he performed a half-turn as he ran, clutching at his mouth. He skidded and knocked something – a calendar or picture – off the wall. As he reached for the back-door handle he was simultaneously juggling with that absurd something, instinctively trying to catch it and prevent it falling. And all the time his back twitched with the anticipation of a bullet.

Afterwards, lying in the snow and savouring the icy air in his mouth and nostrils, he began to feel better. He wiped himself with snow, then smeared his hands along the sleeves of his battle dress.

She was standing in the doorway, the gun still in her hand.

He wanted to thank her for not shooting him in the back, but it seemed to be the wrong thing to say.

'Sorry,' he muttered. 'Really, very sorry about this. I think I must have eaten too quickly. First solid food in days, you see. I'm sure it wasn't anything to do with the bread or the sandwich. Nothing wrong with the meat. Quite tasty, really, although a bit different than what you'd come across in England. But I just couldn't handle it. Rotten waste, I know, and things aren't easy, of course . . .'

There he was, chattering away again, like some gramophone record that wouldn't turn itself off. Was it the presence of the gun? In some vague way, he seemed to feel that it wouldn't shoot a man as long as he was still talking.

He clambered to his feet and made a half-hearted attempt to brush the snow from himself.

That was when she said, 'Go. Go now.'

He stared at her.

'Go? Are you sure you mean that?'

She nodded. 'Go,' she said.

Her voice had an odd tone to it. Almost pleading. He scratched his head. Nothing made sense any more.

'You want us to *go*?' He pointed to the forest.

'*Ja.*' More nodding.

His head swam. He wondered if he was going to be sick again. He swallowed. His mouth tasted like the bottom of a birdcage.

He explained, 'I can't very well go without Mr Woods-Bassett, can I?'

'Ah.' She had forgotten about him. 'But,' she declared, 'it is impossible that you stay here.'

Why wasn't she busy telephoning the police or the Gestapo? He almost asked her the question, but something stopped him.

He told her that Woods-Bassett was too ill to move.

'I cannot help you,' she said.

Help? She didn't *have* to help, for Pete's sake. Perhaps she was a bit dim. That might be the answer. She didn't look dim, but one couldn't always tell about such things by appearances. On the other hand, she could be a hermit who had lived in the forest for years and didn't know there was a war on and so didn't think of Pollard and Woods-Bassett as enemy soldiers. But it had to be admitted that she didn't look the hermit type. Was he supposed to explain the facts of wartime life to her? 'You see, Madam, a state of war exists between Germany and Great Britain and it is therefore your responsibility to notify the appropriate authorities of our presence here, since we are members of the enemy's armed forces, to whit, the RAF.'

Instead of saying that, he said, 'I'm very sorry for causing you all this trouble. We only broke into your house because Mr Woods-Bassett was so ill, you see.'

'*Ja,*' she said, nodding carefully, frowning, worrying.

She had a pleasant low-pitched voice; the German accent sounded good on her, it put him in mind of Marlene Dietrich. He realized that she was the first German he had ever spoken to.

'I apologize,' he said, 'for all the inconvenience and everything.'

Without a word, she turned and went back into the house. He followed.

*　　*　　*

Woods-Bassett woke up as they entered. He didn't react to the sight of the woman; he simply stared, then his eyelids closed again and he slept.

The woman stood for a moment, looking down at Woods-Bassett. Then she turned and went upstairs. Bewildered and still distinctly queasy, Pollard sat down. Was she telephoning the police or the Gestapo? He listened but heard nothing. No doubt he should have been doing something. But what? Run? If I run I'll be leaving my superior officer in the lurch, he thought. And if I attempt to take him with me, he'll kick the ruddy bucket. He looked at the pilot. The poor sod's lips fluttered as he breathed; he was mumbling something. Instructions? No; the mumbles made no sense. Pollard wondered what Woods-Bassett would do if their positions were reversed. Undoubtedly it would be The Right Thing To Do Under The Circumstances. The Woods-Bassetts of this world always knew just what to do.

He stood up and inhaled; it made the walls bend a bit but they quickly settled down. He felt better.

Now he could hear the woman moving about upstairs. Dusting, probably. In his experience, women were always dusting. His mother was a prime example; the duster seemed to be a semi-permanent extension of her arm. She was forever flicking the bloody thing at his model aeroplanes, often with disastrous results. When he complained she would shrug helplessly as if the compulsion to dust was far too strong for her to resist. 'They can't be *left*,' she would say. Being left was unthinkable.

He sighed. Presumably he was expected to sit there until the authorities came to take the two of them away to captivity. He knew the routine; he had seen it umpteen times at the camp cinema. Door bursting open, admitting a swarm of steel-helmeted, jackbooted soldiers, rifles and bayonets clattering. Then the officer, slim, immaculate, possibly with a monocle in one eye and a pistol in one hand, barking orders, waving his pistol at the enemies. His innards trembled at the thought. Would the Jerries grab him roughly? And would he squeak with terror? And would he later despise himself? Would he have another shameful example of his conduct to catalogue with all the others? He still cringed when he remembered the surly drunk on the Underground; a red-headed bloke, he had sworn at a middle-aged couple for no apparent reason. Pollard had studiously ignored the incident even though it was happening directly opposite his seat; he had risen at Moorgate and had got out. But Moorgate wasn't his station. Instinctive cowardice. Not worth risking a busted tooth for an unknown couple? Was that it? Hardly anything to recall with pride.

A door opened upstairs. Pollard's heart bounded; he sprang to his feet, fists clenched. The German woman appeared on the landing, behind the ornate bannisters. She looked down cautiously, then she glanced around the room as if to satisfy herself that the place hadn't suddenly filled with more enemy airmen.

She came downstairs, carrying the gun in one hand, a thermometer in the other.

'You,' she said to Pollard, 'will sit there.' It sounded like 'zare'; she indicated a chair in the far corner of the room. Obediently, he went and sat on it.

She examined the thermometer, shook it, satisfied herself that it was registering accurately. She seemed to know what she was doing with the thing. Woods-Bassett stirred, mumbling as she inserted it between his lips. He moved his head but she held the instrument firmly in place.

'Are you a nurse?' Pollard asked her.

She frowned. '*Bitte?*'

Oh Christ. 'A nurse,' he said. 'A lady who works in a hospital. A Florence Nightingale. Someone who looks after you when you're ill.'

She shrugged, still not understanding, but evidently of the opinion that it probably wasn't important anyway. She studied her wrist watch, then she removed the thermometer.

'His *Temperatur*, it is high,' she announced.

'I thought so.'

'He is very sick. He should be in a . . . *Krankenhaus*.'

'Hospital?'

She nodded.

Pollard thanked her for what she had done. She shook her head, looking at him again. Then she went into the kitchen, returning a minute later with a bowl of water and a flannel cloth. She soaked it and applied it skilfully to the patient's brow.

'He must be kept . . . *kühl*.'

'Cool?'

'*Ja*.'

'Do you want me to help?'

She nodded. 'This cloth must be kept wet. It will perhaps bring down his fever.'

'Mind if I get up?'

'*Bitte?*'

'You told me to sit here.'

She half smiled as if momentarily forgetting that he was the enemy. '*Natürlich*. Come here, please.'

Woods-Bassett was sleeping. The white flannel on his forehead made him look like something out of a Victorian battle painting where there were never any missing limbs or spilling brains, only tranquil wounded heroes with spotless bandages.

The German woman tucked the blanket around Woods-Bassett.

She turned to say something to Pollard.

At that moment he took the gun from her.

5

It was easily done. She had put the weapon on the table beside her; all her attention had been directed to the sick man. Pollard simply stepped forward and picked up the gun. He did it without thinking, without hesitating; the Luger was safe and sound in his hand before she had time to react.

He stepped back into the middle of the room.

She looked at him, then at the gun, her teeth set as if to bite her lower lip; the fingers of her left hand still held Woods-Bassett's blanket.

'Sorry about that,' said Pollard.

'Sorry?' She frowned, perplexed. 'You are sorry?'

The pistol felt enormous in his hand. A formidable weapon – but would it fire if he wanted it to fire? God knows. Was there a safety catch that had to be released before it would work? He felt at its projections with his left hand.

'Right,' he said, hoping she knew even less about the workings of the gun than he did. She hadn't moved; her hand still touched the blanket. He said, 'I don't mean you any harm. Honest. You've been kind and I appreciate it.'

'So,' she said. The single word seemed to ask why, then, was he acting as he was?

He took a deep breath, and another. Now that he had the gun he didn't know what to do with it. He had no intention of shooting the German woman or anyone else for that matter. But it suddenly occurred to him that possession of the weapon automatically made him a target for other people with guns. Already he hated the bloody gun.

Think!

'Have you telephoned the police about us?'

She shook her head.

She was lying; she had to be lying. No. Perhaps not. Perhaps she didn't possess a telephone.

'Do you have a telephone?'

She nodded without hesitation.

'Where is it?'

She pointed. There it was, on a small table close to the front door. Why hadn't he seen the thing?

'Is it working?'

'Working?'

'Is it . . . good?'

'Good?'

Christ . . . He went to the telephone, snatched it from its cradle and listened. The line buzzed. It was working. The question was: had she used it to summon the police? The other question was: if she was telling the truth and hadn't rung the police, why hadn't she? Wasn't it the natural thing to do when your house is invaded by members of the enemy's armed forces? He remembered the moment when he was lying in the snow; she had urged him to run. She wanted him to escape? Why?

'Do you have a car?'

She seemed to find the question faintly amusing. She shook her head.

'A horse and cart? Anything like that?'

Again she shook her head.

'How do you get to the town?'

'I go by bicycle.'

'You live alone?'

'Yes.'

'How far is the nearest town?'

'Perhaps twenty kilometres.'

Was a kilometre more or less than a mile? Pollard couldn't remember. In any event, it sounded a hell of a long way to go to the shops. 'You cycle all the way by yourself?'

She shrugged. 'Before the war there was a car here,' she said. 'But it is not here now. The army took it. I cannot help you, except to give you food. Will you have some food – and then go?'

Pollard scratched his head. 'I'd like to go,' he said. 'Honest. But I can't leave him, can I?'

'I will look after him,' she replied.

'You?'

She nodded.

He almost believed her. He wanted to go. He would make it this time. He would take sufficient food and he would wear a couple of blankets wrapped about his middle; free of Woods-Bassett, he would get through to the Allied lines.

But it wasn't that simple – and he didn't know whether it was because of loyalty or fear of the consequences. Woods-Bassett would probably get better. Eventually he would return to a hero's welcome in Britain. Again the BBC interviewer with the watery eyes and wobbly chin:

'I understand, Squadron Leader Woods-Bassett, that another member of your crew was at one time in the house with you.'

'Yes, chap named Pollard. Flight engineer.'

'What happened to him?'

'Did a bunk. Left me in the lurch, ill and helpless . . .'

'A dastardly thing to do, sir.'

And yet, if the situations had been reversed, would the Squadron Leader have stayed because of the sergeant? Hardly likely, was it? 'Poor fellow was frightfully ill, quite helpless. Really not much point in two of us being captured, so I decided to do something about it.'

'Excellent, sir, excellent.'

'So, as soon as I made sure that he was warm and being as well looked after as possible under the circumstances, I decided to continue my journey.'

'Very sensible, sir, very sensible.'

If you were a Squadron Leader you were dead right, no matter what you did. He motioned for the woman to sit down.

'What's your name?'

'Trude Müller.'

'Miss? Missus?'

'*Bitte?*'

'Are you married?'

She shook her head. 'I am not married.'

'Why are you living here, alone, miles and miles from any-where?'

'It is my home.' Defiant tilt of the jaw.

'It's a nice place,' he agreed. 'Do you have any cigarettes?'
She shook her head.

Enough of the niceties. He pointed the gun at her. 'You'd
better tell me the truth. You have called the police, haven't
you?'

She shook her head. 'No.'

'You've called *someone*.'

'No.'

'Why the hell not?'

'*Bitte?*'

It was exasperating, trying to explain the obvious. Pollard
said, 'That's what a bloody telephone is *for* . . . to use to call
for help when your house gets filled up with enemy soldiers!'

It took her a moment to absorb that. When she did, she
shrugged. She had an expressive shrug. It said: If I choose not
to do the conventional thing, it is my affair.

Pollard sighed. He was getting nowhere. Literally. He had
to think this out. If indeed she hadn't telephoned, then they
were safe for the time being. No, not necessarily; she might be
expecting someone. He asked her. She shook her head. He was
no wiser. He looked about him. If she was lying and had telephoned the police or the army, they would shortly be putting
in an appearance. And the first thing they would do would be
to get a sniper to put paid to that RAF sergeant holding the
pistol on the brave *Fräulein*. Christ. He gulped, fear galloping
around his innards. It was barmy; he was worse off with the
bloody gun than without it. Why the hell had he taken the
thing in the first place? He felt like giving it back to her.
'Here, lady, here's your pistol. Just my little joke. I never
meant to take it.' But he didn't move. Failure, heavy and
sickly, lodged somewhere in the region of his abdomen. A
typical Pollard balls-up.

She said, 'Will you now kill me?'

He was shocked. 'Of course not. What an idea.'

'You kill women and children in your aeroplanes.'

'That's different.'

'Is it?'

'Yes. Anyway, I don't drop bombs or shoot guns. I'm an
engineer.'

'So?'

'I keep the motors working . . . and look after the fuel supply . . . things like that.' He rubbed his eyes. The ruddy woman was sitting, peaceful as can be, hands together in her lap, as if she was about to have afternoon tea. He said, 'Where's the nearest car?'

'*Bitte?*'

'Car. Who has a car?'

'Ah. *Auto.*' She shook her head. 'There are none. Only the army has cars.'

'What about motorbikes?'

'No. There is no *Benzin.*'

'What's *Benzin?*'

She explained. 'It is what you put into the *Auto* . . .'

'Ah, petrol!' Yes, she was probably telling the truth; according to the experts Germany was critically short of fuel.

'What about your bicycle?'

At last she nodded. '*Ja,* it is in the shed.'

'One bicycle?'

'No. There are two.'

Two! One each! It wasn't much but it was better than nothing. For a moment Pollard was elated. Then he glanced at Woods-Bassett. His delight evaporated. The pilot couldn't get on a bicycle, let alone ride the thing for seventy or eighty miles. Besides, when you thought about it you realized that cycling had built-in problems. Cycling meant sticking to roads. And roads meant trouble, in the form of police, soldiers and barriers.

She said, 'Will you take the bicycles and go?'

He shook his head. 'I'll think about it.'

She nodded, resigned, as if she hadn't placed much faith in the notion in the first place.

'It looks as if you're stuck with us for a little while,' he told her. 'Mr Woods-Bassett is too ill to move.'

'You are right,' she said. 'But I cannot help you. He must have a doctor.'

'I know that.' Jesus Christ, why was she so bloody dense? 'That's the reason I brought him here in the first place . . . so that . . .' Oh hell, it was no use trying to explain it to her; for some weird reason she just didn't want to understand. He stood up. 'I think you'd better show me over the rest of the house.' He nodded toward the upper level.

'There is nothing there,' she said. 'Just bedrooms.'

'All right, let's have a look at them then.' That was more like it. Brisk and military. It seemed to be proper procedure to look the place over thoroughly. It was just the sort of thing that Woods-Bassett would have done. A recce of the territory.

She nodded, took a deep breath and got to her feet. She glanced at Woods-Bassett, then turned toward the stairs. Pollard followed her. She had nice legs, he noted as the two of them ascended the stairs.

She opened a door. The bathroom – *Badezimmer* – was full of ornate tiles and gleaming pipes. Pollard studied it for a moment, then he nodded. 'Right, next one, if you please.'

She sighed and opened the next door. It revealed a bedroom, sparsely furnished with only the essentials. 'Who uses this room?'

'It is not used.'

'Nice room.'

'Please?'

'I like the room.'

'*Ja*,' she agreed, 'it is good.'

For an absurd moment, Pollard felt like a man inspecting a piece of property with a view to purchasing it. Stupid. But it was all a part of the vague unreality of the whole thing. He, Ronald Pollard, had no business threatening women with guns and traipsing around their houses like some invading warrior . . . He glanced out of the window. It looked over the rear of the house. Snow was falling again. A few yards away, the forest loomed, black and forbidding. The wind had picked up. It pressed against the house: a million insistent hands trying to move it bodily into the trees. The structure creaked like a ship in a heavy sea.

'The next one?'

She hesitated. 'It is my room.'

'I have to see it.'

'It is not . . . *ordentlich* . . . orderly.'

'That's OK,' he said, 'my room at home's not very *ordentlich* either.'

Her lips tightened as she turned to lead the way.

She opened the door.

He caught a glimpse of a rumpled bed, a tray bearing the remnants of a meal, books and papers scattered about a small table.

Then it happened. The gun seemed to leap from his hand as if it had suddenly acquired a life of its own. He had time to see the fist. But he didn't have time to duck. It came hurtling at him like an Underground train coming out of a tunnel at Golders Green. It collided with the side of his head. And went straight through, tearing a great, gaping hole. Debris flying. Fragments of egg shell, spinning, tumbling. He was back on the end of that bloody parachute again. He was landing on the Edgware Road, near the Gaumont State, dodging the cars. One hit him. In the chest, crushing every bone to pulp. And squeezing every cubic inch of air from his lungs.

An instant later the man swung the cricket bat at him. Its great white surface came rushing at him. No time to avoid it. No chance.

But it wasn't a cricket bat. It was the wall.

The realization took time. Time spent sliding down the thing, hands splayed over its surface. An hour, two hours, for the untidy bundle to reach the floor.

End of journey. He gasped for air. Gradually, painfully, his reeling senses stabilized. He touched his face. No hole.

Somewhere, a mile or two behind him, two people, a man and a woman, talked in a foreign language. Urgently.

He came to the conclusion that he could taste the wall. Then he understood why. His mouth was open; his upper lip was curled back and had presumably wiped the wall on the way down. He moved; his head fell forward loosely as if his neck was broken. You'd better make sure, he thought deliberately. He tried to move his head. It responded.

'Thank Christ,' he muttered.

A hand took his shoulder. He felt himself being heaved about like a sack of vegetables at Covent Garden. His head banged against something. The wall, he realized. It was at his back now; it felt good there, solid and reassuring. He blinked. It was as if he was adjusting the focus on a camera. The lines sorted themselves out; the components slid into place.

A tall man.

He stood in the centre of the picture, chest heaving, legs apart. One hand gripped the Luger; the other was clenched, the knuckles straining, almost bursting. The man wore a white turtle-necked sweater and dark trousers. His face was lean and hard: a study in angry lines. He had cold, grey eyes that never left Pollard for an instant. A scar ran vertically through his left eyebrow.

Pollard gulped. A formidable looking bastard. The odd thing was how badly his hair was cut: all lumps and jagged ends.

Behind him, the woman stood against the bed, her fingers intertwined.

The man's foot prodded Pollard.

'Get on your feet,' he snapped. 'And be quick about it.'

For a moment, Pollard thought he had encountered another Allied serviceman. Then he detected the slight accent. A Jerry, of course, but he spoke English well.

'Get up,' the man repeated.

Nodding, anxious to obey, Pollard clutched at a dressing table and pulled himself upright.

The man's grey eyes travelled Pollard from head to toe, moving methodically left to right, then down to the next area. An autocratic bastard, he clearly despised the sight before him. Pollard was all too conscious of his baggy, unpressed battle-dress, his grubby shirt, twisted tie, unshaven face: a thoroughly dismal representative of the armed forces of the British Empire. Pollard wanted to point out that he couldn't help it; he had been jumping out of burning aeroplanes and trudging in forests. But he remained mute.

His face started to hurt. He wondered about his teeth. Were any broken or loosened? It was no time to find out.

The man continued to gaze at Pollard. The skin was white where the scar went through his eyebrow.

Pollard gulped. The man's hatred was almost palpable. That sod could *kill* me, he thought, the realization crystallizing in an almost leisurely fashion. He had to explain. 'Look,' he said, 'about the gun . . . I wasn't going to do anything with it actually, I didn't know how to fire it, even . . . I mean, I just took it without thinking, in a way . . . and, actually, after-wards – right afterwards as a matter of fact – I wished I hadn't . . .'

It all sounded so lame, so stupid, so unbelievable.

The woman said something. The man nodded but his eyes never left Pollard. He unfolded his arms and did something to the breech of the pistol. Was he putting it on safety or readying the thing for action?

Pollard's insides seemed to turn to liquid. He clutched at his mouth, afraid that he was going to vomit.

'I wouldn't have hurt her,' he said. 'Honest. It's true. I couldn't possibly have pulled the trigger . . . She was kind . . .'

The woman said something else. He answered, shortly. Then he stepped back a pace, stiffly, as if he was on the parade ground. But the pistol still pointed in Pollard's direction.

'You will go downstairs.'

'Yes, sir.'

The pistol barrel indicated the door. 'If you make any sudden movement, I will not hesitate to kill you.'

'Right,' said Pollard, nodding. 'I understand. Yes. No problem.' He squeaked with fright as the man thrust the pistol in his back, jarring his spine. God, this was *horrible*! One false move and he would be done with. His life, his precious life, was in the hands of a cold-blooded bastard who clearly considered it of no importance whatsoever.

On the stairs, Pollard held tightly to the banister, terrified that he might stumble and give the man an excuse for shooting him. When he reached the ground floor, he stood still, waiting for further instructions.

Woods-Bassett slept peacefully, blissfully ignorant of it all.

'Sit there,' ordered the man, nodding at a chair.

Pollard did as he was told. His mouth was dry and his body had become a mass of aches. Gingerly he felt at his ribs. He wondered if any were cracked. The side of his head throbbed as if an engine was running inside.

'Your name?'

Pollard told him: name, rank and service number.

'And this man?'

'He's Squadron Leader Woods-Bassett. I don't know his number but it'll be on one of his identity discs.'

The man considered this intelligence. He turned to the woman. '*Major.*'

She nodded, her eyes fleeting from the man to Woods-Bassett, then back again.

'You were shot down near to here?'

'No sir. A long way, near Cologne, I think. We walked for three or four days . . . or nights, rather. We walked at night, you see, and rested up during . . .' He lapsed into silence, conscious that he was babbling again.

'There were two of you in the aircraft?'

'No sir. Seven altogether. Pilot, bomb-aimer, navigator . . .'

'What about the others? What happened to them?'

'One's dead. We found him. I don't know about the others.'

'No one followed you here?'

'I don't think so.'

'This Squadron Leader, he was your pilot?'

'Yes sir.'

'And you?'

'Flight engineer.'

'Why did you choose this house?'

'We didn't exactly choose it. We just came across it. We were going through the forest and we simply came to it.' He nodded toward Woods-Bassett. 'I had to get him somewhere warm or else he'd die.'

'Did you think there would be medical aid available in this house?'

'No sir. But I thought . . .' He took a deep breath. 'I thought whoever owned the house would telephone the police or the army or somebody and have us arrested.'

'And that was the way your Squadron Leader would get his medical aid?'

'Yes.'

'You were prepared to submit to captivity to save the life of your Squadron Leader, is that correct?'

'I didn't have much choice, did I?'

The man fixed his grey eyes on Pollard's. 'I ask the questions, Sergeant. You answer them.'

'Right, sir.'

'So you just happened to come across this house.'

'Yes sir.' Christ, he'd already told him that. How many times was he supposed to repeat it? His voice had become croaky; he had to clear his throat. 'Look, I'm sorry I had to break into your house . . . although I didn't exactly break in, did I? I mean, the back door wasn't locked. I just opened the door . . .'

'And entered.'

'That's right, sir.'

'And threatened my wife's life.'

His wife? She had said that she was unmarried. 'I hadn't any intention of using the gun, sir. It was, sort of, *there* . . . and I picked it up. As soon as I had it, I didn't know what the hell to do with it.'

'But you continued to hold it on her.'

'I thought I might get a car or even a couple of bicycles . . .'

'A bicycle? For him?'

'Well, I hoped he might get better.' Pollard shrugged helplessly. 'I don't know. I don't think I'm very good at this sort of thing. I haven't had much practice.'

The man studied him for minutes. His grey eyes were as cold as ever, but perhaps there was a subtle softening of the lines around his mouth. He was, Pollard guessed, in his mid-thirties. Tough and wiry. He placed the pistol on the chair beside him. Studiously, Pollard avoided looking at it.

'I came very, very close to killing you, Sergeant.'

'I know that, sir.'

Grey Eyes was dressed in civvies, but he had a military manner about him: his bearing, his manner of speech, his handling of the pistol. Perhaps, thought Pollard, he's an officer home on leave from the Russian front. So you can't really blame him for getting a bit shirty when enemy troops come in his house and start waving guns at his wife or girl friend or whoever the hell she is. But, he wondered, why didn't he come downstairs, instead of the woman? Why did he stay up in the bedroom all that time? It was all very puzzling.

The man had a closer look at Woods-Bassett.

'Do you know what is wrong with him?'

'No sir. I think he must have hurt himself when he baled out of the kite. He was in a bad way when I found him, but he wouldn't admit it. After that, we started to walk.'

'Stupid!'

'It wasn't my idea, sir,' said Pollard. 'He wanted to do it.'

'You should have dissuaded him.'

'He's a Squadron Leader,' Pollard explained. 'I'm a Sergeant.'

With an impatient, irritated sigh, the man bent over Woods-Bassett. He loosened the pilot's clothing and began to press lightly on his body. The patient stirred, groaned and tried to move away from the probing fingers, but he did not wake.

The man straightened up. He shook his head with a curt movement, as if angered by what he had just seen. 'I am not a doctor,' he said, 'but I have some experience of wounds. I believe this man has some internal injury, the result, I suppose, of his parachute jump. He also has a high fever which is no doubt due to your insane attempt to walk halfway across Europe.'

Pollard nodded.

'He needs proper medical aid immediately.'

'Yes sir. I know.'

For a long moment, the German said nothing. His jaw worked slowly, methodically; he glanced at the woman then back at Pollard.

'You came to the wrong house, Sergeant.'

'Pardon, sir?'

Pollard's obtuseness seemed to infuriate the man. 'Damn it, you idiot, don't you understand? I cannot help you!'

Pollard stared. No, frankly, he didn't understand. Why couldn't the man help? All he had to do was to telephone the police, for God's sake . . .

6

The morning light was like some viscous liquid that dribbled into the room a drop at a time. Slowly, painstakingly, it filled the room, gradually replacing the colour that the night had stolen from the walls and furniture, the books on the shelves, the cushions on the chairs. Aching and stiff, Pollard watched it. Minute after minute. It was like some incredibly drawn-out opening to a play; vaguely he expected actors to come striding in from the wings at any moment . . .

His back seemed to creak when he moved; his ribs stung and jaw felt as if it had been cracked in half a dozen places. Was that front tooth looser than it had been yesterday? Would it drop out at any moment?

Sod that Jerry!

Bastard.

A bloke could be permanently deformed, banged about like that. It wasn't called for. But the Jerry probably enjoyed doing it. He was the type.

Woods-Bassett had thrown his blankets aside during the night. He lay on his back, his mouth open, mumbling in his sleep. His breathing was heavy; it had an odd, rather nasty, rasping sound. Pollard pulled the blankets over him. The pilot opened his eyes, but they didn't focus.

'. . . can't do that . . . out of the question . . .'

'You take it easy, sir. It'll be all right.'

'. . . matter of the highest priority . . .'

Delirious, poor bugger.

His forehead felt hotter than ever. The fever was getting worse, no doubt about it. How long would he last? An hour? A day? Christ, he might pop off in the next minute or two.

Pollard bit his lip. I don't know what the hell to do, he told the pilot silently. I wish I did. But this bloody Jerry won't call the police; don't ask me why; I haven't a clue . . .

'. . . extremely serious matter . . .'

'You're dead right there, mate,' Pollard muttered gloomily.

He stood up. The house was perfectly still. He looked outside, peeping through the corner of a shutter. The sun was rising; the sky was a metallic blue. A fine day shaping up.

A fine day for getting out of this house and running like hell.

But what about the skipper?

He couldn't run like hell.

Sod it.

Woods-Bassett's colour worried him. The man's flesh was like putty, yet his eyes were unnaturally bright.

Beside the couch was the flannel that Trude had used to bathe the pilot's head. All right, he'd continue the good work. He'd go into the kitchen, get some water, soak the flannel and see if he couldn't get the skipper's temperature down a bit.

'. . . insane methods . . . quite valueless . . .'

Woods-Bassett mumbled on, his brows dark with anger, his fists clenched as if he was about to strike out at someone. His head turned from side to side; his hair was plastered damply over his forehead.

Pollard touched his shoulder; the skipper was still for a moment; he looked vaguely surprised; he opened his eyes, then closed them. The thrashing began again.

'Take it easy, mate,' said Pollard. 'You'll wear yourself out.'

He sighed, anxiety gnawing deep within him. What if the skipper died? Could it honestly be said that he, Ron Pollard, had done everything possible to save him? Would there be an investigation? Would Sergeant Pollard be brought up on the carpet to explain every action? And could he? Christ almighty. It wasn't fair. He shook his head, automatically pushing back the lock of hair that tumbled in front of his eyes. There ought to be a law.

He picked up the flannel.

'Back in a jiffy.' Feeble attempt at cheery hospital-bed tone. 'Don't go away.'

On tip-toes he made his way across the room to the kitchen.

Still no sign of activity upstairs, thank the Lord.

He pushed open the door.

And found the German.

'Blimey!' Pollard exclaimed, recoiling as if the sight of the man had been a physical blow. 'I didn't know you were here. Thought you were upstairs. Asleep.' The flannel had dropped from his fingers. 'I was going to put some water on that. For the skipper. Cool him down a bit, you know. Sorry to disturb you . . . didn't realize you were there . . .' The words bubbled out of him; he had to tell himself to shut up.

The man said nothing. He was sitting at the table, leaning forward on his elbows. The Luger lay before him, its black barrel pointing at the door.

Pollard stopped to retrieve the flannel. He apologized for dropping it. Still Grey Eyes said nothing.

'Sorry to disturb you . . . I'll get out of here . . .'

In his confusion, he slipped and bumped into the door, closing it.

The German's lips twisted irritably. He motioned toward the taps.

'Get your water,' he said.

'No, it's all right . . . I can come back . . .'

'Get it!'

Pollard nodded. Yes, of course, he'd get it right away. He thanked the German, his voice husky with fear. To think the sod had been there, watching, waiting, all night long, probably . . .

He found a mug and filled it, trying with only moderate success to keep his hands from shaking. That grey-eyed bastard put the wind up him, no denying it. The trouble was, you didn't know what he might *do*. He sort of *simmered*, as if he was always on the point of exploding. How the hell could you handle anyone like that? And why hadn't he rung the police? Wasn't that the obvious thing to do, the sort of thing that any citizen in his right mind would do?

But perhaps he wasn't in his right mind. Perhaps he was a homicidal maniac. A Jack the Ripper type. A Bluebeard. A Dr Crippen. It was possible, wasn't it? Pollard gulped, his spine tingling. Homicidal maniacs didn't just *disappear* when there was a war on, did they?

Deep breath.

'Sir.'

'What is it?'

The Jerry didn't turn. He waited for Pollard to walk around to the front of the table and face him.

Another deep breath. 'Sir, Mr Woods-Bassett is worse this morning. Hotter. We've got to get him to a doctor . . . so would you please ring the police or someone and have us, er, taken away. We're prisoners of war, you see, and . . .'

'I am aware of that.' Snappy, bitten-off words.

'Well then . . .'

'Well then, what?'

'Well, it's sort of your, er, *duty* in a way . . .'

Anger spots at the cheekbones; mouth a fierce straight line.

'I am aware of my duty, Sergeant.'

'Yes sir . . . sorry, sir. Didn't mean it quite like that. Not a bit. But I'm very worried about Mr Woods-Bassett; I'm afraid he's going to die if he doesn't get proper medical attention . . .'

He trailed into silence. The German was gazing through him, no longer listening. The icy bastard just didn't give a damn, couldn't care less that a bloke was dying in his house. *Hun.*

'I'm going to take the water to him.'

No response. The water slopped over the sides of the mug as Pollard carried it back to the front room. Woods-Bassett was asleep again, breathing noisily, his lips fluttering as he exhaled. He didn't react when the flannel was applied to his forehead.

He's bloody barmy, Pollard silently told the Squadron Leader. I don't know what the hell to do about him. He won't get the police. Christ knows why. He seems to hate the sight of us, and yet he doesn't want to let us go. Don't ask me what he wants with us. Haven't a clue. And I'd rather not think about it, he added.

He shook his head. It throbbed. Then he realized why.

He hadn't eaten anything since the unsuccessful sandwich of the previous day. God knows how many hours ago that was. He listened to his stomach complaining, clamouring for nourishment. He closed his eyes and pictured a steaming plate of sausage and mash. Every nerve in his body ached; he felt brittle with hunger. He had to escape. It was the only solution. Get out of this madhouse and run like blazes and keep on running until he found a village or town. Surrender to anyone who'd have him. Tell the authorities about Woods-Bassett. And about this house. And hope the poor bugger was still alive when they got to him . . .

Yes. It made sense. He had to do it. He was momentarily cheered. He had decided what he had to do. But how to escape? When would Grey Eyes stop watching? And where were the flying boots and jackets? Yesterday, on entering the house, he had tossed them aside, the jacket on a chair, the boots on the floor. Over there, near the kitchen door. He remembered distinctly. But they weren't there now. Someone had moved them. Brilliant deduction. Was that sadistic Jerry bastard chuckling to himself at this very moment: a good game – See If The Dim-witted Sergeant Can Find The Boots And Jacket?

He glanced up at the sound of footsteps.

The woman, Trude, was descending the staircase. She wore the same plain dress that she had worn the day before; her hair was again pulled back into a simple bun at her neck. It was as if she set out each morning to make sure that she looked as dowdy as possible. But she failed. She was still remarkably sexy. Pollard realized that this was the first time he had thought about sex since leaving England. There, with WAAFs and copies of *Men Only* all over the place, he thought of practically nothing else.

'Morning,' he said, glad to see her.

She nodded carefully, then glanced at Woods-Bassett.

'Your comrade, he is better?'

'Don't think so. Fever seems worse. I just got some water to bathe his head. Is that all right?'

'Oh yes.'

She had a gravely deliberate way of nodding. And a nicely shaped neck. And, he fancied, a splendid pair of tits under that horror of a dress.

This, he told himself, is one hell of a time to start thinking about tits.

'It is good that he sleeps,' she said.

'Shall I keep putting the damp flannel on his forehead?'

Another nod. '*Ja.*'

She went into the kitchen. The door closed behind her. There were words but they were low-pitched, and German.

Were his flying boots and jacket upstairs? Were they in that cupboard near the front door? Christ, they could be in a hundred places. And he couldn't start looking for them, could he? He shook his head, agreeing with himself.

The kitchen door opened.

'*Essen?*' she asked him. 'You wish to eat?'

God, yes. 'Thanks. Don't mind if I do.'

She handed him a plate on which lay three thin slices of dry cake. Pollard wanted to wolf the cake down but he forced himself to consume it slowly, fragment by fragment. That way, the meal lasted a little longer. He pressed the plate with the tips of his fingers, picking up every last tiny morsel. Delectable fare. But insufficient. He felt hungrier than ever.

'You wish coffee?' she called to him from the kitchen. 'Come.'

Pollard tried not to look at Grey Eyes, but it was difficult. Instinct seemed to scream at him, telling him to watch him constantly for fear of what he might do.

'There is no sugar,' said Trude.

A marvellously everyday statement. Pollard felt like grinning at her; she represented sanity in this madhouse. 'It doesn't matter about sugar,' he assured her. 'I like it without sugar. In fact, they say that's the right way to drink it. Better flavour and all that. Course in England we drink a lot of tea and I must say I do like a bit of sugar in my tea, but when it comes to coffee . . .'

Put a bloody sock in it, mate! You're babbling! No wonder she's looking at you as if you've gone off your rocker. And perhaps you have. Hardly surprising, under the circumstances.

'Sit,' she said.

'Thanks.'

The coffee was bitter, but hot and delicious – nectar to Pollard who hadn't had a hot drink since the cup of tea out of the thermos en route to the target. The heat of it spread to every part of him. He swallowed greedily, and in a moment it was gone. He wanted more but he dared not ask.

'You are very kind,' he said, 'to give me this.'

She shrugged. 'It is nothing.'

'It's part of your ration, isn't it?'

'Ja.'

'Well then, thanks very much.'

Grey Eyes drank his coffee without evident enjoyment or interest. He might have been a machine being refuelled. He put the cup down carefully, guiding it into the saucer's concavity.

He *was* up all night, Pollard thought. His eyes are red; he's fagged out; he can hardly stay awake.

Would he doze off in a moment? And would that provide an opportunity for escape? Of course! No trouble at all! Just ask Trude for his jacket and boots and off he'd go, sauntering away to Belgium and a wild welcome from the British army, or the Americans, or Canadians; he didn't care, as long as they spoke English.

Odd, how he kept forgetting that Trude was an enemy. She had no reason to help him. He'd held a gun on her, hadn't he? God, how he wished he'd never picked the ruddy thing up . . .

They were talking in German again. Short sentences, incisive gestures. What to do with these damned Englishmen? The morning light set Grey Eyes' features in sharp relief; his face might have been cast in bronze. A good looking man in an icy sort of way. Well shaped face with prominent cheekbones; a wide brow, strong mouth.

And a terrible haircut.

Silence. Discussion over – apparently without having solved anything. The problem remained, half of it sitting right there at the table. Grey Eyes sighed. Pollard stole a glance at him. The German had folded his arms and was pulling them tightly as if to absorb the tension in his body. His mind was miles away. What on earth was he thinking about? Whatever it was, it did nothing to cheer him up. For a crazy instant, Pollard felt almost sorry for him. The German was utterly, completely downcast, an end-of-the-world look in his eyes, resignation in the set of his mouth. Pollard remembered a Flight Sergeant who had worn an expression like that. His fiancée had sent him a Dear John letter; she had met an Australian captain; they were, she explained, madly in love and she was very sorry about everything but that was the way things sometimes happened, didn't they, and she hoped he would understand. When someone with the best of intentions told the Flight Sergeant that he was better off without such a faithless bitch, and that there were plenty more fish in the sea, a fight had ensued, with bloody noses and a couple of chipped teeth.

Trude poured more coffee. Pollard revelled in the sour stuff; it was gone far too quickly. He felt hungrier than ever.

'You wish more?'

A generous and beautiful lady, even if she was a Jerry. Pollard thanked her fervently for the slices of cake and the third cup of coffee. She half smiled and gave him another slice of cake.

'That's marvellous . . . honest, I really appreciate it.'

'You were very hungry?'

'I'm all right now,' he assured her. 'Besides, I'd better not eat too much, had I?' They smiled: their private little joke. 'Don't want to overload the works. Best to eat so that you could always manage a bit more; that's what I read in some Yank magazine. Blimey, I thought to myself, I've been doing that for as long as I can remember! Anyway, according to that paper, everyone's eating too much in America even with the war on. Must be nice, eh?'

She nodded.

Grey Eyes took no notice of their inconsequential chatter; he was still lost in his own gloomy thoughts. A weird one, Grey Eyes. There was definitely something mental about him; that was what made him doubly frightening. You didn't know what the sod might do next. And that horrible Luger still lay on the table in front of him, beside his cup and saucer, innocently, as if it was pretending to be just another item on the average breakfast table.

Pollard cleared his throat.

'Is it all right,' he asked, directing the question to the corner of the table between Trude and Grey Eyes, 'if I go upstairs?'

The man looked up sharply. 'Upstairs?'

Pollard shrugged, feeling his cheeks burn. 'I want to go to the lavatory,' he explained.

*   *   *

God, but it was good to be out of Grey Eyes' presence. The lavatory was a secure little haven, a place to savour solitude and relative safety.

And it possessed a window.

Pollard looked at it and wondered. Should he give it a go? Did it really matter about his jacket and boots? If he ran fast enough he'd get warm – and hell's bells, he'd keep on running until he found someone to surrender to. And he'd tell that someone about Woods-Bassett. And hope . . .

Insides bubbling with the thought of it; heart pounding; palms sweating. Was it the best course of action? Best? It was the *only*! You've got to do it, he told himself. He nodded. He agreed. But he was scared, even more scared than when he had climbed the oak tree near the school and couldn't get down, even more scared than when he had been cornered by the Wilkins gang from Camden Town or when he had clambered aboard the kite in preparation for soaring away and dropping bombs on people. But there wasn't anything else for it, was there? He asked himself the question and he replied in the negative.

He tried the window latch. Stiff, but it moved. The frigid air flooded in as he gingerly pushed the window open. He leant out over the sill. It was snowing. There was a sizable drift immediately below the window. Would it break his fall? Or would it break his leg? There was a tree nearby; if he could reach the nearest branch he could get down easily. But could he reach it? He tried to gauge the distance. It was difficult; the whiteness and the falling flakes played tricks on a bloke's eyes; you couldn't sort out how far away anything was.

He stood on the lavatory seat and clambered out onto the sill. The wind hit at his bare hands and slid uncomfortably up his back. He tightened the battledress buckle around his waist and surveyed the situation once more. Yes, the tree seemed to be the best bet. One good leap should do it. Difficult? Errol Flynn wouldn't even give it a second thought.

He hesitated, gnawing at his lip. You've got to do it, mate. You've *got* to! His muscles felt as if they were dissolving from sheer, unashamed funk. You've got to, he said again. And jumped.

The cold air embraced him. His trouser legs fluttered like frightened birds. He heard himself gasp as the wind swept up the length of him.

He hit the tree. He grabbed at the branch, missed it and fell, spreadeagled, into a drift of snow.

The snow was in his mouth and nose and eyes. He kicked and struck at it; he was drowning in the bloody muck. It was snuffing the life out of him; he didn't know whether he was upside down or the right way up. A steel band was tightening about his chest. Then he felt something solid. He pushed against it. Suddenly, surprisingly, he found he could breath. He was free. He gulped the icy delicious air. It filled his lungs. Gasping, he heaved himself to his knees.

And turned.

And looked into the muzzle of the Luger.

Grey Eyes stood there, rigid with anger, his shoulders braced, his free arm drawn back as if he intended to deliver a punch.

'You,' he declared, 'are a damned nuisance.'

Numbed, gasping, Pollard could only stare at the muzzle of the Luger: the unwavering circle of metal that would in a moment or two put paid to his existence. There were tiny scratches on the dark metal; one was V-shaped. V for victory.

Grey Eyes pressed the gun against Pollard's forehead. The cold metal seemed to bore a hole through the wall of bone, deep into his skull. He squeezed his eyes shut. Held his breath. Braced himself, every nerve taut.

Somewhere, miles away, a train went rumbling along. Pollard listened intently; it was the last sound he would ever hear. A train full of people and not one of them knew what was happening. No one cared. It wasn't fair.

'Carl!' Trude's voice. Shrill, urgent.

He heard Grey Eyes sigh, irritated.

'Get inside!'

Pollard opened his eyes. To his surprise, the German was

standing a few feet away and the gun was dangling at arm's length. Pollard touched his forehead; he still seemed to feel the muzzle pressed against his flesh.

Grey Eyes gestured with the Luger.

'Did you hear me? Get inside.'

Pollard nodded weakly and struggled to his feet. His legs felt rubbery. He slipped and sprawled full length, scooping snow into his collar and up his sleeves and inside his trousers. He tottered to his feet again. He listened; the train had gone. He followed Grey Eyes into the house, starting to mumble something about falling out of the window accidentally. But it sounded stupid and unbelievable even to him. He lapsed into silence. Grey Eyes pointed to the front room; Pollard went in. He heard the German shut the door, then stride into the room behind him.

'You are not very intelligent, Sergeant.'

Pollard said nothing; there seemed to be nothing to say.

The German sat down and crossed his legs. 'But you must also think that I am equally stupid.'

Pollard denied it. Nothing was further from his mind; the thought had never entered his head. He was very sorry for all the trouble he had caused; he regretted it . . .

'Be quiet, Sergeant.' Grey Eyes' voice had an edge, and yet he spoke quietly with a kind of deadly calm. 'You presumed that the possibility of your escaping through the lavatory window wouldn't occur to me.'

'I don't know . . .' Pollard shrugged helplessly. 'I didn't think about it.'

'That is why you are a fool.'

'Yes sir.' Agree with him, whatever he says.

Grey Eyes regarded him coldly, his face an unmoving mask. A clock ticked nearby: an incongruously cheerful, clockwork sound.

'Did you know what direction you would take?'

'No sir.'

'You were simply going to run.'

'Yes sir.'

'You have no boots on.'

'I know.'

He felt the snow melting around his neck, running in chilly rivulets down his back. One ear seemed to be packed with snow; he wanted to finger it out but he dared not move. To the right, Woods-Bassett was sleeping, oblivious to everything. Lucky sod. Pollard kept remembering being lectured by teachers; they talked like Grey Eyes: all-knowing, all-righteous, voices crisp and cutting. He looked down. Snow was running over his feet, collecting in little pools beside him.

'I'm sorry,' he said. 'I'm making a mess here, all the snow . . .'

Grey Eyes ignored the remark. The muscles around his mouth worked ceaselessly, as if he was restraining himself with difficulty.

'Where did you intend to go?'

'I don't know.'

'You had some plan in mind.'

'Not really . . .'

'You intended to run to the nearest village and surrender to the police. You would report that your Squadron Leader was injured and was being kept here in this house. Is that not basically correct?'

'I s'pose so,' Pollard admitted.

He heard the man and woman talking in German, their voices low. She sounded frightened. Of what? Of what he might do? Was she as scared of Grey Eyes as he was? Why did she stay with him? Was he keeping her here against her will?

Woods-Bassett stirred, mumbling, grunting. The woman went to him and stooped over him. She touched his forehead; he was calm.

The wind sighed its way about the eaves of the house, pressing at the windows and rattling the shutters. Pollard shivered. God, what a rotten way to end up! Stuck in a madhouse with a lunatic with a gun. A bloke deserved better than this. What was the *point* of surviving the bloody plane crash? Life had to have a point, didn't it? It had to be more than just a collection of *events* taking place without reason. But this didn't make any sense at all. Grey Eyes was silent now, gazing at the floor, thinking God only knows what thoughts.

Pollard said, 'Do you mind if I sit down?'

The man stared at him for an instant, as if suddenly reminded of his presence. He nodded.

'Ta.' Pollard sat, his clothes cold and damp against his skin. No one spoke.

Pollard swallowed. His stomach growled. He tried to brace his stomach muscles to stop the noise but it didn't help. The gurgling continued unabated.

Trude's eyes caught his. The corners of her lips twitched into a smile.

'Sorry,' he apologized. 'I can't turn it off.'

At which she burst into laughter, explosively, as if she had stored it up for too long.

Pollard found himself giggling. It was idiotic, childish, but he couldn't help it. And every fresh gurgle from his abdominal regions generated new paroxysms of mirth. His eyes ran; he had to hold his sides.

And through it all, Grey Eyes sat unmoved, simply glancing at each of them, then apparently losing interest in them and returning to his own thoughts.

The merriment expired at last, leaving the pair of them red-eyed and panting.

Trude said something to Grey Eyes. An apology, by the sound of it. He shrugged. Cold fish.

Pollard took a deep breath. The moment seemed reasonably propitious. 'Sir,' he said, 'I really appreciate your hospitality but I think we should surrender to the proper authorities, so that . . .'

'It is not possible,' Grey Eyes replied, quietly, levelly.

'Why? I don't understand.'

'Perhaps not.'

'But it doesn't make any sense.'

Grey Eyes didn't respond.

Pollard persisted: 'If I don't get Mr Woods-Bassett to a doctor he's going to die.'

Grey Eyes nodded. It was possible. An unfortunate fact of life, but one that was beyond his control.

And then Pollard realized the truth.

Grey Eyes was a deserter!

Of course! It was obvious! Plain as the nose on your face! Why hadn't he tumbled to it before? It explained everything. If you've decided to let the army get along without your services, the very last people in the world you want to ring up are the authorities! In fact, he thought, you avoid 'em like the plague! Grey Eyes, he reasoned, was probably home on leave from the Russian front and had simply refused to go back. Instead he had settled down in this house stuck deep in the forest: the ideal spot in which to wait out the war.

'I think I understand,' he said.

Grey Eyes looked up. 'And what do you understand, Sergeant?'

Pollard congratulated himself on his perspicacity. Yes, that was an officer talking, all right, asking what a mere sergeant could possibly understand. Woods-Bassett and this sod would get along famously. Soul-mates.

'You don't want the authorities nosing around here, do you?'

The German flushed. His eyes narrowed. 'You presume a great deal, Sergeant.'

'I could be wrong,' Pollard admitted.

'Yes, you could.'

Deep breath. Calculated risk. 'But I don't think I am.' Pollard shrugged, hands spread wide. 'Look, honest to God, it doesn't matter to me. I won't tell anyone about you. All I care about is getting help for Mr Woods-Bassett. I can keep mum. I had a mate once. He did a job on a petrol station one Easter Sunday. It wasn't a big thing at all. Actually he'd had a couple of pints too many and I don't think he really knew what he was doing, if the truth was known. He had a bit of a wild streak, but he wasn't really bad, if you know what I mean. Not the criminal type at all. So I didn't say anything when the rozzers came asking their questions. I wouldn't have said anything even if they'd really grilled me, given me the third degree. Live and let live, I say . . .'

He trailed into silence.

Grey Eyes said, 'If you don't keep your mouth shut, Sergeant, I really believe I may shoot you. Do you understand?'

Pollard nodded. He understood.

7

The key turned. Pollard stared at it, folding his arms, then unfolding them again and thrusting his hands in his pockets. The door handle rotated as Grey Eyes tried it from out in the corridor, testing it, making sure it was secure. There was a moment's pause as if he was waiting for some response from within, then he moved away and down the stairs.

Pollard managed a smile at his reflection in the mirror. 'They always said you'd land up in jail,' he said. A brave smile; it quickly disappeared. He didn't feel brave. He felt small and frightened.

He sat on the bed. It was comfortable, soft, with an inordinately fluffy eiderdown on top. That was something. At least he could look forward to a good night in the pit. But, on second thoughts, could he? How, he asked himself, are you supposed to get a satisfactory kip when you're in the same house as a Jerry with a Luger who hates the sight of you?

He sighed. It was all so bloody bewildering. How was a bloke supposed to know what to do next? What *could* he do next? He wondered and shrugged at his reflection. What choices did he have? None, as far as he could determine. Was Grey Eyes' plan to keep the RAF types under lock and key until the Allied armies arrived? Did he regard them as his passport to good treatment? No, that didn't make sense, not if he continued to deny Woods-Bassett the treatment he needed. So what was it all about?

An odd one, Grey Eyes. But Pollard was beginning to have doubts about the German being a deserter. He simply didn't seem the type. Perhaps he had had a nervous breakdown. Couldn't face going back to Russia. Probably burst into tears. People did, all sorts of them. Bomber Command types too. LMF they called it in the Air Force. Lack of Moral Fibre.

Sounded as if you had a part missing. And as far as the authorities were concerned, you had.

Was the skipper still alive? Poor sod. Hell of a thing, just letting him die down there. Pollard rubbed his brow trying to think of some way in which he could help the pilot. In the back of his mind lurked the fear that when it was all over, some pasty-faced wingless wonder would say 'Well, good God, man, why on earth didn't you do so-and-so?' and his innards would lurch under the awful impact of the obvious.

The window overlooked the front of the house. There was no tree on this side, nothing to help you get down. Just as well, he decided; he had no wish to incur Grey Eyes' wrath again. He shivered, remembering. Just a little squeeze on that trigger and it would have been curtains. He shook his head in distaste at the sight that popped into his mind: his own corpse, twisted and awkward, pumping blood into the snow with Grey Eyes standing over it, smoking pistol in hand, one foot in the small of the departed's back, like a big game hunter in Africa.

He got to his feet and looked about him.

It was an attractive bedroom. Blue walls. White door. Brass bed. Pictures of sheep and deer. He searched the drawers and wardrobe but there was nothing to provide a clue to the identities of Grey Eyes and Trude. The room was as anonymous as a transit billet at RAF Padgate.

He decided to ask for a pad and pencil. He would start a journal. 'Being An Account of How I Was Incarcerated By The Enemy.' It would be witty and wise and would be published after the war and would make him a millionaire. Then, all this would have been worth while; it would have had a *point*.

*　　*　　*

They came a couple of hours later with a plate of bread and cold meat and more of that bitter coffee.

'You are comfortable?' Trude enquired in her direct way.

Pollard nodded. 'Bit bored, though. Nothing to read. I'd like something to write on, if you wouldn't mind.'

She said she would see what she could do.

'How is Mr Woods-Bassett?'

At the door, Grey Eyes said, 'His condition appears to be unchanged.'

'Thanks very much,' said Pollard.

He got a curt little nod for a response.

He felt a curious relief; it was as if the responsibility for the Squadron Leader's condition had now been assumed by the German couple. There was nothing that he, Pollard, could do. He had only himself to worry about.

He wondered if Trude fancied him a bit. There was no getting away from the fact that she looked at him with a certain *intensity*. He contented himself for a few minutes with delicious imaginings: Trude tapping at his door in the middle of the night. Urgent, passionate tappings. Trude entering, wearing diaphanous night attire, her splendid breasts stirring gently, generous nipples thrusting toward him, manifestly aching for his touch. Trude, finger to dewy lip – no words of endearment, not with *him* in the next room – slipping into bed beside him, simultaneously sliding the nightgown off her shoulders. Trude, joyfully melting into his arms, galvanizing his flesh with hers.

'Just the job,' he murmured appreciatively. That'd be the way to while away the winter. Pretty hot stuff, the *Fräuleins*. An old warrant officer at OTU claimed they were the sexiest women in the world. He knew all about them, he'd been with the Occupation Forces in 1919; given the slightest encouragement he would recount his conquests by the hour.

'Downed Flier Finds Love Nest in Hun Home.'

The *News of the World* would like that one. Juicy stuff for the home front. And it would provide him with just the right sort of credentials for civvy street. Girls would nudge each other in the street and say, 'That's *him*, the one in the paper. The one who spent the whole war *shagging*.'

Gloom followed the brief enchantment. It was silly, thinking up fantasies involving Trude. A waste of time and energy. Even if Clark Gable was locked in this room, would any woman in her right mind misbehave when Grey Eyes and his Luger were just around the corner?

You, he chided himself, should be trying to think of something *constructive*.

True. But what? Set the house on fire and attempt to escape in the confusion? Smashing idea, but how to get the fire started? Overpower Grey Eyes, grab the gun from him? He grimaced; it was singularly an unattractive proposition. And what about Woods-Bassett?

He sighed, weary. In a moment he was asleep.

*   *   *

He was permitted downstairs to join them for the evening meal.

'Jolly kind of you,' he said, tucking into the stew.

'It is dull for you in there alone, no?' she asked him.

He agreed that there was little to do but think.

'And what,' Grey Eyes wanted to know, 'do you think about, Sergeant?'

Pollard flushed, remembering the train of his imaginings. Did the bastard suspect? He said, 'Home, mostly. And Mr Woods-Bassett, of course. And the war and everything. But mostly home.'

'Where is your home?'

'London.'

'You are married?'

Pollard shook his head. 'Can't afford to keep myself,' he said, 'let alone anyone else.'

Neither of them smiled, Trude because she probably didn't understand what he was saying, Grey Eyes simply because he was too frosty to smile at anything.

'You live with your parents?' Trude asked.

'That's right.'

'You have brothers or sisters?'

'No. I'm the only one. They gave up after me.'

'What is your father's profession?'

'He's an office manager in a shipping company.' Not quite accurate, but he could be said to be in charge of part of the office. 'Quite a big office too. I went there once, when I was a nipper.'

'A nipper?'

'Yes, a kid, a child.'

Grey Eyes sighed, as if irritated by the vagaries of the

English language. 'Your parents will be concerned about your fate. It is regrettable that you can't inform them that you are alive.'

Pollard nodded, weighing the advisability of pointing out that if he became an official POW, his parents would be informed. He decided against it. That subject had been pretty adequately covered.

'My brother,' said Trude, 'was a pilot.' She said it softly, reflectively. 'He was killed in Greece. He was twenty-one.'

'Too bad,' Pollard muttered. The automatic response.

'He was a nice fellow. A good sense of humour.'

'That always helps,' said Pollard.

Trude said, 'I would like very much to fly one day. It is an . . .' She turned to Grey Eyes. '*Ehrgeiz* – *was* . . .?' He told her the English word. 'It is an *ambition* of mine. In England do many women fly?'

Pollard nodded. 'Some of them deliver aircraft from the factories to the squadrons. I think they do a bit of test flying, too.'

'Does it take a long time to learn?'

'Not too long,' said Pollard expansively. 'It's all a question of balance, you see. A bit like riding a bicycle, in some ways.'

'It sounds very difficult.'

'Not once you get the hang of it.'

'But,' said Grey Eyes, 'you are an engineer, are you not?'

Bugger him for remembering and spoiling his tiny moment of glory. Typical. 'But I've done quite a lot of flying,' he declared. 'You see, most pilots teach their engineers to fly so there'll be someone to get the kite back in case they get hit. Hatch spent hours and hours teaching me.'

'Hatch? He is the Squadron Leader?'

'No, sir. Sergeant Hatchford. He was my pilot. But he and the rest of my crew got the chop a few weeks ago. I was in bed with laryngitis. I missed the trip.'

'You were lucky.'

'I thought so then.'

'But now,' said Grey Eyes, 'you are not sure, so?'

'You are lucky,' said Trude, 'as long as you are alive.'

*　　　*　　　*

They gave him a German–English dictionary and a pile of old magazines and newspapers. At first he found it amusing, trying to sort out the meaning of the foreign words, but he quickly found it hard, tedious work – and enormously frustrating because of the German script and because so many of the words he sought weren't in the dictionary.

He began a journal. He described the events leading to his present predicament, then he described the room. (Initially he had planned a scathing description of Grey Eyes, but prudence prevailed. The subject might all too easily find the pages.) After that he dried up. There was nothing more to say because nothing more was happening. Woods-Bassett continued to sleep and groan, his temperature still at a frighteningly high level; the hours dragged themselves along; food was brought; he consumed it; he was permitted to use the toilet facilities, even obtaining the temporary use of one of Grey Eyes' razors. But he was denied the use of the bath; there was, they told him, a severe shortage of hot water. He had to be content with a lukewarm sponge-down. Afterwards he was appalled by the colour of the water in the basin. It looked like gravy. I must have smelt like a ripe rhinoceros, he thought.

Again he joined them for the evening meal. But the conversation was harder this time. Grey Eyes said little and seemed to withdraw into his own doleful world; when he did speak the words were sharp and irritable.

Trude appeared not to notice; she answered him levelly. How, Pollard wondered, did a girl like her ever get mixed up with a bastard like him? And why did she stay with him? For a few delicious moments he conjured up a scenario: brave English sergeant rescuing sensuous *Fräulein* from wicked master, fleeing with her across snow-covered plains and reaching the Allied lines.

But he'd conveniently forgotten about Woods-Bassett.

Sod him.

Trude was saying that it was the coldest December she could remember. Often, she assured him, it was mild enough at this time of year to go walking in the forest in shirtsleeves. One Christmas, flowers still grew near the house.

'Just my luck,' Pollard commented.

She smiled.

It snowed all that night. In the morning the snow still fell; at times the forest disappeared from view and the house seemed to be floating in an ocean of snow. Damn the bloody weather. Pollard hated it. It had stopped the Allied advance towards Germany, delayed the winning of the war. The front was static; God knows how many thousands of troops on both sides were huddling in foxholes fighting to stay warm instead of fighting each other. The snow stopped. The low grey clouds moved off to the east. The sun broke through, shimmering on the whiteness. The forest looked as if it had been spattered with icing sugar.

Then from downstairs came the noise of Woods-Bassett's coughing. Agonizing, racking coughs.

Pollard listened, shaking his head. The poor bugger sounded as if he wasn't much longer for this world.

When Grey Eyes and Trude brought his coffee and cake they reported that the pilot's temperature was unchanged.

'But now he coughs so much,' Trude said, frowning.

'I can hear him.'

'He had a little piece of soup,' she added; her English was occasionally quaint.

Pollard looked at her, saw the genuine concern in her eyes, then he glanced at Grey Eyes standing in the doorway with his pistol.

'Listen,' he said, 'I'm afraid Mr Woods-Bassett may die. Let me get him up and put some clothes on him. We'll shove off and you won't have to worry about us ever again. We won't tell anyone about you. I promise. You can trust me. It'll be much better for you if we go. We won't be eating your food and everything; I mean, I know rations are short, it's the same in Britain. My mother says if things get any worse she's going to take up burglary as a sideline – and go for Sainsbury's instead of banks. Sainsbury's are food shops,' he explained lamely. 'Of course, she didn't mean it really; it was just a joke.' He shrugged; no one was smiling. 'But anyway, what I'm saying is, you don't have to worry. We won't tell anyone about you. Honest.'

Grey Eyes said, 'And how will you explain the fact that you are washed and shaved? It is obvious to anyone that you have spent some days in a house. The interrogators will want to know what house and where.'

'I'll make something up,' said Pollard. 'I'll tell them anything you want me to tell them. I don't care. You tell me what to say. I'll say it.'

Now Trude was talking to him, half turning away from Pollard as if to prevent him overhearing. Grey Eyes didn't respond. A moment later the two of them went out of the room, locking the door behind them.

Pollard sighed. He shrugged at his reflection in the mirror. I tried, didn't I? I couldn't do more, could I? The reflection seemed to agree.

*　　　*　　　*

His German was improving. He recognized *bitte* and *danke*, *entschuldigen* and *guten Tag*. *Essen* meant grub, *trinken* meant drink. He succeeded in translating small items from magazines. It was a laborious business but it occupied him.

The magazines were, in the main, musty old things dating back to the early days of the war when things were going swimmingly for the Germans. Page after page was crammed with illustrations of Jerries blasting their way through Norway and France. Cheerful looking blokes. Their expressions put Pollard in mind of advertisements showing holidaymakers at Butlin's camps. Wish you were here. Machine gunners, infantry or Stuka aircrew, they seemed to be having the time of their lives. War was great fun apparently. But of course you had to be a Jerry to enjoy it. The enemy bods were glum, dishevelled and dirty. Inferior types. No match for the Master Race. Through it all Hitler was prominent, poring over campaign charts, presenting medals to heroic warriors or patting nippers on their blond Aryan heads.

The articles were repetitive. Pollard started yawning, his interest waning. The Jerry papers needed a Jane to liven them up. He began to flip quickly through the pages; he could almost predict what each one would have in store for him.

He went right past the picture before it registered fully. He stopped. No, he must have been mistaken. *Must* have. Carefully, page by page, he retraced his literary steps. Obviously he was wrong; it was just one of those things you think you've seen, an optical illusion, a trick created by the fleeting pages.

Nothing on this one, nothing on the next, or the next. It didn't exist. He had imagined it. Silly . . .

Then he found it. Top of page twenty-four.

His mouth dropped open. He blinked and shook his head. He looked once more.

'Blimey.'

If it wasn't Grey Eyes in that picture, it was his twin brother.

And there was Adolf himself, shaking hands with him.

Pollard reached for his dictionary. It took him twenty minutes to make a rough translation of the caption, looking up every word, writing it all out, then trying to knock some sense into it. In the end it was done. It read: 'A Hero Meets His Führer: Captain Carl von Eisner, outstanding tank commander, receives the Iron Cross First Class for his bravery in the fiercest battles in France and Belgium. Captain von Eisner was born in Leipzig.'

Pollard emitted a long, reflective whistle. It *was* Grey Eyes. He looked a bit younger and his hair was neatly trimmed but there was the same scar in the middle of his eyebrow, the same jutting cheekbones and determined mouth.

Captain Carl von Eisner.

Von. Same as Baron *von* Richtofen. *Von* meant he was an aristocrat, like an Honourable in England. A somebody. With an Iron Cross First Class. Personally presented by Hitler.

Christ almighty.

It hardly seemed believable. Yet it was, wasn't it? He looked again to make sure.

Yes, the man *was* Grey Eyes.

A deserter. No wonder he didn't want to call the bobbies.

What would they do to him if they caught him, an officer and a *von*? Summary execution out there in the snow, with Trude looking on?

Pollard shook his head. If Grey Eyes – von Eisner – wasn't such a prickly sod you could almost feel sorry for him. He was utterly and completely up the creek without any oars, and no mistake. What would make a bloke like that desert? What would make Woods-Bassett do a bunk? Their sort just *didn't*.

A search through the other magazines revealed no more pictures of Grey Eyes. Pollard wondered why a copy of the magazine photograph wasn't prominently displayed in the house with all the other family pictures. If I got a medal from King George, he thought, Mum would have enlargements of the snaps all over the place, even in the lav probably. But perhaps, under the circumstances, Grey Eyes was too ashamed to display it. Then something occurred to Pollard. One individual was conspicuously absent from all those family pictures on the mantelpiece: Grey Eyes himself.

Odd, that.

*   *   *

The key turned. Grey Eyes beckoned from the doorway.

Suddenly Pollard realized why his hair was so lumpy.

He couldn't go to the barber. He daren't leave the house, so Trude had to cut his hair.

Grey Eyes said, 'Come, Sergeant. I think your comrade is worse.'

As Pollard hurried downstairs he heard Woods-Bassett's breathing; it was harsh and laboured, punctuated by violent coughing.

Christ, Pollard thought, he's going to die.

Trude stood beside the pilot; she looked up as Pollard approached.

Automatically Pollard asked Woods-Bassett how he was feeling; the skipper showed no sign of hearing the question.

Sick at heart, Pollard sat down. He gazed bitterly at Grey Eyes. Stupid sod, he had caused all this.

'It is quite obvious,' Grey Eyes said, 'that the Squadron Leader's condition is deteriorating. Therefore I have come to a decision.'

Pollard's heart missed a beat.

'It is clear that he must receive medical attention immediately.'

Pollard brightened. 'You're right there, mate.' That, he

added silently, is what I've been bloody well telling you all along, you square-head git.

'I think it can be accomplished without too many complications,' said Grey Eyes in his deliberate way. 'But I shall need your cooperation, Sergeant.'

'OK.'

Grey Eyes said, 'We shall arrange for the police to come and arrest the Squadron Leader. In that way I trust that he will receive adequate medical attention without delay.'

Pollard nodded. 'OK,' he said again. 'What about me?'

'You will remain here.'

'All right,' said Pollard. He wasn't sure whether he was glad or sorry.

'If we all do our parts properly, I believe it can be accomplished.'

'I understand,' said Pollard. 'Thanks very much, sir.'

Grey Eyes ignored that. 'What we will do,' he said, 'is to make it look as if the Squadron Leader has just broken into the house, alone.'

'I see.'

'My wife will telephone the police. She will say that she has just found the man. They will come and take him away.'

'Yes sir.'

'You and I will keep out of sight, Sergeant.'

'Right.'

'For this purpose we must get him up and put on the clothes that he was wearing when the two of you arrived.'

Pollard glanced at the pilot. Unshaven, dishevelled, the poor sod looked as if he'd been thrashing about in the forest for a couple of weeks. 'He won't be able to tell them anything about this house,' he assured Grey Eyes. 'He's been half out of his mind the whole time.'

'I trust you are right.'

'I am right. Honest.'

'We will see.' Grey Eyes gave a curt little sigh. He massaged his jaw. He seemed to be going over his plans, ensuring that he had forgotten nothing. 'I can rely on your cooperation, Sergeant.' It was more a statement than a question.

'Yes, sir. I'll do whatever you say.'

'Good.'

'When do we do it?'

'At once. There is no time to waste. My wife will telephone the police as soon as we have made your comrade ready.'

Woods-Bassett was hardly aware of what was being done. His eyes would open and he would mutter incomprehensible sounds, his hands clutching at air, then releasing it, the fingers thrusting out at awkward angles as if suddenly paralysed.

Pollard kept talking to him, soothing him, telling him that everything was going to be all right now, that soon he would be in a proper hospital bed with doctors and nurses looking after him, that in a little while he would be himself again.

Trude brought the pilot's flying gear and boots, battered and scarred mementoes of the long trek in the snow. Pollard thought of Meade. Had anyone come across his body yet? Hell of a way for a bloke to end up, lying alone in the snow. With bare feet.

It was an awkward, tedious business getting Woods-Bassett into his clothes; he kept slithering out of sleeves and legs and slumping back onto the couch, in an oddly liquid way. He had to be heaved back into position and propped up like some hefty but poorly balanced doll while the work went on.

Pollard was perspiring freely, but at last it was done.

Woods-Bassett lay back, arms flung apart, head rolling from side to side.

On an impulse, Pollard felt for the string of the pilot's dog-discs; he broke it and slipped a disc into his pocket. Evidence for the prosecution in case Woods-Bassett simply disappeared.

'It's going to be all right, mate,' he said quietly, patting the man's clammy hands.

The two Germans were pacing about in the front room, pointing, gesticulating. They were rehearsing their stories. It went on for ten minutes. Then they seemed to be satisfied. It would work. It had to work.

Grey Eyes went into the scullery.

'Your Squadron Leader crawls on his hands and knees from the forest. He finds the back door unlocked. He crawls inside and collapses here. It is feasible, yes?'

'Yes,' said Pollard.

'You would believe the story, Sergeant?'

'Yes sir.'

'Then you would be an idiot, Sergeant.'

'Sir?'

'You will observe that the sun is shining. There has been no snow for the last twelve hours. How do you suppose your Squadron Leader arrived at the house? Did he fly and land at the back door like an eagle? Tracks, Sergeant! He would make tracks in the snow, would he not?'

Pollard nodded, reddening. 'Sorry.'

'Do you think that he would have walked from the forest to the house?'

'No sir. He was too ill. He would have crawled.'

'I agree, Sergeant. You are correct. Now our problem is to produce the marks of a man crawling from the forest to the house.'

'I'll do it, sir.'

'Thank you, Sergeant.'

'S'all right.'

'How do you propose to make these marks?'

'I'll just walk over there and then turn around and get down on my knees . . .' Pollard clutched his jaw as if to make it stop talking. 'The trouble is, there'll be footprints going out as well as coming back.'

'Very good, Sergeant. We need one set of prints only, do we not?'

'Yes, sir. You're dead right.'

'What is your suggestion?'

Pollard thought. He never had been any good at puzzles. 'Is there some way we can get out and go around and . . .'

'Not without creating tracks in the snow.'

'No, I suppose not.' He scratched his head. 'Then I don't see how we can do it.'

'There is a very simple way,' said Grey Eyes in the infuriating manner of teachers, parents, officers and all others who possess answers. 'I am surprised it does not occur to you, Sergeant.'

I'm not surprised, Pollard thought.

Grey Eyes said, 'You must crawl *backwards*, Sergeant. Then, when you have reached the forest, you must simply return, being careful to place your hands and feet in the marks you have already made. In this case I don't think it will matter very much if the marks are smeared. In his condition, I believe the Squadron Leader would have made a rather untidy path through the snow.'

Pollard had to nod in admiration.

'Very clever, sir. I've got to hand it to you.'

Grey Eyes shrugged. It was nothing; an elementary solution to a minor problem.

*   *   *

When Pollard returned from making tracks in the snow, he helped Grey Eyes to hoist Woods-Bassett to his feet and half led, half dragged him to the scullery behind the kitchen. The pilot muttered, sweat streaming down his waxen cheeks. Pollard kept apologizing silently. It was a hell of a way to treat a patient. He was sorry, but there was nothing else to be done, he did see that, didn't he?

They put him against one wall. At first he was propped up by the wall, but he slid sideways and fell asleep, arms thrown forward as if he was preparing to jump.

Grey Eyes regarded the back door and Woods-Bassett; he moved his limbs so that he was lying at an angle to the door.

Pollard was impressed. The sod was thorough; you had to give him that. The scullery looked precisely as if it had been invaded by a sick, weak man who had crawled halfway across the floor and had then passed out.

Grey Eyes busied himself with the latch of the back door, then he scattered handfuls of snow on the floor, and on Woods-Bassett's boots and uniform. The snow quickly melted. He studied the scene critically, like a stage director, biting at his lower lip, moving a chair here, a table there. At last he nodded, satisfied. He said something to Trude in German. It was time. It had to be done. She smiled bravely, bracing her shoulders. She was ready.

'*So*,' he muttered.

Pollard knelt beside Woods-Bassett. The pilot opened his eyes for a moment; he gazed at Pollard without apparent recognition. Another bout of coughing racked his fevered frame.

'Sorry about all this,' Pollard told him. 'Bloody poor do, stretching you out on the floor, in your condition. Don't like to do it. But it's all for the best. They'll have you tucked up in a nice warm hospital in no time. Chin up.'

A hand touched his shoulder. Grey Eyes, impassive as ever, stood over him.

'It is time,' he said, matter-of-factly, as if he was talking about catching a bus. Trude stood in the front room, her hands clasped in front of her.

Pollard cleared his suddenly dry throat.

Grey Eyes studied the scullery once more. Then he beckoned. 'Come with me, Sergeant.'

One last glance at the hapless Woods-Bassett, then he hurried past Trude, smiling briefly, vaguely, at her, then through the front room and up the stairs. At the top, Grey Eyes turned.

'What we will do, Sergeant, is to climb up into the roof. You see the trap door?'

'Yes sir.' Obediently.

'That is the way into the roof. That is where we will hide. We will not make any noise, is that clear?'

'Yes sir.'

'Very well.' He turned to Trude and said a few words in German. The odd thing was, he suddenly seemed more interested in life; there was an alertness about him now; he had an immediate, engrossing challenge, a purpose.

'She will ring the police.'

Pollard gulped as he watched Trude pick up the telephone. The conversation took only a few moments, after which she replaced the receiver, with exaggerated care, as if she was afraid the thing might give her an electric shock.

'*Sie kommen. Sie werden in zehn Minuten hier sein.*'

Grey Eyes acknowledged the message, briskly, as he must have acknowledged messages on the French battlefields.

'Our friends will be here in ten minutes,' he told Pollard.

'OK.' Voice a bit croaky.

'Come.'

Grey Eyes placed a chair directly beneath the trap door. With the assurance of someone who has rehearsed the action many times, he stood on the chair, reached up and opened the trap door; then swung himself easily up into the aperture.

'It's quite simple, Sergeant. Step up on the back of the chair and then you can grasp the ledge. I will see that you don't fall.'

When Pollard had clambered up into the roof, Grey Eyes said something to Trude below. She took the chair and put it back into one of the bedrooms.

'*Wiedersehen, Liebling!*'

Grey Eyes closed the trap door. He took a torch from a ledge on one of the roof trusses and switched it on, projecting a powerful beam of light among the dusty beams.

'So.' He wiped dust from his hands. 'We will go now to the other side. You will follow me.'

'All right,' said Pollard without enthusiasm. The air was heavy and dry with dust. It seemed to cake in his nostrils and lungs.

'Be careful. Walk only on the beam.'

Gingerly Pollard followed, shuddering as the beam creaked under their weight. Grey Eyes stopped and crawled on all fours into a dark corner where several large beams met, forming a deep pocket.

'We can hide here,' said Grey Eyes. 'If we crouch low behind these beams we cannot be seen from the trap door. I know. I have tested it.'

'Yes sir.'

'I doubt that they will explore the whole attic, but it is possible.' He placed the Luger on the beam before him. 'You will be absolutely quiet while the police are here.'

'Yes sir.'

Grey Eyes nodded. '*Gut.*'

Privately, Pollard shook his head in wonderment at life. Who the hell arranged things? How did he manage to get himself in this predicament? How was he ever going to get himself *out*?

He glanced at the German, crouched tense ready to spring. A strange contradictory character: threatens to bump you off then does this, for an enemy.

Pollard said, 'I appreciate what you're doing for Mr Woods-Bassett.'

Grey Eyes dismissed the comment with a flick of his head.

'I appreciate it anyway,' said Pollard. 'You're taking a hell of a risk for him.'

'It is necessary,' said Grey Eyes simply.

Then they heard Trude's voice. Urgent, harsh with anxiety. 'What . . .?'

Grey Eyes scrambled to his feet and hurried back along the dusty beam to the trap door. He exchanged a few words with Trude, then closed the trap door again.

'Damn it!'

'What's wrong?'

'We forgot this thing!'

It was Woods-Bassett's battle-dress blouse, complete with badges of rank, pilot's wings and gongs. Pollard shuddered. When they had fastened Woods-Bassett back into his flying clothes, they had forgotten the blouse. Completely, utterly.

'There's no time to put it on him now.'

'Never mind,' said Pollard. 'Aircrew types often fly without their jackets.'

'Yes?'

'Sometimes,' he said, not very convincingly.

Grey Eyes clicked his tongue in annoyance. A stupid mistake, inexcusable.

Pollard wiped his brow. But he didn't finish. His arm stopped in the middle of the movement as if suddenly frozen.

There was the sound of a motor.

8

The raps on the door were brisk and authoritative. A moment's silence, then Trude could be heard crossing the hall, opening the door. The sound of the wind swept through the house. Then they came streaming in, dozens of them by the thud of their boots and the clattering of their rifles. Steel helmets, fixed bayonets, eager to get at the hated enemy. Involuntarily Pollard closed his eyes and clamped his hands over his mouth, scared to death of the men below and doubting his ability to remain quiet and still. Everything was all upside down. He *wanted* to be captured! Being captured would be a bloody picnic after being a prisoner in this loony bin. He just wanted a bit of peace and quiet; it wasn't too much to ask, was it . . .

More orders, loud and harsh. Boots thumped about the house; doors opened and slammed; voices seemed to come from every corner of the place.

'They've brought the army,' Grey Eyes whispered. 'They must think him dangerous!'

The notion seemed to amuse him.

Pollard stared. There was nothing to say, nothing to do but wait and hope. But he wasn't sure what to hope for.

Trude was replying to a man's questions. A rude sod, by the sound of him. He seemed to be blaming Trude for something. She answered in the clipped, angry way of people who resent government-backed bullies.

Grey Eyes nodded, as if approving of her conduct.

Pollard swallowed. It was maddening, not knowing what they were saying. The talk was just so much mumbo-jumbo – and yet it was incredibly important, therefore he found himself trying to understand, straining to make some sense of the sounds, all to no avail. He wanted to ask Grey Eyes, but he daren't make a sound.

Suddenly there was a sound behind them.

The trap door! Someone was pushing at it, trying to open it.

Heart thumping, Pollard flattened himself against the beam. God, should he jump up, hands held high? If he didn't he was liable to be cornered, then skewered on a bayonet. His flesh crawled at the thought; every nerve and muscle tightened within him; he lay there, rigid with terror.

Grey Eyes' voice was little more than a breath.

'Not a sound, Sergeant.'

Pollard nodded, jerkily, several times.

An untidy clatter. The trap door opened. Voices. A grunt of exertion. Pollard pictured burly German soldiers heaving themselves up into the attic, rifles slung across shoulders.

He could hear them, breathing heavily after their exertions, muttering as they peered around the dusty attic.

'*Verdammt noch mal – hier ist nichts als Staub!*'

'*Lass uns abhauen.*'

'*Hilf mir 'runter.*'

'*Gut. Komm jetzt.*'

They thumped and clattered their way out of the attic; the trap door slammed, sending shivers through the wooden beams.

Grey Eyes raised a cautioning hand. No movement yet. Wait. Be patient.

Pollard's heart bumped against his ribs. He clenched his fist until his arms trembled. Blimey, he was going to have a heart attack! He was! He could feel it!

Below, heavy boots banged their way down the stairs; the last orders were bellowed, repeated, travelling from officer to sergeant, from sergeant to corporal, from corporal to private. Pollard wondered about Woods-Bassett. Were they taking him away now? Would he recover? Perhaps, after the war, he would bump into the skipper on Oxford Street. What a meeting that would be! Cause enough for a pint or two. Pollard found himself shrugging modestly. It was nothing, anyone would have done it, given the same circumstances . . . piece of cake, old boy.

Trude could be heard talking to the raspy-voiced sod, the officer probably. Officious bastard by the sound of him, puffed up by his own importance.

The door slammed.

Grey Eyes stirred. Carefully he raised himself onto one elbow.

'*So*,' he murmured, as if closing the file on the job.

Pollard breathed again. He felt weak. Fighting tension was as bad as having a couple of rounds with the PT instructor.

'Are you *sure* you haven't got any smokes hidden away somewhere?'

Grey Eyes shook his head.

They heard the truck rumble into life. Squeaking and groaning, it pulled away. Only the wind disturbed the silence.

Then Trude's light step approached. She sounded buoyant with relief.

'*Es ist schon gut. Sie sind weg.*'

Grey Eyes' nod was matter-of-fact.

'Our friends have departed. Let us hope they don't return.'

*   *   *

They sat at the kitchen table. They had shared an ordeal and it had created a kind of bond between them.

Pollard said, 'You did a very brave thing for Mr Woods-Bassett.'

Trude said nothing. She was calm, too calm. Her lips were tightly compressed and her shoulders were rigid.

Shrugging, Grey Eyes said, 'He would have died if we had left him.'

'I know,' said Pollard. 'But you didn't have to do anything. That's the point.'

'It is to be hoped that he will recover.' Grey Eyes pressed his hands over his forehead, deflated, it seemed, now that the excitement was over. 'It is also to be hoped that he doesn't talk about this house.'

'He won't,' Pollard assured him. 'He didn't know where he was. When we got here he was delirious. Thought we were in Belgium, poor sod.'

Trude nodded in a jerky, mechanical way, as if responding for the sake of courtesy rather than because she believed in what was being said.

'I think,' said Grey Eyes, 'that we will find out soon

enough how much the Squadron Leader knew about this house.'

There was a moment's silence.

Pollard placed his two hands flat on the table and stared at them. 'I know who you are,' he said.

The German didn't say anything for a moment. Then he looked up. 'And who do you think I am?'

Pollard had to clear his throat. 'Your name's Carl von Eisner and you're a Captain, at least you were in 1940.'

Startled, Trude started to say something in German. Still looking at Pollard, Grey Eyes raised a hand; she lapsed into silence.

'And what makes you believe this, Sergeant?'

'I saw your picture in a magazine.'

'What magazine?'

'I forget the name, but it was one of the lot you let me have to read. I can find it again.'

'Don't trouble, Sergeant.' Grey Eyes spoke quietly, almost disinterestedly. 'It is of no consequence. You are mistaken.'

'I don't think so,' said Pollard. 'You were getting the Iron Cross. From Hitler.'

Grey Eyes shook his head. 'You are wrong.'

'It wasn't you?'

'Of course not. I do not have the Iron Cross. I am not a soldier. I am a civilian. And I intend to remain a civilian. That is why I avoid the police; that is why I did not wish them to come to this house.'

'And your name isn't Carl von Eisner?'

'No.'

'Sorry,' said Pollard.

'You are satisfied, Sergeant?'

Pollard took a deep breath. 'No sir, I'm not.'

'You still think I am this Carl von Eisner?'

'That's right.'

'But if I was in the army and a holder of the Iron Cross would I not be with my regiment instead of here?'

'Perhaps you've had enough of it.'

'Had enough? What do you mean? I ran away?'

'I don't mean exactly that, sir.'

'Then what exactly do you mean, Sergeant?'

'Well . . .' He groped for the right words. 'Sometimes a man wants to do something but . . . well, his nerves won't let him.'

'Nerves? You think I had a breakdown?'

'I don't know, sir.'

'You presume a great deal, Sergeant.'

'I suppose I do, sir. But I don't really care about that. All I want to say is that I know it was a hell of a risk for you to take for, well, an *enemy*. Because that's what Mr Woods-Bassett and I are; we're enemies. And I'm sorry we came along and buggered things up for you. But I'm sure it'll be all right now. Mr Woods-Bassett won't tell them anything about you because he doesn't know anything.'

Trude said, 'What do you know about Carl von Eisner?'

Pollard shrugged. 'Just what it said in the magazine: that he was a tank commander and that he did a good job in France and so Adolf gave him an Iron Cross.'

'That is all?'

'That's all it said, at least all I could sort out.'

She spoke to Grey Eyes in German – the name 'Hitler' cropped up several times. She started to sob in the middle of it; for a moment there was a note of hysteria but she quickly controlled herself.

Grey Eyes rose and stood behind her; he took her shoulders in his powerful hands; her head lolled to one side and rested against his arm. She closed her eyes; it was as if she was drawing strength from him.

Then she opened her eyes.

She said, 'He is Carl von Eisner. And he is a great man. He is a patriot. He attempted to kill Hitler so that Germany could raise its head again in the world.'

She spoke the words with pride and a kind of joy.

For a moment it didn't sink in. Pollard stared at her. Was she delirious? Was he hearing things properly? He opened his mouth to speak, but Trude and Grey Eyes – von Eisner – were already talking again in German. Curiously, it was a low-pitched conversation; they might have been discussing the price of beetroots or cabbage.

Then Eisner turned and crossed the room, to gaze out of the window.

'I am glad,' Trude told Pollard, 'that I have said this to you. I cannot tell you how much I admire this man. I am happy that someone knows now.'

Pollard gaped.

Hitler? *The* Hitler?

'You mean . . . the bomb in the conference room? Back in the summer?'

She nodded.

'Christ almighty,' breathed Pollard. He didn't know what to say. It was fantastic. He mumbled, 'Pity it didn't . . . er, *work*. Hell of a pity. Have you been here since then?'

Trude nodded. 'Five months almost.'

Pollard said, 'I won't tell anyone. You can count on me. Honest. I mean, I think it's bloody marvellous that you at least . . . well, *tried*.'

'You're very kind,' said Grey Eyes heavily.

'And they've been looking for you ever since?'

'Of course.'

'Blimey.'

'It has been a difficult time,' said Trude. 'But I tell myself that one day Carl will be known as a great hero by every German.'

Eisner exclaimed in German. He was evidently tired of this topic of conversation.

Pollard wiped his brow. He remembered reading the story in the paper. Everyone talked about it at the time. Shaking their heads and saying things about old Adolf having the luck of the devil himself. An item of fleeting interest, to be forgotten quickly in the welter of news pouring in from France and Russia. Old Adolf got away with it that time but it wouldn't be long before he finally got his lot . . .

'I think that we can rely upon you,' said Trude.

'Of course you can. No question about it.'

'You are the only person in the world who knows where we are.'

'I understand.'

'If you did tell anybody, it would mean certain death . . . for us.'

'I know that,' said Pollard. 'You don't have to say that to me. I wouldn't ever split on you. I've never even seen either of you. Wouldn't recognize you if I bumped into you. Honest. Perfect strangers, the two of you.'

Trude smiled, a wry sad smile. 'Thank you,' she said.

Pollard thought of the *News of the World*. 'But you won't mind if I tell anyone after the war, will you? I mean, it won't matter then, will it?'

Grey Eyes – von Eisner – turned.

'No, Sergeant, after the war it will not matter at all.'

* * *

The British sergeant now accords me an almost ludicrous degree of respect. He keeps telling me that he doesn't know what to say; but he still manages to keep talking for most of his waking hours. He is a tiresome individual, a perky study in irritating mannerisms, ill-educated and totally lacking in finesse. And yet the man – boy, really – possesses a dogged, persistent courage and loyalty that is commendable.

I lock him in the bedroom. He thanks me as if I am doing him a favour. Then, through the door, he informs me that it was a hell of a good show. He might have been commenting on the performance of his local football team. In his eyes I have been elevated to the rank of ally; he seems convinced that we are now on the same side. No doubt he wonders why I lock him up.

Trude waits downstairs. She is contrite. The apologies tumble out. She realizes that she shouldn't have told the British sergeant the truth, she doesn't know what came over her. It was wrong, terribly wrong, she says, but suddenly she found herself talking, revealing the truth – *glorying* in it, she says.

Secrets imprisoned so long seem to generate a kind of spontaneous combustion; they have to escape.

'You did no harm,' I tell her. 'Don't concern yourself.'

'He can be relied upon,' she says, her eyes still pleading for forgiveness. I know her so well, this splendid woman; she longs to be held tightly and comforted. I take her hand and manage a smile. I sit down. I fear that our flimsy structure of security is finally disintegrating. Soon the jackals will be upon me. And upon Trude.

Never has the house seemed cosier and more inviting. I have come to love this place. It has been a haven for an incredibly long time, far longer than I ever imagined, even in my wildest dreams. When we arrived here, I thought that we would stay a few days, a week or two at the most, lying low until it might be possible to move elsewhere. But we stayed. Weeks became months. Almost half a year. No one came near the place. Apparently the human race had forgotten our existence. Then the sergeant and his pilot arrived.

Now? I fear that the deadly process of suspicion has been set in motion. Police and the army know about this house. Officious, inquisitive bureaucrats will begin to wonder why an attractive young woman lives alone deep in the forest. Curious. Worthy of investigation. A report must be prepared. Name of the female in question? Trude Müller. Married? Widow. Husband, Lieutenant Albert Müller, killed near Leningrad in 1942. Employment record of subject? Until the middle of 1944 the Müller woman was an administrative assistant in the War Office on the Bendlerstrasse in Berlin. Subject resigned in July 1944, came directly to this secluded house and took up residence. Owner of the property? Her uncle, Johann Esser, an artist of some reputation. Died 1943. No family . . .

And doubtless those tireless officials would want to know why the Müller woman would suddenly leave a responsible, important position, to live alone in the country. To escape the bombing? Or to escape something else? And then how long would it take them to unearth the interesting intelligence that when in Berlin she had upon occasion been seen in the company of none other than Colonel Carl von Eisner, plotter, traitor?

'Some *schnapps*, Carl?'

Why not? There is little point now in hoarding the stuff. I accept the glass and drain it. The *schnapps* warms me, almost in spite of myself.

Trude assures me that everything will be all right.

'Of course,' I say, as if I agree.

Women seem convinced that all they have to do is believe with sufficient intensity in order to make their dreams come true.

What to do now? Sit here and hope that no questions will be asked? And hope that the retreating *Wehrmacht* will spare this place, leaving us to await the arrival of the Allies?

Or should I try to reach the Allied lines and surrender?

'I claim special treatment because my name is Carl von Eisner and I was one of the plotters against Hitler. If you place me with the other officer prisoners, I fear that I will almost certainly be murdered by zealous Nazis.'

A sorry end for a career that used to be described as 'brilliant' and 'full of promise'.

Am I the only surviving conspirator? Stauffenberg, Beck, Goerdeler, Stieff, Olbricht, Quirnheim, Haeften, Hoepner and the others, God only knows how many of them. Earnest, gallant men. But they were better at dreaming than plotting, better at talking than acting. They were amateurs when what was needed was totally ruthless professionals. Endlessly, Goerdeler had discussed the Germany that would be *afterwards*. He organized the cabinets for the new German governments; he assessed the position of the opposition parties, the labour unions, the press, the army. But the killing and the takeover were what mattered immediately. And somehow the vital decisions were never taken, the essential plans were never completed. Vaguely, everyone seemed to feel that if Hitler was killed the rest would all fall magically into place.

The man had to die – the man to whom every officer had sworn a sacred oath of loyalty, the fifty-five-year-old man with an extraordinary talent for survival, the man who had already foiled several assassination attempts by his habit of continually altering his schedules, seldom arriving when and where he was expected, frequently cancelling appearances altogether. Early in 1943 he visited the Russian front. This time, the conspirators thought, he will not escape. They secreted a bomb on the Junkers 52 taking Hitler back to Germany; it was disguised as a bottle of Cointreau, a gift, it was explained, for General Stieff. The weapon simply failed to explode. Hitler landed safely. Later in the year Stauffenberg decided to kill

Hitler at a military conference. He placed a bomb in his brief-case; he went to the conference, but Hitler didn't. The man's luck was awesome. But at Rastenburg, in July 1944, it seemed that nothing could go wrong. Again Stauffenberg carried time bombs in his briefcase: two of them, each weighing about two pounds. The mechanism was elementary, but reliable. In order to activate the bombs, a small glass capsule containing acid had to be broken; the acid would eat through the wire holding the firing pin away from the percussion cap. The acid would work in complete silence, taking precisely ten minutes. The pin would then connect with the percussion cap, detonating the hexite. An admirable device, perfect for the mission in hand. Stauffenberg – handsome, idealistic Stauffenberg – forgot nothing; he even packed a pair of rubber-handled pliers with which to break the capsule of acid. There would be no mistake this time.

It all went so incredibly smoothly. The day was cloudless, the still air sweet with the scent of pines from the forest. Stauffenberg flew to the Wolf's Lair from Rangsdorf Airfield near Berlin. On his way to the *Lagerbaracke* where the conference was taking place, he went to the lavatory; there he broke the glass capsule and closed the briefcase again. The bomb was primed. It would explode in exactly ten minutes. When Stauffenberg entered the conference room Hitler was listening to General Heusinger, Deputy Chief of the General Staff. Stauffenberg was informed that he would be required to present his report as soon as Heusinger had finished.

Two dozen men, senior officers, adjutants and stenographers, sat at the eighteen-foot-long table which was supported by two massive oak slabs. Stauffenberg placed the briefcase on the floor, beneath the table, close to the right-hand corner. No one observed the action. The conference continued while the acid silently but diligently ate its way through the wire. In a few minutes it would complete its work; the explosion would blow Hitler in half. At that instant a new era would commence for Germany and for the world. Stauffenberg slipped out of the conference room, saying that he had to make a telephone call. He was elated. Surely nothing could go wrong now. But while Stauffenberg was out,

Heusinger's Chief of Staff, a colonel named Brandt, touched the case with his foot. It was in his way. He reached beneath the table, gripped the case and moved it. The distance was insignificant, a foot or two, no more. But Brandt had pushed the case to the other side of the oak table support, unknowingly finding a shield for his *Führer*.

Heusinger was droning on about the Russians advancing west of the Duna and of the advisability of withdrawal by the army group at Lake Peipus.

And then the room erupted. Walls and ceiling disintegrated. The huge table went spinning into the air. The scorching air was filled with wood splinters and concrete shrapnel. Men were torn apart; limbs hurtled in every direction; hair burst into flames; chests collapsed like crushed eggs. And yet, incredibly, some men were unharmed. Hitler suffered only cracked eardrums, a few minor burns and shock.

He had escaped again.

The Gestapo moved, mercilessly. In a few hours it was over; it had all been for nothing, a monstrous waste of time and effort and, ultimately, lives.

And what had it achieved other than to provide Hitler with further proof of his immortality? Providence was again protecting him so that he might continue his divine mission for the Fatherland.

Trude is holding the bottle, smiling in her slightly hesitant way.

'A little more, Carl?'

I smile back at her. 'A lot more,' I tell her.

9

The firm, strong hand shook Pollard back to wakefulness.

'Wake up, Sergeant! They're back!'

Pollard blinked the sleep out of his eyes. His confused senses absorbed the fact that it was early morning, barely light yet; and there was the sound of a motor vehicle approaching.

With a single motion, Eisner ripped the bedclothes off the bed.

He rapped out orders. 'Collect your things and go up into the attic. And hurry. Don't leave anything in this room. Do you understand?'

Dazed, frightened, Pollard nodded as he scrambled off the bed. The floor was cold to his bare feet.

'Be certain that you take everything,' Eisner told him, turning the mattress upside down. He hurried out, the bedclothes bundled in his arms.

Pollard nodded. Suddenly the room looked empty and forlorn. He picked up his clothes as the truck stopped, as men jumped out. Someone yelled something.

Pollard bit his lip. Hard.

'Quick, man!'

Eisner was in the doorway, beckoning. Pollard followed him, into the corridor where the chair was waiting beneath the open trap door. In a moment they were in the attic; Trude appeared to remove the chair and to give them a last wave as they fastened the trap door in position.

An instant later came the banging on the front door.

Eisner and Pollard made their way across the roof structure.

Eisner had thrown the bedclothes into their hiding place in the corner of the attic.

'The bedclothes were warm,' Eisner said with a shrug. 'Difficult to explain, no?'

Pollard nodded unhappily. Difficult to explain, yes. Fear was a chilly hand that roamed his innards, pulling here, pushing there. How much could a bloke be expected to take? One more shock to his system and he would be sick, there and then. Now he knew how rats felt when they were backed into corners. Already the attic seemed to be closing in, the great beams creating a tomb for him. The Jerries were sure to find him this time. They knew the truth; they were coming back to do the job properly. Had Woods-Bassett babbled something incriminating in his delirium? Had the poor sod seen more than they thought he had? Curtains! It was then that he realized that he was in his underclothes. He wasn't wearing uniform! Spy! His bare legs looked ridiculously thin and white in the gloom. As if they already belonged to a corpse. Hastily he wriggled into his battle-dress blouse and pulled on his trousers.

More rapping below, louder, even more officious.

Eisner cocked the Luger.

Trude could be heard, walking to the front door. She opened it.

Voices: hers, controlled yet cool. His, harsh, bully-boy.

Eisner whispered, 'He says they must search the house again. They think there may be more Allied airmen hiding in the area.'

Pollard nodded, closing his eyes, squeezing them shut as he huddled down behind the massive beam.

'Here they come.'

The house reverberated with the banging of boots and the rattling of equipment.

This time they'll get us, Pollard thought bleakly. The dusty blackness seemed to curl about him like soft lace curtains. In a few moments he'd know. One way or the other. Not much more waiting, wondering, hoping, praying. All over soon.

Trude was almost shouting at the man. The words were incomprehensible to Pollard but the tone was unmistakable. Damn him for his intrusion! How dare he come marching into the house! She would have the law on him! Number eight. Mrs Delaney. Palsied old fist shaking at the bailiff. She had lived in the place for fifty years; in some weird way she had become convinced that it belonged to her; there was no need for her to pay rent . . .

What the hell ever happened to Mrs Delaney?

Pollard tried to remember, forcing his mind back to those days when he was a child and when there was no real world outside the street. Mrs Delaney had been good for a chuckle. No one had given the poor thing a thought afterwards.

Was this his punishment?

Boots thudded on the stairs immediately beneath him. They sounded like drum beats. A military tattoo. He clutched his throat. It was burning: dry, horribly dry. He swallowed, almost choking in the process. Ron Pollard, you are condemned to die here in this great coffin, smothered by dust!

A noise very close. Muffled voices. Fumblings. He froze. The bastards were going to come up into the attic again! They would search the place properly! There'd be no escape!

'Let us be extremely quiet,' Eisner breathed. He sounded quite calm.

Pollard clamped a hand over his mouth. He refused absolutely to give in to the desire to clear his throat. No, throat, you'll have to wait a bit. You've got to put up with it. It won't kill you, having to wait; it's not the end of the bloody world just because you can't cough. And it may *feel* as if the throat is filling up with phlegm and vomit and all kinds of other lovely things but it isn't. It's your silly mind. Imagining it. So if the mind can imagine it, it can also *un*imagine it . . .

He heard the Jerries, grunting as they shoved at the trap door. Someone cursed. Then with a cracking sound, the trap door opened. It banged against a roof beam.

Pollard felt the tremor.

More grunting and heavy breathing as the soldiers pulled themselves up through the narrow opening. The beams creaked and groaned under their weight.

Shockingly, a torch beam broke the gloom; it traversed the attic, glancing off the dusty beams, darting into dark corners.

To Pollard it looked as if the entire attic was suddenly illuminated. The light stung his eyes as it swept over him. He held his breath and squeezed his eyes shut again. He didn't want to see. He prayed. He was sorry he hadn't prayed for so long but it was simply forgetfulness, not because he didn't *believe* . . .

The soldiers were moving about the attic. All they had to do was to come to one corner and look *down* into the corner. In a moment they'd do it. They had to. It was their job.

The cold hand tightened on his stomach, squeezing it, contorting it.

That was it, then. In a couple of seconds they'd come this way. They'd clamber over the beams and shine their torches and that would be that for ever and ever, amen . . .

Don't shoot, though, Pollard silently begged the soldiers. Give me a chance to surrender. That's all I want to do, surrender. I don't have a gun. Not me. This man does, but I don't. Honest . . .

There was a thump of a falling body. The attic shuddered and squeaked as if in pain. A man cursed. Bind, bind, bind; soldiers were the same the world over. A second man chuckled. More grunting and panting as the first man got to his feet. Pollard didn't understand a word of it, but he'd heard it all before.

Again the torch threw its light, darting about the attic, picking out the cobwebs and the caked dust. Surely the Jerries would notice the spots where the dust was disturbed; surely it was glaring, obvious as hell, just pleading to be seen, surely . . .

The light snapped off. The soldiers had had enough of the attic; one man kept sucking in air and exhaling it noisily, far more interested in his pain than in continuing the search. They called to a comrade below. Time to get down from out of this hellish place; nothing to be seen up there but dust and spiders . . . and how the hell was a man supposed to get his uniform clean after this sort of caper?

It took them an age to get out of the attic. Someone had moved the chair. Where was the damned chair? Idiot!

They didn't bother to close the trap door. Their voices floated up into the attic. Still binding.

Eisner moved at last, turning, exhaling softly. A peep over the top of the beam. All clear.

Pollard fingered his throat. Oddly enough, he no longer wanted to clear it. Mind over matter. Where the cold hand had been exploring his insides now everything seemed empty and airy, as if it had all dissolved.

'They're going,' Eisner whispered.

'Bloody lucky, that bloke tripping and falling.'

'It wasn't entirely luck,' Eisner replied softly. 'I fastened pieces of wood at strategic points along the beams. I hoped that they might discourage all but the most diligent searchers.'

They heard Trude berating the soldiers for intruding, for dirtying her clean house with their great big boots, for wasting her time and theirs looking for British airmen who weren't to be found. Why didn't they have the sense to listen to what she had told them the first time?

The door slammed.

*　　*　　*

Pollard coughed and spluttered as the *schnapps* wended its fiery way down his throat.

'Blimey,' he gasped, 'that's rough stuff to start the day on.'

Trude smiled as she sipped. 'I think we have earned it, no?'

Eisner drained his slim glass and rose. He went to the window.

'Anyone around, sir?' Pollard asked.

The German shook his head. 'But I have a strong feeling that they will come back, perhaps not to search the place again, but simply to keep it under observation. That *Leutnant* is, I believe, keenly interested in this house. He wonders. He asks himself questions. He looks for answers.'

'He is a pig,' Trude declared.

'I know the sort,' Pollard told her.

'Because he wears a uniform, he thinks he owns the earth.'

Pollard nodded understandingly. 'We've got 'em too.' He sipped his drink. Odd, how all of a sudden these two Jerries had become almost like family. He trusted them and they trusted him.

Eisner sat down. He stroked his chin as he gazed at nothing.

'I think,' he said at last, 'that it is too dangerous for us to remain here in this house.'

Trude stared. '*Was?*'

Eisner shrugged. He spoke to her in German, then he

turned to Pollard. 'I have a very strong feeling that they are asking questions about this house and about my . . .' He paused and nodded in Trude's direction. 'We are not married,' he said in a rather formal way.

'I see,' Pollard murmured. He didn't know what else to say.

'We knew each other in Berlin,' Eisner went on. 'Eventually they will succeed in unearthing that fact. Then they will realize the truth. They will come with a regiment of troops to tear this house apart.'

'I'm sorry,' said Pollard. 'It was my – our – fault. You were snug as bugs in rugs until we came along.'

Eisner didn't respond. He poured more *schnapps*, lifting his glass to Trude and then to Pollard. He downed the drink in a single gulp, turned to Trude and spoke to her in German. Pale faced, she nodded but said nothing. Eisner told Pollard: 'She will go to a cousin in Wiesbaden. She will be safer there.'

'What about you, sir?'

'I don't know.'

'Don't you have any friends or relatives?'

Eisner smiled mirthlessly. 'When you have done what I have done, you have neither friends nor relatives.'

'So what are you going to do?'

'I am not sure.'

Trude sat beside him, taking his hand in hers. He must go to Wiesbaden also. *Please!* He shook his head. No: impossible. Tears sprang to her eyes; she buried her head in his chest.

Pollard looked away, embarrassed. An awful sense of responsibility descended upon him. It was all his fault. He'd got them into this mess; wasn't there some way he could help them out of it again?

'If you can't stay here, you've got to go *somewhere*, right?'

'That, Sergeant, is obvious.'

'Well, what I mean is, you've definitely decided to leave this place.'

'Correct.'

'And you don't know of anywhere to go in Germany?'

'There is nowhere I can go.'

'All right, then, that means you've got to go somewhere *outside* of Germany.'

'A remarkable observation, Sergeant.'

Pollard persisted. 'What I'm getting at is that you and I are sort of in the same boat. We both want to get out of Germany and across to the Allied lines.'

Trude began to sob, soundlessly. Eisner spoke to her, his voice low and gentle.

Suddenly she ran out of the room, sobbing still.

Eisner stood up as if to follow her; he reached for her; then his arms dropped to his side.

'She wishes to come with me,' he said. 'But I cannot permit it. I want her to survive this.'

He sounded as if he believed only one of them had a chance.

Pollard said, 'I bet we could get through to the Allied lines.'

'We?' Eisner looked at him. 'The two of us?'

'Why not? That's what I was doing with Mr Woods-Bassett, only he wasn't in very good shape. Besides . . .' A notion had occurred to him. Barmy, of course. But . . . 'Your problem is that if you get picked up you'd be recognized, isn't that right?'

Eisner nodded. 'The Gestapo are looking for me everywhere.'

'There's one place the Gestapo wouldn't look for you,' Pollard said.

'Where's that?'

'In a POW camp.'

'What? You mean a camp for British and American prisoners?'

'Yes.'

Eisner smiled sadly, then shook his head.

'An ingenious thought, Sergeant. But there is a fundamental problem. I am a German officer.'

'I know that,' said Pollard, excitement growing with him. 'But we've got Woods-Bassett's jacket. He was about your size. It'd fit. You speak English bloody well.'

'Yes, but I would hardly pass for an Englishman.'

'No – but the RAF's full of Poles and Dutchmen and God knows what else. All sorts of 'em. I met a South African navigator who sounded a bit like you. Drank like a fish.'

'But I couldn't wear a British uniform.'

'Why not?' Suddenly the wild notion had become the only

intelligent course of action. 'Seems to me you haven't got much of a choice. If you make a dash for the front line you might make it. Good. But if you get picked up you've had it. No question about that. *Except* if they think you're an RAF type. Then you're just another airman trying to escape.'

'I couldn't possibly convince anyone that I was an Englishman, or even a Pole or Dutchman.'

'Not if you were by yourself,' Pollard agreed. 'But if you were with me, you'd stand a *chance*. And a chance is a bloody sight better than nothing.'

'Impossible!'

'Why?'

The German shook his head, 'I appreciate your concern, Sergeant, but it is out of the question.'

'The only bloody question,' Pollard responded, 'is how to get you out of the country.'

'It really doesn't matter very much. In a way I have no country now.'

'Trude thinks it matters. And I agree with her.'

Eisner said, 'It is kind of you, Sergeant. But it is impossible. I disagree with you that I would have any chance if we were picked up. Disguises would be of no value whatever. I would be spotted as an imposter immediately.'

'Why?'

'Because I know nothing of flying or of the RAF.'

'I'll brief you. Pack you full of gen.'

'Gen?'

'First lesson,' said Pollard. 'Gen is information. Air Force slang.'

Eisner rubbed his forehead with his fingertips. 'No, Sergeant, I cannot agree to this. All you will do is cause a great deal of trouble for yourself – more, perhaps than you realize.'

'I know all about that,' said Pollard. The words slipped out so easily. He heard them as if someone else was saying them. 'Fair's fair, isn't it? You took a risk for Mr Woods-Bassett; I'll take a risk for you.'

Eisner regarded him levelly. 'You are an unusual young man.'

'Just a bit weird,' said Pollard.

Eisner half smiled.

'What did you do before you became an airman?'

'I worked at the United Dairy.'

'Dairy? In a farm?'

'No. In London. United Dairy's a big company.'

'And what did you do at this big company?'

'Carried cups of tea around, mostly. Office boy, you know. Nothing much.'

'And will you return to this job after the war?'

'Dunno. Hadn't thought much about it. The first thing is to try and get through the war in one piece.'

Eisner sat back, his hands clasped behind his head.

'It's a mad scheme, Sergeant.'

'I know. But it's worth a go, isn't it?'

Eisner nodded slowly, reflectively.

He said, 'And do you think the Squadron Leader's jacket will fit me?'

*   *   *

You're bloody well potty, mate. Round the bend. Up the flue. Barmy. Do you really know what the hell you're *doing*?

I've got to do it.

Only because you bloody well babbled yourself into it. Your tongue took over. You're probably going to get *killed*, mate, shot at dawn, blindfold and all, just because you couldn't keep your bloody yap shut.

I sort of owe him something.

What do you owe him? Five quid for meals and accommodation? Give him a cheque. An IOU. Anything. But don't get any more involved in the thing. You can't afford to, mate. You're giving aid and comfort to the bleeding enemy!

Christ, no!

Christ, yes!

*   *   *

It was odd, seeing Woods-Bassett's tunic on Eisner. With the pilot's wings, gongs and rank badges, the German suddenly became another RAF type, someone to salute, an authentic hero for the girls to ogle.

Pollard suggested that he wear a white turtle-necked sweater beneath the battle-dress. 'It'll keep you warm, and it'll look right. A lot of the lads wear them on ops, especially in winter.'

'And the trousers?'

'Any dark pair will do. Your uniform trousers could have been ripped to shreds when you baled out. You had to steal a pair, from a farm house, let's say. You'd better cut all the labels off them, and your underwear too. And for God's sake don't carry any documents or letters.'

Eisner said, 'It was not my intention to do so, Sergeant.'

Pollard scratched his head. There were so many things to think of, any one of which could trip them up. 'What do you want to be, Englishman or Canadian?'

'I don't understand.'

'I've got an identity disc from our navigator. A Canadian. Meade, his name was. I've got Mr Woods-Bassett's discs too. And mine, of course. Perhaps you'd better be Meade. For one thing, he was a year or two older than Mr Woods-Bassett. And there's a French part in Canada, isn't there? They've got pretty thick accents, the blokes who come from there.'

'My accent is not French, Sergeant.'

'I know that.' He thought rapidly. 'So if we do get caught, you're going to have to be ill, like Mr Woods-Bassett was.'

'Ill?'

'Yes, you got banged up when we baled out. All right? You hurt your back. You're in agony from it. A bloke in sick bay told me once if you want to pretend to be sick, tell 'em it's your back. And squirm and groan like hell. They might think you're lying but they can't prove it. He was right, you know. I tried it once when I wanted to get an extra couple of days' leave. Worked like a charm.'

Eisner took the identity disc.

'I am Earl James Meade,' he read. 'Protestant. Born 1914. But this man was thirty years old. I am thirty-eight years.'

'Pain makes you look older,' Pollard countered. 'Look, I haven't got a big selection of those things. We've got to make do with what we have.'

Trude stood in the doorway, watching the two men, holding her hands to her cheeks. She accorded Eisner a wan smile and spoke to him in German. He considered, nodded and turned to Pollard.

'She points out that it might be best for me to be the Sergeant and you the Squadron Leader.'

Pollard stared. 'Me?'

'Yes. If we are unlucky enough to be picked up by German forces, they will, I suspect, be far more interested in asking questions of an officer than an NCO, particularly one who is injured.'

Icy fingers again. Pollard gulped. The trouble was, it made sense.

'Do you think anyone's going to believe I'm really a Squadron Leader?'

Eisner shrugged. 'I don't know. Do you?'

Pollard picked up Woods-Bassett's battle-dress blouse. He put it on. It was a little big for him, but it would do. In a mirror on the far wall, Pollard saw himself. Begonged. Bestriped. Squadron Leader Ronald Pollard, DSO, DFC and a few others for good measure.

'Blimey,' he said, 'a promotion at last.'

* * *

In a curious contradictory way it is a relief. I have cowered in this rabbit warren far too long, waiting, hoping, praying. Oddly enough, it is the longest period I have spent in one place since the beginning of the war. Now it is time to become a moving target once again.

We sit, waiting for evening. My arm is around Trude's shoulder. Her head is close to mine. I can feel the soft touch of her breath on my cheek. I want to tell her things: that she is the only reason that I try so hard to stay alive, that she is the bravest and most delightful companion that a man could wish for, that one day I will return to marry her. But we do not talk. The time seems too precious for words.

* * *

Pollard wrapped a blanket around his middle, pulled on his flying boots and fleece-lined jacket. He felt as if he was being embalmed. God, it was a hell of a thing to look forward to: another midwinter hike. But this time there would at least be warm clothes, a reasonable supply of food and a good map.

Eisner was of the opinion that the biggest hurdles would be the rivers: first the Rhine, then two of more modest proportions, the Erft and the Ruhr. He planned the routes; first they would go south to avoid Cologne, then strike out westward to the Belgium border and the front line.

Pollard shook his head in despair at the reflection in the mirror. What the hell had he got himself into?

The bloody barmy thing was, he was doing all this for someone he didn't particularly like because that someone who he didn't particularly like had done a good turn for someone else he didn't particularly like.

Where the hell was the sense in that?

His reflection couldn't answer.

10

He was in that nightmare forest again, thrusting blindly through the darkness, running the endless gauntlet of trees and bushes that tore at his clothes and jabbed at his eyes with their spiteful fingers.

Eisner strode in silence, setting the pace, checking directions from time to time with the aid of a compass and a road map.

At the first glimmer of light, they stopped and ate.

'Perhaps fifteen kilometres,' Eisner announced after consulting his map.

'I believe you,' Pollard muttered. His legs were stiff and his head throbbed with fatigue. He looked behind, half expecting to see platoons of troops in hot pursuit. But the woods were still again, wrapped in winter chill.

They made a kind of tent, fastening one of the blankets between two trees; they wrapped the other blanket around themselves and, in snug proximity, they slept.

It was early afternoon when they stirred. The weather was considerate: chilly but dry and sunny. A small animal, a squirrel perhaps, bounded through the leaves behind them. They turned, startled, Eisner reaching for his Luger.

'False alarm,' said Pollard, heart thumping.

Eisner put the pistol down. 'We must remain here until nightfall. Perhaps you would be kind enough to continue your instruction.'

Pollard sighed. It was hard work thinking up the sort of morsels of gen that Eisner should know if he was to pass even the most elementary interrogation. And it was irritating, the way Eisner expected him to cough the stuff up to order.

'Who's Harris?'

'I have no idea.'

'He's head of Bomber Command. Air Chief Marshal, I

think – anyway, a hell of a lot higher up than me. Even now. His nickname is "Butcher".'

'Harris. Good. I have it.'

'His office is in High Wycombe.'

'Where is High Wycombe?'

'Near London.' Pollard yawned. 'What's a sprog?'

'An untrained airman.'

'OK. What about a prang?'

'Ah yes. A crash, I believe.'

'Very good.' The Jerry was an apt pupil. 'What does "Going for a Burton" mean?'

'Getting killed.'

'And what about a "tour"?'

'It is so many operations.'

'How many, for a bomber boy?'

'Usually thirty, if I remember correctly.'

'Right. How many trips have you done, Sergeant Meade?'

'I don't know. Shall we say fifty?'

'No. Too many. You'd have been promoted by now. Probably commissioned – you're a Canadian, don't forget. They're as bad as the Yanks for promoting people. Better make it twenty.'

'Very well.'

'What sort of aircraft were you flying when you were shot down?'

'A Lancaster.'

'What engines?'

'Four Rolls-Royce Merlins.'

'Armament?'

'Twin Brownings in the front turret, two in the mid-upper and four in the back.'

'Crew?'

'Seven. Pilot, flight engineer, navigator, wireless operator, bomb aimer and two gunners.'

'What's your trade?'

'I'm a flight engineer.'

'How do you start a Lanc?'

Eisner winced with the effort of remembering Pollard's instructions.

'Ground/Flight switch on Ground; set the throttles and put pitch in full fine . . .' And on and on through the checklist: idle cut-off, supercharger, air intakes, radiator shutters, fuel tank selection, booster pumps, ignition . . .'

'Ten out of ten,' said Pollard admiringly. It must have been a fantastic job for Eisner to learn all that technical jargon. The trouble was, when you sat down and thought about it logically and sensibly, the whole process was probably a ruddy great waste of time and effort. How long would the Jerry last, confronted by genuine air force types? Five minutes? Five seconds was more like it. And then what? He gulped unhappily. It was all very well talking glibly about a POW camp being the safest place for the poor bugger, but was there really any hope that he would ever actually get *into* one?

They had to reach the Allied lines.

But in order to get to the Allied lines, the German lines had to be crossed. Eisner had talked about 'slipping through' as if it was a minor problem. Pollard kept remembering scenes from 'All Quiet on the Western Front': heroic soldiers dragging wounded comrades to safety across the hell of no man's land, shells bursting, machine gun bullets lacerating the air.

Hatch said, 'And you're doing all this for a bloody Jerry? You must have gone a bit funny in the noggin, chum.'

Chilling, that. It was just as if his old pilot had been standing there in the forest beside him, his big face wearing a sardonic grin. Pollard shivered. Perhaps Hatch was there. Doing a bit of haunting to while away the time.

Sod off, Hatch. I've got enough problems without you barging in.

'Pity about the house,' he said.

Eisner looked up. 'House?'

'Seems a shame just to leave it. It's a nice place.'

'A house is not important.'

'That's not what my dad says. In fact, that's about all he ever talks about. It's sort of his life, if you know what I mean.'

'His life? I don't understand.'

'Well, owning that house is the only really big thing he's ever accomplished. In five years, no, four and a half now, he'll have paid for it. It'll be his. But it's a rotten little dump, really. And it won't *really* be his because he doesn't own the land it's on. Funny, eh?'

'Very,' said Eisner.

'I suppose you had a big house when you were a nipper.'

Eisner shrugged. 'It was not so very big.'

'Servants?'

'One or two.'

'Was your father in the army?'

'Yes, my father and his father and his father before him.'

'All officers, I suppose.'

'Yes, they were officers.'

'I thought so. And you lived in Leipzig?'

'Yes, when I was a child. How did you know?'

'It said so in the magazine. Is someone living in the house now?'

'My mother, perhaps, I'm not sure. I cannot risk her safety by trying to contact her. You ask a lot of questions.'

'Sorry, sir,' Pollard said. 'I'm interested. I've never met anyone like you before. I've got cousins and uncles and lots of pals in the services – but not one an officer. Tells you something, doesn't it?'

'What does it tell you?'

'It tells you something about our places in the world.'

Eisner smiled wryly. 'Well, now that is all changed. You are the officer, I am the NCO.'

Just before dark, a pack of Typhoons came streaking by, looking for something tasty to fire their rockets at. Pollard's heart ached as he watched them disappearing westward, heading for their comfortable bases and a spot of tea and cake before supper. Lucky sods. Who the hell arranged things so that they should be up there and he should be down here?

'We will be seeing the *Autobahn* soon,' Eisner announced soon after they started marching again. 'A few kilometres beyond it we must turn west.'

'Go west, young man,' Pollard commented.

'What?'

'Never mind. Just an expression.'

They trudged on, shoulders hunched against a chilly damp wind that had developed as the sun went down. Clouds began to occupy the bleak sky. They heard the sound of traffic. Soon they were through the trees and into open country. The ground was soggy and spongy beneath their feet. They no longer had the protection of the trees. The wind lashed them.

A truck came clattering along the road, its headlights masked to mere pinpricks of light.

Cautiously they approached, crouching, like infantry going in to the attack. They had almost reached the road when the convoy materialized. It was a seemingly endless procession of trucks packed with troops and equipment; it thundered by, showering the huddled figures at the roadside with dirt and stones, setting the earth shivering beneath its awesome weight.

What'll happen now, Pollard thought, is that the RAF will decide to have a go at this convoy. Then everything will stop and all the soldiers will jump out and take cover at the side of the road and find us and we'll have one hell of a lot of explaining to do.

But, thank God, there was no attack. Finally, the last truck rumbled away to the west. Pollard sniffed. He wondered if he was getting a cold.

Eisner beckoned.

'It's safe to cross now.'

'Coming,' Pollard responded, wearily dragging himself to his feet.

They hurried across the solid roadway, then they were in open fields again. It began to rain; soon the precipitation became a mixture of ice and sleet. They were drenched and chilled, but they had to keep going, slogging on through the muddy, slippery mess.

Pollard's – Meade's – boots were beginning to deteriorate. Soft and comfortable, they had been designed for use in aircraft, not on long-distance hikes. Cracks had appeared; water seeped in to soak his chilled feet. If the Jerries don't get me, he thought, the rheumatism will.

The wind was too strong for them to make their tent. They had to wrap the blankets around their bodies.

*   *   *

Pollard awoke. It was still snowing. For a terrifying instant he half dreamed, half thought that he had died. For surely he was too incredibly, unbelievably cold to be in the land of the living. He felt solid, as if his body had become a hunk of frozen meat, something to hang up at the butcher's. His eyes seemed to crack when he opened them. He didn't attempt to move a limb, scared that it might snap and fall off. Gingerly he lowered his gaze. He could just see the shape of one gloved hand on his snow-covered chest. But he couldn't feel the thing; it might have belonged to someone else.

Then he realized why. Eisner had rolled over in his sleep and had taken the blankets with him.

Sod him! Angrily, Pollard reached out to retrieve the precious coverings. He startled Eisner into wakefulness. The German swung toward him, Luger in hand.

'*Was* . . . what is it?'

Pollard tried to tell him. The words of outrage boiled within him. But he was unable to utter them. His jaw wouldn't work. He emitted a series of strangled mumbles. Then at last he found his voice.

'You stole my bloody blanket!'

'Sorry,' said Eisner shortly.

Pollard gaped. The bastard had the temerity simply to turn over as if the subject was closed.

'I bloody nearly froze to death!'

Eisner shrugged. 'And you very nearly got a bullet in your middle. A word of advice, Sergeant: never wake a man suddenly if he has a gun.'

'Balls,' said Pollard, aggrieved. He jumped up and down. God, why didn't he have a smoke? Was it so much to ask?

Eisner watched him for a few moments. He was clearly irritated. 'Let me remind you that it is still daylight.'

'I don't care. I've got to get warm. I'm chilled to the bloody marrow!'

Eisner seemed unimpressed. 'It has been my experience that one can discipline one's senses with a little effort. Extreme cold and heat seem to lose their sting if one refuses to give in to them.'

Pollard stopped jumping. 'You forget, mate, I'm not a member of the master bleeding race!'

'Indeed,' said Eisner, nodding.

'So when I get cold I *feel* cold, through and through!'

'I'm sure you do.'

Pollard glowered. The sod was agreeing with him. It was infuriating of him.

He continued to run on the spot. His feet were beginning to tingle, telling him that they were coming back to life.

It was then that Eisner suddenly reached out, grasped his ankle and tugged him off balance. He fell with a thump in the slushy leaves.

'What the . . .'

Eisner's finger was pressed against his mouth. He pointed. Pollard froze.

The boy came trotting between the trees, trailing a piece of string, alternately chatting to himself and humming a rambling tune. He was about ten.

His small feet beat a tattoo on the sodden ground. He passed within a dozen feet of the two men, then went on his way, apparently oblivious of their presence.

'I apologize for tripping you,' Eisner murmured, his eyes following the boy as he made his way through the trees.

'Don't mention it.' Pollard brushed the damp, chilly leaves off his uniform. 'What the hell would we have done if the little bugger had seen us?'

Eisner shrugged. 'I was wondering the same thing.'

* * *

Daylight was fading. Soon it would be dark, time to be on the move again. Pollard said, 'D'you mind if I ask you something?'

'No, of course not.'

'What made you decide to . . . well, have a go at Hitler?'

Eisner smiled in his distant way. 'An odd expression, "Have a go".'

'You know what I mean.'

'Yes, I know what you mean.'

'You don't have to tell me if you'd rather not.'

'I don't object. It is ancient history now. Soon, I think, it will be completely forgotten. It deserves to be. It was a miserable failure, a farce. When I think back, I realize that it was always doomed to failure. Too many men were involved, all with their own opinions on how things should be handled. The planning and the plotting went on for ages. It is fantastic that we were not all arrested years ago. Goerdeler in particular was incredibly outspoken; he lost no opportunity to criticize Hitler. I often wondered why the Black Bastards – that is the Army's name for the Gestapo – I wondered why they didn't act. I believe now that it was because Himmler himself thought a coup likely. And, I suppose, he reasoned that it might be successful. He was being his usual two-faced self, ready to be loyal to whoever might be in control.' He turned to Pollard. 'You are a soldier. Does it shock you, the idea of a soldier attempting to assassinate his commander-in-chief, a man to whom he has sworn a sacred oath of allegiance?'

'Not when the commander-in-chief is *him*. You did the right thing.'

'You knew about Stauffenberg's attempt?'

'Yes, it was in all the papers in England. Big headlines. Everyone said it was a shame it didn't come off. What's Hitler like?'

'He is an extraordinary man,' said Eisner. 'He has an amazing personality. I can personally vouch for that fact. For some reason that I can't explain you have to listen to him; you have to absorb what he tells you. He is a sort of hypnotist. But he has power over an entire country, not just individuals; that is the terrible thing.' He sighed. 'It has for some time been obvious to anyone with the most elementary grasp of military matters that Germany has lost the war. We are steadily being overwhelmed. Defeat is inevitable. It has been inevitable for a long time. A year ago I became acquainted with a group of officers with similar views. We considered that our duty to our country transcended our duty to Hitler, an individual. Do you agree, Sergeant?'

' 'Course I do.'

'And would you do the same, if our positions were reversed?'

'If I had the guts.'

Eisner nodded, a thin smile on his lips. 'It was something I asked myself many times,' he said. 'The enormity of what we were proposing was frightening. I began to doubt myself. Was I doing all this for reasons of personal ambition? Was all this talk about duty to country merely a means of covering up the truth? I wondered. We planned. We made several attempts on Hitler's life. I'm ashamed to say that we failed every time. It makes me doubt the existence of God. I simply cannot believe that a thinking, caring God would protect the man in this way.'

'How did you escape?'

'I was in Berlin at the time. Stauffenberg was flying back from Rastenburg. It was believed that he had succeeded. But no one was certain. Everyone hesitated; everyone was reluctant to act decisively. Except the Gestapo. They were decisive enough. Himmler bet on Hitler. I was lucky. I was driving towards Bendlerstrasse when I saw the Gestapo moving in. I realized what had happened. I telephoned Trude. She begged to come with me. She said her uncle's house was vacant. We could go and hide there. And so we left immediately. We left the car at a village because of course every policeman in the country was looking for it. We came the rest of the way by train and by bus. And we stayed there, in hiding.'

'And then Woods-Bassett and I showed up.'

'Correct.'

'Sorry.'

'It's not important now. One individual's fate doesn't matter. The whole country is in imminent danger of total destruction. And once Germany goes, so goes Europe's last hope against the Russians.'

'The Russians?' said Pollard, remembering the posters in London. 'The Ruskis are all right.'

'Stalin intends to take over Europe.'

'Old Uncle Joe?'

'Unquestionably. Our idea was to seek an immediate peace

with the British and Americans, so that we could all face the Russians together.'

'What, us turn on the Russians?' Pollard was genuinely shocked. 'Can't do that; they're our allies.'

Eisner smiled. 'Does it shock your British sense of fair play?'

'Yes,' said Pollard, 'I think it does.'

'You must try to be realistic about the world. Unfortunately it is not peopled by good fellows and bad. Every country is a mixture of the two. Even England. And most certainly Russia. Stalin's aim is to infect the whole world with his communist ideology. Europe will be first.'

Pollard shrugged. The blokes had talked endlessly about communism and capitalism. 'Perhaps it wouldn't be such a bad thing. Time for a bit of a change, if you ask me.'

'Why?'

'Because there's been far too much privilege for too few people – far too bloody long, that's why.'

'Well said.'

'Thanks,' said Pollard.

'Has it occurred to you that you might be considered one of those privileged people?'

'Me? My dad's a clerk in a shipping company. A nobody.'

'Nevertheless, the commissar might decide that anyone who doesn't work at manual labour is one of the privileged few. Your standard of living might come down, Sergeant.'

'That,' said Pollard, 'would be one of the seven bloody wonders of the world.'

*   *   *

When he saw the river, Pollard whistled in dismay.

'It's a big bugger.'

Eisner nodded soberly.

Pollard peered through the bushes. Was it the Rhine or was it the North Sea? If it had another side, it was invisible, wreathed in wintry mist.

'How wide is it?'

'A kilometre perhaps.'

'Christ.' Pollard munched his stale bread. His stomach

complained. Was he developing an ulcer? It wouldn't surprise him; a bloke needed hot meals, regularly, not a lot of dry, cold muck all the time.

'We must avoid the bridges,' said Eisner. 'They will be guarded.'

'It looks a bit much for wading,' Pollard commented.

Eisner wasn't amused. 'We must find a suitable boat.'

Pollard sniffed. If Superman needed a bloody boat, no doubt Superman would find a bloody boat. An odd sod, Eisner. Infuriating at times. Typical Jerry.

'When it gets dark we will see what we can find.'

'If you say so.'

Eisner looked up sharply. 'You do not agree?'

''Course I agree. Why wouldn't I agree? You're the one who knows where the hell we're going: I haven't got a clue. I'm just going along as a sort of passenger.'

'I wouldn't say that, Sergeant.'

'No, but you'd think it,' Pollard countered.

Eisner shrugged. 'This seems to be a totally unproductive conversation.'

'In that case,' said Pollard, 'we'd better put a sock in it, hadn't we?'

Eisner frowned, puzzled. 'A sock?'

*   *   *

They searched the bank for hours, trudging along in the darkness, heads bent low against the wind, bodies chilled and soaked by the driving sleet.

Then, when they were ready to give up in despair, they found the dinghy. It was on the shore, upside down beside a wooden shed. At first they thought it had been brought on land for repairs; but they ran their hands over the snow-covered hull; it seemed sound enough. Pistol in hand, Eisner listened at the door of the hut. No sign of life from within. Nothing outside either. Eisner nodded. Time to move.

It was hard, exhausting work, heaving the boat upright, then dragging it bodily through the snow. Pollard felt as if his arms were being torn out of their sockets; pinpoints of light kept flashing before his eyes as he tugged, straining with all his might to keep the bloody tub moving.

At last they reached the water's edge.

'Thank Christ for that,' Pollard gasped. 'Let's get the sod in the water.'

'I think our progress will be more satisfactory if we take oars,' Eisner observed. 'Wait here, Sergeant. I believe I know where they are.'

Pollard crouched beside the boat. I knew we needed bloody oars, he told himself. Anyone could see that. Obvious.

He caught his breath. Was that the sound of glass breaking? It was hard to be sure with the wind whining in your ear.

He waited, biting his lip. Where the hell was Eisner? Just like him to go dashing off on his own leaving a bloke stranded nursing a ruddy rowboat without oars. He huddled against the boat but the wind came curling around behind him, sneaking down his neck and up his trouser legs. The moisture on his clothes was beginning to freeze; soon he would be covered in ice, preserved for all time like some prehistoric monster. God, what the hell was Eisner *doing*?

He'd run into trouble. That was it. The police – or the Gestapo – had got him. Now the Black Bastards were looking for the second man, the Englishman. They were fanning out, forming a semicircle. In a moment they would come charging through the sleet, bayonets fixed, each one eager to run the *Engländer* through . . .

But it was a pair of oars, not bayonets, that emerged through the gloom; Eisner carried them, one in each hand.

With difficulty, Pollard resisted the temptation to tell the German how glad he was to see him and how he had been worrying about him. He straightened up and nodded.

'Back already, eh?'

'I thought it best not to linger,' Eisner replied, placing the oars in the boat. 'Come. One more push.'

The boat splashed into the water. Pollard clutched at its gunwale to prevent it drifting away. He went up to his knees in frigid water. Then, gasping, he clambered aboard and flopped damply into the bottom of the boat. Eisner was already on the forward seat, sorting out the oars.

That was when Pollard realized what was missing. The

boat had no oarlocks! Stupid sod, Eisner, he spent all that time looking for oars which could only be used as paddles!

He opened his mouth to tell Eisner. But he closed it again without uttering a word. The German was already tugging the vital oarlocks out of his pocket. Carefully he inserted them in the sides of the boat.

Bastard.

*   *   *

The water was rough, driven by a strong wind. The boat bounced and flopped as if it had no more weight than a leaf.

The two men sat side by side, each pulling an oar. Their progress was erratic. One moment an oar would plunge deep into the water, the next moment the boat would bob wildly, horribly, and the oar would miss the water altogether.

They soon lost sight of the shore. They were surrounded by angry, tossing waves, lashed by the wind and sleet.

Pollard was terrified. He had no idea that a river could be so violent. It was like being on a helter-skelter at Hampstead Heath fair – but much, much worse because there was no solid iron structure underneath, just more grey greedy water, Christ only knows how many fathoms of it. He couldn't swim. If the boat sank he'd go down like a stone. Why the rotten, sodding hell did he ever get himself mixed up in this madness? Why couldn't he be captured and sent to POW camp like any normal bod? It wasn't too bloody much to ask of fate, was it? Perhaps it was.

Water sloshed around in the bottom of the boat; more splashed in with every wave.

Eisner had to yell to make himself heard:

'I will row! You try to get some of the water out!'

Pollard nodded. But he was scared of moving, of letting go of the oar; he might be tossed bodily out of the boat.

And now he was beginning to feel sick. His visceral regions were lurching about in protest at the unfamiliar and thoroughly unpleasant motion of the boat.

God, what the bloody hell had he ever done to deserve this misery?

Kneeling in the water, one arm tightly encircling the

forward seat, he scooped with a drinking mug they had brought from the house. A normal bloke would say no, not on your bleeding life mate, go and have a go yourself but don't drag me along. Why hadn't he said that? Why, why, why? It wasn't *his* fault that Eisner had half the bloody *Wehrmacht* after him. If he, Ron Pollard, had taken it into his head to have a go at Churchill, would he expect some ruddy Jerry to help him out?

It wasn't fair. Not the slightest bit fair.

Numbed by the cold and his own terror, he kept bailing. Hopeless, absolutely hopeless, any fool could see that. He simply couldn't bail fast enough. They were going to sink. It was only a matter of time, no matter how frantically he dipped and tossed, dipped and tossed . . .

The boat touched bottom. Pollard turned, startled. He saw tall trees looming over him.

'Told you we'd make it all right,' he said shakily.

*   *   *

Exhausted, they slept until the middle of the next day. They awoke to find fog moving in, shrouding the tops of the pines.

'The next time I do this,' said Pollard, 'I'm going to make sure it's the middle of summer. And I'm going to bring a spare pair of boots. Mind you,' he added, 'these boots are very nice in their own way. They're specially designed so that your feet don't get too bleeding hot.'

Eisner was busy studying his map.

'We are, I think, somewhere in this region. If I am right then we can expect this forest to continue for a good distance. Following the forest there will be a stretch of open country; after that, more forest.'

'And then we'll be there?'

The German nodded. 'We will have to slip through the lines. But I believe it will not be too difficult. This area is heavily wooded. I know it well. I do not expect the forces to be too numerous.'

*   *   *

They trudged on, mile after mile, through forest and field,

chilled, exhausted, groggy from hunger. They lost track of the hours and days; their motion became mechanical. Life consisted only of placing one numbed foot in front of another. It snowed, it thawed, it rained, it froze, it snowed again. Still they pushed on. They saw convoys of trucks moving up to the front. They saw Allied aircraft: the bombers high overhead, the fighters snarling low, just clearing the trees as they searched for prey.

Then, one foggy morning, Eisner announced that they were only a kilometre or two from the front line.

At that moment the artillery opened up.

11

It was an awesome, mind-numbing din; a thundering cacophony. The air recoiled, shocked, shattered; trees trembled, shaking their branches as if in terror.

Confused, frightened, Pollard could only stand and stare. What the hell was it all about? Where was it coming from?

Eisner grabbed his arm.

'Get down! Lie flat!'

'What's going on?' He had to repeat the question; the first attempt was drowned in the din. He flattened himself on the slushy ground. 'What is it? Are they bombing us?'

Eisner shook his head. 'Artillery. Fifteen centimetre howitzers, I believe.'

'Ours?'

Again he shook his head. 'German guns.'

Christ! Pollard winced, gasping. The detonations exerted a kind of physical force. They would squash the life out of him; they were *hitting* him. His ears ached. He clapped his hands over them as he tried instinctively to burrow into the earth, seeking shelter from the nightmare of noise. The whole world seemed to echo with it, shuddering under its merciless impact.

Eisner peered to his left then to his right. 'Fantastic,' he yelled. 'It sounds as if they're firing all along the front!'

Wincing, cringing, Pollard didn't care. Sod the Jerry and his professional observations! Hell, the bloody world was being blown to bits! And what for? Wasn't the front supposed to be tranquil now? Wasn't everyone supposed to be comfortably snuggled in for Christmas? The ruddy Jerries had no business *shooting*. They were supposed to be just about beaten, cowering behind the Siegfried Line, attempting to reorganize their forces in preparation for the Allied assault on Germany itself: so said all the experts.

Eisner crawled a few yards, then scurried back.

'Come! Quickly!'

'What . . .?'

But there was no time for explanation. Eisner dragged him to his feet. They fled through the forest, through the gauntlet of sound. Then, abruptly, Eisner stopped. He pointed. 'There!'

It was maddening, the stupid sod wouldn't say what he was doing. Again the strong fingers grasped Pollard's arm. Commanded him. Propelled him. Pollard found himself lying in a ditch, in six inches of cold, dirty water.

'What the hell . . .?'

Again Eisner pointed.

'See for yourself!'

They came thrusting themselves through the forest. Great, slab-sided monsters: 45 ton Panthers with the huge barrels of their 75 mm guns reaching ahead like antennae, 60 ton Tigers, armoured tractors hauling mobile steel pillboxes, Wasp 10 cm assault guns, half-tracks. Before them trees fell in their scores, as if in supplication, consumed by the armour, disappearing beneath the lumbering, lurching, roaring hulks without a sound; their death-cries, their cracking and splitting drowned in din.

'Head down!' Eisner shouted. 'Stay flat against the bank!'

It was as if an entire colony of metallic creatures was on the march, gigantic things, swarming out of some subterranean hiding place to invade the world. Beneath them the earth shuddered and quaked. Tanks, half-tracks, self-propelled guns: they kept crashing out of the shadows, demolishing, crushing everything in their path, slithering down slopes, tracks spinning, screeching, grinding back into motion, to disappear into the night.

Where did the Jerries find all these tanks? Hadn't the papers gloated about the almost total destruction of the Panzer forces after D-Day? And fuel: it was said to be as rare as butter. What were the Jerries running all these contraptions *on*, for God's sake?

What the hell was going on?

Eisner was shaking his head as if disbelieving the evidence

of his own eyes. An endless procession of armour. The very latest thing in military hardware.

Pollard felt a twinge of pity for the poor sods who would have to face all this stuff. Yank or Limey, they were in for one hell of a shock.

Quickly the air became polluted; rolling clouds of waste gasses merged with the fog and clung to the trees as if trying to poison every form of life in the area. The noise had become a single totally consuming, utterly ennervating roar that battered your brain and your being until you could feel your sanity splitting like a rotten tomato. All you could do was cower and attempt to dig a hole for yourself with your bare hands. And try to hold on. It had to end. But when? They kept coming. And how would they ever be halted? Were there enough guns in the world to stop them?

Suddenly, strangely, it was relatively quiet.

The last of the behemoths waddled away into the shadows, leaving their stench and their exhaust fumes hanging in the still air. The barrage ended.

Drained, Pollard shook his head.

'I think,' he muttered, 'that the rotten bastards have just moved our front line.'

The forest was a shambles; a hurricane might have swept through it. Carcasses of fallen trees littered the ground, forming a series of pitiful paths to mark the progress of the armour.

Eisner, mud-spattered, exhausted, looked about him, remembering. 'This is the way we came in 1940,' he said, as if talking to himself.

'When you went into Belgium and France?'

Eisner nodded.

'Here we go again,' Pollard said inconsequentially.

Eisner wiped the dirt off his face. 'It's incredible,' he declared. 'They must have kept back enormous reserves; now they have mounted a counter-attack – and a massive one at that – when everyone least expected it. Audacious!'

Pollard sniffed. Was the sod glad or sorry about it?

*   *   *

Through the patches of fog, they could see the explosions: fountains of dirt and snow and bits of trees and God knows what else, flung high in the air to tumble back to earth in an untidy shower. Some poor blokes were getting a bloody awful pasting over there, no question about it. The air reverberated with the insistent rap-rap-rap of guns; fires burned unchecked among the pines; through it all the dull roar of the tanks' engines was still audible.

The fog persisted.

'He has the devil's own luck,' Eisner muttered.

'Who?'

'Hitler,' said Eisner. 'Your fighter-bombers could create havoc among those tanks. But they cannot even take off in this fog. They are powerless.'

'The fog won't last forever.'

'Let us hope not.'

Eisner was peering into the distance; his jaw worked incessantly. Was he thinking over the old victories? Remembering dead comrades? Regretting everything that had happened since?

Pollard pulled his collar tighter around his neck. The icy fog seemed to worm its way through every layer of clothing. Eisner pored over his map.

'I think we have crossed the border,' he said. 'I believe we are now in Belgium.'

'I always wanted to visit Belgium,' Pollard muttered.

Eisner looked up in surprise. 'Why?'

'Just a joke,' said Pollard.

Eisner frowned. Evidently he could see nothing the least bit amusing in the remark.

Ten minutes later, they found the three Americans in a ditch. One was a corporal, the others were privates. Bullets had riddled their bodies. Their smooth young faces wore expressions of surprise and disbelief.

'Poor buggers,' Pollard murmured.

A Jeep lay upside down like some metallic beetle on its back. If it hadn't been for the bloody Jerry counter-attack, *this* would have been home. Allied territory. Handshakes, K-rations and Lucky Strikes from the Yanks. Congratulations on the prisoner. Telegrams to Kilburn. Hero son safe and sound.

But hero son was still a fugitive, still shivering in a damp uniform that didn't belong to him, wandering about a battle-field, looking at the piteous remains of blokes from New York and Arkansas. Hero son patted the dead Yanks' pockets. But every one was turned inside out. The victorious Jerries had made off with all available smokes. His eyes travelled down to their feet. Bare. The Jerries had taken a fancy to their boots too.

*   *   *

The snapping of a twig woke him.

He opened his eyes. And caught his breath.

Two men approached cautiously, holding Sten guns, fingers curled around the trigger.

One man was about forty; he wore a fur collared jacket and a soft cap pulled low on his forehead. The second man was younger, not more than twenty; a beret sat at a rakish angle on his dark head and he possessed sullen good looks. He glared suspiciously at Pollard, then at Eisner, then at Pollard again.

Beside Pollard, Eisner suddenly groaned.

'My back,' he hissed.

'What?'

The penny dropped.

'OK,' Pollard breathed.

Stomach turning to liquid once more, every nerve twitch-ing. Who were these men? Why were they carrying Sten guns?

'You are English?' the older man asked.

'Of course we are.' Pollard's voice was husky and strained.

The older man looked at Eisner; he muttered something to his companion in what sounded like French.

'Are we in Belgium?' Pollard enquired.

'You are,' the man replied in a curiously formal way.

'Thank Christ for that. We've come a long way.'

'What is wrong with your comrade?'

'He hurt himself when we jumped.'

'Jumped?'

'By parachute. We were shot down. We had to jump out of our aeroplane. I'm . . .' God! He almost said he was *Sergeant* Pollard! 'I'm Pollard. Squadron Leader.' It was easy. Came naturally. 'This chap is Sergeant Meade. He's a Canadian.' Why the hell did he say that? No need for it! Calm down! Don't say any bloody more than you have to!

Eisner was writhing in simulated agony, his face contorted. To make matters worse he kept groaning. The performance was horribly unconvincing. But he kept at it. Pollard shuddered inwardly. The silly bugger couldn't convince a half-witted infant, let alone these tough characters. Why the hell did he have to be so good at everything except acting?

'It's his back,' Pollard explained hastily. 'Very painful, back injuries. Something to do with the spinal column. Poor chap can hardly stand up.'

The Belgian looked incredulous. 'And he has walked, so?'

'Rather,' said Pollard, reminding himself to talk like a Squadron Leader, to enunciate with clarity, to replace his natural, comfortable cockney with crisp Oxford. 'The pains seem to come and go. It's always at its worst when he wakes up, poor chap. But he's a stout fellow. Doesn't complain.'

More hasty words between the two Belgians. Incredibly, Eisner's performance seemed to convince them. Sympathy replaced suspicion on their faces.

'I think, Squadron Leader, that it would be unwise to remain here one moment longer than is necessary. The *Boche* may return.'

'We saw all the tanks,' Pollard said. 'What's happening. Are the Jerries attacking?'

'Indeed they are, sir. They have launched a major assault. The Americans are retreating.'

'Retreating?'

A shrug. 'They have retreated from this area, that is all we know.'

'Poor show.'

'As you say. Come. We will assist your comrade. This way.'

*　　　*　　　*

It was dark when they reached the village: a tiny place, a cluster of cheerless looking buildings huddled on a bleak, windswept road. The Belgians led the way, following a frozen stream that ran parallel to the road. Opposite a brick house they waited, watching, listening. A light flickered in one window.

Satisfied, they moved forward, crouching like advancing soldiers, entering the house through a side door. It was dark inside. Pollard heard the door squeak and close with a clatter. A light was switched on. A heavy-set man with a large flowing moustache took Pollard's arm and indicated a narrow damp-smelling corridor. Pollard followed the man. Behind him, the two Belgians assisted Eisner.

The plump man wore a dark suit with an old fashioned winged collar; he had short arms which stuck out at an angle and bounced lightly as he half walked, half trotted along the passage, down a few stone steps, through another door.

He stopped, turned and held out a well-fed hand, indicating the room. For an absurd instant, Pollard thought he expected a tip.

The room looked like something out of the Tower of London: forbidding brick walls with massive columns in the centre of the bare floor. There was a table and a few chairs, a couple of army cots in one corner and a large and rather ornate wireless in the other. Wooden crates were piled against the far wall.

Eisner was helped onto one of the cots. His groans were piteous.

Pollard attempted to catch his eye, to convey his opinion of the histrionics. But the Belgians were crowding around the cot, full of concern for the gallant Sergeant. Where was the pain? Was there something the Sergeant wanted? Was he able to take a little wine? Coffee? Food? A cigarette?

Pollard's ears pricked up. Who had the cigarettes?

But the plump Belgian was busy introducing himself. 'My name is Pierre Lebrun. It is an honour to welcome you to my house.'

Pollard assured him that it was an honour to be there.

The door opened. A middle-aged woman and a moderately pretty girl of about nineteen appeared in the doorway. Lebrun spoke to them; they glanced quickly at Pollard and Eisner. Pollard turned a smile on the girl. She reddened. She looked prettier with a reddish hue.

'There is great confusion,' said Lebrun apologetically, throwing up his hands as if he no longer had control of them. 'The *Boche* are meeting with some success, it would appear.'

'I see,' Pollard murmured, still eyeing the girl, who managed a shy smile in return. Then the two women withdrew.

'There are many rumours,' Lebrun droned on, 'but it would seem to be true that the Americans have fallen back many kilometres. We in this village were liberated and now we have been overrun once more. Ah, what a world!'

'Unfortunately,' said Pollard sagely, 'it's the only one we have.'

'How true, Squadron Leader, how very true.'

Pollard thought quickly. He realized that he had spent most of his life waiting to be spoken to; now that he was suddenly a Squadron Leader he seemed to be expected to establish the conversational directions. 'Jolly good show,' he observed, 'running into you chaps.'

'Indeed, you were most fortunate, Squadron Leader. My associates ventured into the forest merely to investigate the situation in general. They were not expecting to find Allied airmen, I assure you. Tell me, have you walked far? Where were you shot down?'

'Near Cologne.'

'You have travelled a long way.'

'Bloody right,' said Pollard. He mentally kicked himself. A bit too slangy, that, for a two-and-a-half striper. Watch it! He noted the Belgian eyeing his boots and uniform. The old bugger was asking himself whether this indeed was a man who had walked such a distance in the middle of winter.

'You had no food?'

'We borrowed some,' Pollard told him.

For a moment Lebrun frowned, puzzled. Then he understood. He nodded, his ample cheeks wobbling. 'I think it must have been a most difficult journey, Squadron Leader.'

'It was no picnic,' Pollard agreed.

'Picnic . . . ? Ah!' Another flurry of nods as comprehension dawned. 'If you do not object to my saying so, Squadron Leader, you seem so young to be such an important officer.'

Pollard's heart hesitated, then pounded. The stupid disguise! It was failing already! He should have stayed a sergeant. He belonged among the Other Ranks. He was the sort. It was his *station*. Ordained from birth. But it was too late to change now. He had to keep up the bluff. Somehow. Anyhow.

'Young?' A casual – too casual – shrug. 'In Bomber Command all you have to do is survive. The promotions come along. Really nothing to it.'

A finger wagged. 'I think you are not telling me the truth.'

Somewhere deep in the house, a clock chimed. One, two, three, four, five. Pollard's hands were clammy. He wanted to run. Now! He cleared his throat.

'Truth? What do you mean?'

Lebrun nodded, as if agreeing with himself; with every nod a bulge of flesh oozed from either side of his chin, great globules of fat that seemed about to fall off.

'You are,' he declared, 'a very brave young man but like so many of the British, too modest.' He pointed at Pollard's chest. 'Look, you have so many medals.'

'They're nothing at all,' said Pollard, his voice reedy.

Lebrun shook his head; his jowls trembled like a cow's udder. 'No, Squadron Leader, the British do not give many medals like the Americans. I think you must do a great deal to win one.' He leant forward; beaming, he pointed. 'What is that one, Squadron Leader?'

Pollard coughed. It occupied a moment. 'I got it for being on time for breakfast every day last year.'

The Belgian's laugh was an explosion. The joggling cheeks turned bright pink; he looked as if he was about to suffer an attack. At last the eruption subsided. 'Ah, you have much humour, Squadron Leader. And so modest. Truly a great warrior. What age have you?'

'Twenty-two,' Pollard said, adding a couple of years.

'Amazing,' breathed Lebrun. 'And yet we must not forget that Alexander the Great was but twenty-one years when he crossed the Hellespont, having defeated Greece and the Balkan Peninsula. He was, you see, about to start his campaign against Persia.'

'Of course,' Pollard murmured.

'I am a student of history,' Lebrun announced. 'I think sometimes that I feel more secure in the past than in the present. You were born in England, Squadron Leader?'

'London,' Pollard told him.

'A great city. I have visited London many times.'

'You speak English jolly well.'

'Thank you. You are most kind. And the sergeant? He is English too?'

'No, a Canadian. From Montreal.'

'Poor fellow. I do hope he is not badly hurt.'

'He'll be all right if he rests up a bit.'

'Were there other airmen in your aeroplane?'

'Seven altogether. We found one. Dead. God knows what's happened to the others.' No, for Christ's sake, that didn't sound right. Too unconcerned. He was supposed to be the *skipper*. Skippers *cared*. 'I do hope they got down safely. Good lads, all of them.' Clipped, upper-class phrasing. Wizard prang and all that. A regular Noël Coward. 'Can you help us to get to the Allied lines?'

Again the pudgy hands were spread. 'I do not know, Squadron Leader. The situation is quite difficult at the moment. We are not even sure where the lines are, you see. Everything has happened so suddenly, so unexpectedly. The *Boche* concealed their preparations with great efficiency. None of us here was aware that anything unusual was about to happen. We were all fast asleep in our beds when the attack took place – except perhaps Jean over there,' he added, indicating the glowering young man they had met in the forest. 'It is possible that Jean was in someone else's bed; in fact, knowing him as I do, I think it is highly likely.' More detonations of laughter, more jiggling cheeks and jowls; M. Lebrun enjoyed a good chuckle. Then the laughter died abruptly, as if a switch had been turned. 'Ah, but the situation does not seem to be good. The Americans have retreated. How far they have retreated I do not know, but it is certain that they have gone from here and the fighting appears to have moved some distance to the west. What will happen next? I do not know. It is therefore very difficult for us to tell you how we might be able to assist you. At one time we had a most efficient organization for repatriating airmen. A "pipeline" we called it. We were able to get so many brave men through France to Spain, and from there to Gibraltar and back to England. It was most interesting and satisfying work. But now? We must, I think, wait and see what happens in the battlefield. Perhaps tomorrow the Americans will return. In the meantime, we shall do our utmost to make you comfortable, Squadron Leader. I shall contact an acquaintance of mine, a doctor. He is a good doctor, an experienced man. He will examine your comrade and will do what is necessary.'

Pollard had to clear his throat again; it felt as if an elastic band was squeezing his Adam's apple. 'Good show,' he muttered. Bugger the Belgian for knowing a doctor! And bugger the doctor for being experienced! The sod might take one look at Eisner and immediately brand him for the fake he was. Then what? For all their chuckling the Belgians were a tough bunch, experienced practitioners of the dangerous business of blowing up trains and bumping off German troops. Helping Allied airmen escape was only a sideline, something to while away the dull evenings between blastings and killings. It was all too horribly easy to guess what they would do if they discovered a Jerry in their midst.

M. Lebrun produced a pack of Camel cigarettes.

'You would care for one, p'raps, Squadron Leader?'

Pollard cheered up.

'Don't mind if I do.'

'A pleasure. These are mementoes of our American allies. I hope they are to your liking.'

Pollard was too busy sucking the delicious smoke into his lungs to answer. Beautiful! It was like being reborn, to feel the stuff wafting around inside one, wriggling into all the nooks and crannies, tickling every nerve, every sinew.

'Bloody marvellous!' he said at last.

M. Lebrun inclined his head, like a chef acknowledging a compliment.

The woman returned, carrying a tray. She looked tired and irritable. She handed the tray to Lebrun and departed without a word.

'My wife,' said Lebrun apologetically. 'She seems to blame me for the German counter-attack. I think she believes that I arranged it because I wished to indulge in my Resistance work once more. Ah, women!' He stood up, his stomach swaying beneath his waistcoat. 'We must eat and rest. We shall leave you now. *Bon appetit!*'

The door clattered loosely as it closed. The lock sounded as if it was falling apart. Did a key turn? Pollard couldn't tell. He listened as the Belgians clumped up the steps. A second door slammed. Silence.

He and Eisner exchanged glances. The German raised a cautioning finger. Be careful, he seemed to be saying, they're probably listening to us, perhaps even watching us. Pollard nodded, his stomach gurgling. He looked about the room.

The walls and ceiling seemed innocent enough but God only knows what peepholes those stones might conceal. And the crates against the far wall were the perfect spot for hiding anything from cameras to microphones.

He licked his dry lips. It was all very well not saying anything suspicious, but saying nothing was equally suspicious. Think! Hurry! But his brain wouldn't respond. It refused, categorically. It seemed to be telling him that he had got himself into this predicament without using his brain once; now it was up to him to get himself out of it the same way.

'Jolly good types, these Resistance chaps.'

It was feeble but better than nothing.

Munching his sandwich, Eisner grunted agreement.

'How are you feeling now, old boy?'

'OK,' said Eisner. 'Sir.'

'Good man.' Very Woods-Bassettish. 'Where does it hurt? Same place?'

Another grunt. Good. But how long could he limit his speech to grunts and monosyllables?

The sandwich was tasty: white bread and fresh meat.

'I was under the impression that they were having such a rough time in the occupied countries.'

'Mm?'

'Our friend Lebrun looks remarkably well fed.'

Another grunt.

'He seems to have been living off the fat of the land.' Pollard chattered on. 'Unless he has gland trouble. That can make people fat, you know. They might only eat small portions, but they still get fat because of their glands. Shame, what?'

'Uh huh.'

'That corporal in the orderly room is like that. You know the one I mean, the red-haired chap.'

'Mm.'

'I understand he eats very little, but still he puts on the pounds. Pleasant chap, though, don't you think?'

'Yessir.'

'Is the old back hurting again? Bloody bind. Anything I can do? No? Anything you want? They're getting someone to have a dekko at you. Have you up and about again in no time. Piece of cake.'

Eisner's grey eyes seemed to be telling him to put a sock in it. Don't overdo it! Enough is enough!

Pollard gulped down the words he was about to utter. He was babbling again. Squadron Leaders didn't babble. Squadron Leaders were cool and calm, no matter what the situation. The trouble was, he didn't know how to be cool and calm. Hadn't a clue. He wasn't fooling anyone, for God's sake. It was laughable, this trying to pass himself off as a Squadron Leader. Lunacy. He must have been completely round the bloody bend even to have thought it for a moment. The fat Belgian, Lebrun, wasn't chuckling at his funny remarks, he was having a giggle at the common little cockney sergeant trying his pitiful best to impersonate an officer!

Christ almighty.

That icy hand was running through his innards again; his chest felt constricted as if his vital organs were swelling, bursting to get out.

Imposter!

I'll explain, he thought. They'll understand. We're all allies, aren't we? It's not as if I was trying to do them any harm . . .

Heck no, just bringing in a German officer dressed up in RAF uniform. They'll think it's a jolly fine joke . . .

He sighed, limp with dread. The Belgians were Resistance fighters, men who killed and were killed as a matter of course, all in the day's work. They didn't take *chances*, for God's sake. They couldn't afford to.

He ran his tongue over suddenly dry lips. That dreadful desire swept through him again. He wanted to leap to his feet and yell out the truth. All of it. How he had been shot down with the genuine Woods-Bassett, how he had stumbled upon Eisner, how circumstances had somehow crazily manoeuvred him into trying to protect the German from his own people . . .

The words seemed to bubble in his throat, straining to be uttered. Christ, why should he risk his life for this Jerry? It didn't make any bloody sense. Eisner was an *enemy*. And it was his own damned fault if he decided to try and assassinate Hitler. Why should he expect help from an RAF type?

It wasn't fair.

He sighed. What the hell was? You're a twerp, he told himself. He could see the inscription on his headstone: HERE LIETH RONALD POLLARD, IMPOSTER: HE LIVED LIKE A TWERP AND HE DIED LIKE A TWERP.

12

'Would you mind telling me what was on at the pictures when you left England?'

Pollard stared. The man had a tight little mouth and ferrety eyes. A nasty piece of work, he reminded Pollard of a school inspector from the old days. Lebrun had introduced him as 'a colleague'. Why did the bastard want to know what was on at the pictures in England? It was a stupid question. No, on second thoughts, it wasn't. The Belgians wanted to satisfy themselves that they had genuine RAF blokes in their care, not Gestapo agents.

He coughed, then blew his nose.

'The cinema, you mean?'

'Of course.'

'Right.' Pollard sniffed, trying to remember. He couldn't. 'I saw something with Bing Crosby last month, a stinker about a Catholic priest.' Oh Christ, you've torn it, he told himself. The Belgians are all Catholics. Silly sod. He was on the point of apologizing when he remembered that he was a Squadron Leader; he didn't have to take any nonsense from anyone, except Wing Commanders and up. He yawned. Tiresome, these silly questions. He shrugged. 'I don't visit the cinema that frequently,' he told the man. 'And for the moment I'm dashed if I can recall what's on locally, either on the camp or in the village.'

'Never mind, Squadron Leader, perhaps you will be good enough to tell me the name of the pub most generally used by the airmen from your field.'

That was easier. 'The Running Deer.'

'And approximately how far is it from the airfield to that particular establishment?' The man had an irritatingly pedantic way of talking.

'It's about two miles if you go by the main gate; half a mile if you sneak through the wire down near the MU.'

The man wrote rapidly; the scratching of the pencil was clearly audible in the small room. Three armed men had accompanied the interrogator; they stood against the wall holding their Sten guns loosely, almost casually as if they were no more dangerous than golf clubs.

'How long is it since you were posted to RAF Brocklington?'

'Not long.' Another yawn, a scratching of the chin. 'A few months, if I recall correctly.'

'I see.' More scribbling. 'And would you be good enough to tell me how much a package of Player's cigarettes costs these days.'

'Two and fourpence,' said Pollard. 'And they come in "packets". Our American friends call them "packages", but we don't.'

'Of course. Most interesting. Thank you.'

Pollard was relaxing now. 'I just remembered what was on at the pictures,' he said. 'It was "Love Story" with Margaret Lockwood and Stewart Granger. And last week it was "Orchestra Wives", with that swing band leader; I forget his name; he's in the Yank air force now, a major or colonel or something.'

'Glenn Miller,' said Lebrun helpfully.

'That's the bloke,' said Pollard. But why the hell couldn't he stop saying "bloke"? Squadron Leaders don't say "bloke", they say "fellow" and "chap".

The man had more questions. How much was the railway fare from Brocklington to York? How long did the journey take? Was there a bus service? Where did one catch the bus? Who was ITMA? Who was Jane? Who was Butch?

Pollard had to restrain his smile. Now the bloke – chap, damn it, chap – was asking the same questions that he, Pollard, had been putting to Eisner! It was all a great roundabout, everyone trying to deceive everyone else.

At last, the man put down his notebook. It was, he said, most kind of the Squadron Leader to give him so much of his valuable time.

Lebrun said, 'I too thank you for your patience and co-operation, Squadron Leader. I'm sure you understand the necessity for all these tiresome questions.'

Pollard lit another of the Belgian's cigarettes. 'It's quite all right, old chap. I understand. Any more news of the fighting?'

The school inspector type said, 'Reports are confused but it would appear that the Americans have retreated some thirty kilometres. It is believed that the Germans intend to drive through to Antwerp, thus cutting the Allied forces in two.'

'They won't do it,' Pollard declared.

'It is to be hoped that they will not,' the man agreed.

'The whole thing is a bloody bind,' Pollard declared. 'We've simply got to get back to the Allied lines.' It sounded as if the war could not continue until he returned.

Lebrun was apologetic. 'I'm afraid it is a very difficult situation, Squadron Leader. The front line changes hour by hour. Moreover, I am concerned about your sergeant here. He is not, I think, well enough to attempt a journey by foot.'

Pollard nodded with a show of reluctance. He was not, he pointed out, accustomed to sitting around and waiting for things to happen.

The Belgian assured him that he understood perfectly; as soon as some stability was apparent, the necessary arrangements would be made, the Squadron Leader could be assured of that.

Pollard nodded thoughtfully. He had noticed an interesting thing: because he was a Squadron Leader, people suddenly cared about his reactions to what they said to him. As a mere sergeant he had simply been a sort of receptacle for instructions; no one ever gave a damn whether he approved of them or not.

'What,' he enquired in carefully measured, precisely enunciated tones, 'would you do if I decided to get up and walk out of here? Would you use force to keep me here?'

'Most certainly not,' Lebrun assured him, as if the mere idea was unthinkable. 'But I must tell you that such an action would be most unwise. A battle was fought here just two days ago. We have no way of knowing when the Germans will send more troops. The only safe course of action at the moment is to keep one's head low and stay out of sight. Believe me, Squadron Leader, our only concern is your safety and the safety of your sergeant. You are our friends, and we are your friends.'

Pollard wagged a finger. 'Ah, but you weren't too sure about that, were you?'

Lebrun shrugged in his eloquent way. 'If we have learned anything from the last four years it is to take nothing for granted. We regret deeply the many questions asked by my colleague. You will perhaps excuse us, however, if I tell you that on more than one occasion the *Boche* sent English-speaking Gestapo men dressed in airmen's clothes pretending to be British and American fliers shot down in action. What they really wanted to know, of course, was who we were, how we were organized, how we communicated with London, how we managed to spirit so many Allied airmen back to England. They fooled us for only a short time,' he added, smiling. 'My colleague has become an expert in the everyday things that genuine Englishmen and Americans all know.'

The school inspector type smiled modestly.

Pollard swallowed. 'What happened to the ones who weren't genuine?'

'We disposed of them.'

'Here?' said Pollard. 'In this room?'

'In one or two cases, yes,' Lebrun replied. 'On other occasions we took them for a visit to the forest. You seem very interested in the fate of your enemies, Squadron Leader.'

Pollard's collar had become too tight. It was hard maintaining the nonchalant air. 'All this is quite new to me, you see. Undercover work and all that. Bit different to buzzing about up in the air for everyone to see, what?'

The Belgian held his cigarette delicately, between his thumb and forefinger. He turned to Eisner.

'You are feeling a little better, Sergeant?'

Eisner nodded, long-sufferingly.

The school inspector said, 'I would like to ask you a question, Sergeant, a rather personal question. Would you object?'

Pollard cut in, 'Look, the poor chap isn't feeling well. Let him rest. He's been through a lot.'

'But,' said the Belgian, 'I merely wished to ask his age. A harmless question, I believe.'

'What do you want to know his age for?'

'It is simply that the Sergeant seems to be a little older than most of the British airmen I have encountered.'

'I'm just thirty,' said Eisner. Thank God he took care over the 'th' sound; it was the one that sometimes gave him away.

Pollard tried to sound relaxed. 'We call him "Pop". He's the oldest chap in the crew. But as a matter of interest, he's not the oldest aircrew type on the station. There's a gunner in B Flight who's over forty, they tell me. Comes from County Durham, I believe. Going as grey as hell. He's called "Grandad" on his crew.'

'Remarkable,' was the response. 'Is that not rather too old for operational flying?'

'As long as they're fit, it's all right,' Pollard told him airily. 'The older chaps are usually ground staff types who have volunteered for flying duties. Extra pay, you see. Only a few pence a day, but it all adds up.'

'I suppose it does,' said the Belgian. Again the narrow little head turned toward Eisner. 'I understand, Sergeant, that you are from Canada.'

'Montreal.'

'Ah, I recall a pilot who passed through our hands a year or two ago. He too was from Montreal. He said it is the biggest city in Ontario.'

'He told you wrong,' Eisner snapped. 'It's in Quebec.'

'My mistake,' purred the Belgian. 'Forgive me.'

* * *

The doctor is an elderly man with kind eyes. He speaks no English; the fat Belgian, Lebrun, insists on translating everything, although I understand French reasonably well. The doctor clasps his hands in front of him and tells me that I am a brave soldier and that it is his privilege to assist me. I keep nodding while Lebrun repeats it all in English. It is acutely embarrassing. I am deceiving this poor old trusting soul who is risking his neck to come and attend to me when there is absolutely nothing wrong with me. I keep wondering if Pollard intends to reveal the truth to them. I wouldn't blame him if he did. It might be the best course of action.

I squirm with simulated pain as they help me to remove the Sergeant's tunic and my sweater. I lie on my side with my eyes tightly closed as the old doctor gently probes my shoulders and spine. I cup my hands around my mouth as if to suppress my cries of pain.

It is difficult, appallingly difficult. I must be convincing. I must act superlatively well.

'Does it hurt there? At this spot?' Lebrun asked anxiously, after the doctor has asked him the same question in French.

I nod, jerkily, as if even that modest movement causes me pain.

By the end of the examination, the old man is breathing heavily; his bald head is shiny with sweat. He talks to Lebrun, gesturing with his trembling hands, after which he mops himself with a white handkerchief, sits on the edge of the bed and fiddles with his shirtsleeves while Lebrun translates. It is likely, he tells me, that I am suffering from a severe sprain, in which case the pain should ease in a day or two. But it is possible that I have suffered more serious injury. He hopes it is not so but the possibility cannot be ignored. A complete X-ray examination is, therefore, advisable as soon as I am back among my own people.

My own people! If only he knew the truth! I squirm again, this time in shame while the old doctor rumbles on in his quavering voice.

'The doctor,' Lebrun informs me, 'wishes fervently that he could do more for you but unfortunately he is limited by lack of the proper equipment. It is his hope that you will soon feel well and strong again.'

I nod my thanks to the old fellow. He pats me on the cheek, gently, almost tenderly, then he goes to Pollard and clasps his hand. The doctor, Lebrun declares, was a *poilu* in the Great War. And as if to prove it, the old man salutes us before he turns and wobbles out of the room.

'Nice chap,' says Pollard. 'Reminds me a bit of the old family medico.' God, why doesn't he shut up! He will ruin everything!

Where is Trude! I pray that she has reached her cousin's house safely. My eyes blur with tears when I think of her. She is the only reason that I want to keep on living. There is no future for us in Germany. We must leave. We will go to America, if they will have us. The two of us. A fond and beautiful dream. A new start. A life without war. A life of getting on a bus and going to a job and buying meat and fish and butter and choosing furniture. In New York. Or San Francisco. What was the name of that little dark-haired fellow? He lived in San Francisco before the war. Poor man, he had come back in 1939 to visit his sick mother. Before he could return the war had started: he was in the army. He wanted so desperately to return to San Francisco but he must wait until the war is over. I hope he survives. I hope he gets back to San Francisco. I hope we get there too. 'We.' It will always be the two of us. Without her, the whole wearisome business would be pointless. I have no interest in continuing to live if it is without Trude. Extraordinary. I keep attempting to understand myself. Before Trude, I thought only of great events, of history and how I might change it. I was, I suppose, motivated largely by personal ambition. When I met her, my focus on life seemed to change. At once the things that had consumed my entire existence seemed to shrink in importance. The tragedy was that it was already too late. I was irrevocably involved. And now it has all led to this: lying on a cot in a cellar dressed as an enemy sergeant, pretending to be ill among a group of bloodthirsty Belgians!

The hours drag by. I cannot relax. I must continually remind myself that I am in excruciating agony. How suspicious are the Belgians? I keep expecting to feel a gun in my ribs and to be told that the game is up. No, I must not think like that. I am a Canadian, name of Meade, from Montreal. I am a sergeant, a flight engineer; my panel on the starboard side of the Lancaster's cockpit contains oil and fuel gauges, fuel tank selector cocks, booster pump switches, fuel pressure warning lights, emergency air control and oil dilution buttons.

It sounds impressive. But I haven't the faintest idea what any of it means.

13

'My wife and my daughter would like to meet you, gentlemen.'

M. Lebrun stood like a ringmaster, a pudgy arm extended to bring on the next act, the ladies. His wife, he told them, knew no English but his daughter, Jacqueline, possessed a slight knowledge of the language.

They entered: the same middle-aged woman and pale-faced girl who had made a brief appearance early that morning.

Pollard rose.

'A pleasure, ladies. Delighted to make your acquaintance.' It was funny: as plain Sergeant Pollard he would merely have nodded and said 'How-d'you-do', but as the heroic Squadron Leader he found that a touch of flamboyance came easily.

'May I introduce Sergeant Meade,' said Pollard. 'Poor chap banged himself up a bit when we baled out. He's coming along, though. Be right as rain in a little while, won't you, old boy?'

Eisner grunted assent while Lebrun translated the gist of Pollard's statement to his wife. Her dark eyes travelled from man to man as she absorbed the words.

The girl spoke, her face reddening. 'It is a very nice,' she said shyly, 'to meet you.'

'Same here,' said Pollard with enthusiasm. On closer inspection, the girl possessed a definite charm.

'My father says you are a great *aviateur*.'

'Great? I really wouldn't say that. No, not really *great*.'

'I am glad that you visit this house.'

Her voice had an intriguingly breathy quality; quite beguiling. She was dark, like her mother, but her features were considerably more delicate and attractive. She grew on one. Definitely a bit of all right.

Lebrun poured wine and proceeded to toast Mr Churchill

and King Leopold III, Generals Eisenhower and Montgomery, Joe Stalin and President Roosevelt. The girl's eyes kept meeting Pollard's – once, twice, three times. The fourth time, he winked at her. She coloured charmingly; her lips twitched into a fleeting smile despite the fact that her father was at that moment expounding at length on the dangers created by the German counter-attack. The possibility had to be faced, he declared, that the Allied armies might have to retreat back across the Channel and then attempt another invasion in 1945. Pollard nodded with due solemnity, but he was thinking that he probably wouldn't have winked at Jacqueline if he had been Sergeant Pollard. He wondered why. He supposed it was because he was uncertain how she might react. She might be offended. All right, but mightn't she be just as offended if a Squadron Leader winked at her? Yes, but if she was, the Squadron Leader would chuckle and dismiss the whole thing as an aborted op and think no more about it. Somehow it was all so much easier when you were pretending to be someone else, particularly someone with two and a half stripes on either shoulder plus a cluster of gongs under the pilot's wings.

The wine worked wonders for M. Lebrun's optimism.

'It is my personal opinion,' he declared, 'that, in spite of their initial success, the Germans will fail. The Americans will stand firm.'

'Jolly good show,' Pollard murmured. He was beginning to enjoy himself. The strain of uncertainty was lifting from his shoulders; he felt secure. The Belgians had accepted him and Eisner. Now it was simply a question of waiting until the Allies came back and liberated the village. He might even reveal the truth, if a suitable moment presented itself. He would see about that.

Lebrun poured more wine. Fine wine, he informed Pollard: pre-war stock from Château d'Yquem. He said that in recent years he had frequently thanked Providence for guiding him into the grocery profession, following his esteemed father's footsteps. He said it with a certain reverence, as if talking about taking Holy Orders. Although the war had created difficulties, he had always been able to feed his family adequately. 'Moreover,' he added, 'I was able during the

Occupation to obtain various commodities for the Germans – for which I charged them quite outrageous prices, let me assure you! But, more important, these activities created a sort of relationship between myself and the German officers. I was useful to them, therefore they never bothered me. I was, in fact, carrying on my Resistance work under their very noses!'

'You are a very brave man, M. Lebrun,' Pollard declared, 'I salute you.'

Lebrun shook his head. 'I am but a simple patriot, Squadron Leader.'

'What you have done,' Pollard insisted, 'requires far more courage than what I have done. Yet I have medals and you don't.'

M. Lebrun considered the statement; perhaps he had been too hasty, perhaps he was indeed much more than merely a simple patriot. 'You are most kind, Squadron Leader. A little more wine, perhaps.'

Pollard allowed his glass to be refilled as he engaged in conversation with Jacqueline. How had she fared during the Occupation? Had the German troops ever troubled her? Had she been frightened, seeing the Germans talking to her father? She answered the questions with obvious pleasure, flattered that an important British airman was taking such an interest in her. She rambled on about the school and the nuns and how the Germans had commandeered part of the place for an anti-aircraft post and how they had taken the father of one of her friends and how he had never been heard from again and how the Germans had retreated and how the Americans had entered and how they had in turn retreated and the Germans had swept through once more.

Then she said, 'You are married, yes?'

'I am married, no.' Pollard assured her.

'But you have a fiancée in England perhaps.'

For a shy type, she had a remarkable, direct way when it came to leading questions. Pollard told her that he was totally unattached; she nodded as if mentally cataloguing the information.

'I hope,' Pollard heard himself saying, 'that you will come

and visit London after the war. It will be a pleasure to show you around and I shall try to repay your hospitality.'

She beamed. 'That would be splendid!' she cried; she chattered away in French to her parents, both of whom immediately looked up at Pollard, eyes wide.

M. Lebrun smiled and shook Pollard's hand.

'You are a generous man, Squadron Leader.'

Pollard wondered if he had invited the whole family.

An instant later he was berating himself. What was the matter with him? Who the hell was he to invite anyone to visit him in London? What if they took him up on the invitation? How delighted would they be when they found out the truth: that he was not a Squadron Leader, that he lived in a common little house on a dead end of a street, that his family were nobodies and always would be.

But it was as if someone else was doing the talking for him, chatting easily about the 'town house' and the 'place in the country'.

Lebrun said, 'I have visited London many times. I know it well. In what part of the city do your parents live, Squadron Leader?'

'Our place is in the Maida Vale area,' said Pollard, which wasn't totally untrue; one had to go through Maida Vale to get to Kilburn on the Edgware Road. 'We've been there a long time. Mother likes it. All her friends are in the vicinity. And it's handy for Father, going off to the office.'

'A very excellent location,' Lebrun agreed. 'Have you visited Brussels, Squadron Leader?'

'As a matter of fact, no,' Pollard replied, as if Brussels was the one spot on the map that had somehow, inexplicably, been omitted from countless holiday itineraries. 'But I hear it's most charming.'

*   *   *

I pretend to be asleep, for fear that they might want to include me in their ridiculous conversation. Pollard babbles on, revelling in his drunken fantasies of wealth and influence. He is an idiot; I want to spring off the bed and kick his behind for him. What bewilders me is the way the Belgians swallow it all! They listen, enraptured – perhaps because he is saying all the things they want to hear. Now we have to listen to the gallant Squadron Leader talking about his Uncle Frederick who is so well known in the film industry. God, will it never end?

But I have to ask myself whether Pollard's fantasies are to be criticized more than mine. I dreamt of changing history, of ridding our country of the evil monster, like some knight on a white charger. The sergeant and I are both dreamers in our own ways.

It is a curious fact, no doubt explainable by a psychiatrist, that at times I experience precisely the same emotions as I did when I was a small boy and had done something wrong. I see my mother, miraculously young and strong again. Anger has hardened her classic features. She hits me, expertly, her hand flashing out at me with the speed of a rapier. Her palm stings my cheek. Instantly she is transformed. The blow dissolves her anger. Her eyes become warm; she is herself again, now that she has done her duty and delivered the punishment. In a moment she will insist that we discuss the entire matter: what I did, why I did it, why I shouldn't have done it and why it would be foolish of me to do it again. She is infinitely patient, talking about my misdeeds as if they are a subject of considerable significance for humanity, examining every side of the question tirelessly, meticulously. She always wishes me to understand clearly the reasons why and why not; the reasons for rules, she tells me, are far more important than the rules themselves.

I can almost make myself believe that a quarter of a century has not elapsed. But then M. Lebrun's alcoholic cackles drag me back to reality. My mother is no longer young; she is a widow, she lives alone in that gloomy old house. No doubt the Black Bastards are keeping a watch on the place, but I pray they don't trouble her.

Is she ashamed of me for what I have done? Or is she proud? I wonder if I shall ever find out. I realize with a shock that she doesn't know of Trude's existence. It seems incredible yet it is so. The two most important women in my life, and they have never met.

14

The next morning Jacqueline took Pollard on a guided tour of the premises. He was allowed to peep into the shop and inspect the stockroom; he saw the kitchen and the living quarters; from a tiny garret window he viewed the main street of the village. Snow-dusted and windswept, it looked even bleaker and drearier in the daylight than it had in the darkness.

'Charming,' he lied.

'It is only a very tiny place,' said Jacqueline. 'Not like London.'

'But it has such *character*,' Pollard told her, remembering a line out of a Cary Grant flick. 'Besides, it's lucky enough to have you.'

More pretty blushes. God, it was fantastic being someone else. You could be totally outrageous – and get away with it. No wonder actors were so successful with women.

That he was succeeding with Jacqueline was undeniable. She hung on his every word, her eyes forever on him. Fact of the matter is, he told himself, you've bowled her over. She thinks you're a bit of all right, mate. She's hearing wedding bells. 'Belgian Miss Marries RAF Hero' . . .

Christ, how easy it was to start believing it all! He had to stop and tell himself: You're not a bleeding hero; you're not a Squadron Leader. You're Sergeant Nobody. But somehow the truth had less relevance than the moment.

She was standing very close to him. She wanted him to kiss her. He could tell. The air between them was electric.

He leant forward. Their lips met. Hers felt delightful: soft and warmly moist, like marshmallow. The touch of her sent his blood surging, every nerve tingling.

'I hope,' he murmured, 'that the war lasts a couple of years and that I will find it quite impossible to leave here.'

Jacqueline said she would like that too, please.

She was marvellous in his arms; she had an intriguing way of wriggling without actually moving that did wonders for the various points of contact. Her shyness had disappeared; she held him with firm, proprietary fingers.

His hand found her right breast. He was, she breathed, a very naughty boy. But her grip on his neck tightened encouragingly. His hand slipped inside her blouse and began to explore the fascinating hills and valleys.

She told him that he must not do that. But she made no move to interrupt him.

Blimey, he thought, no wonder old Woods-Bassett had such a reputation with the girls; it's easy when you've got the right trappings . . .

At that moment there were footsteps in the corridor.

A knock on the door.

Hastily Jacqueline straightened her clothes. '*Qui?*'

M. Lebrun's head appeared.

'Ah, Squadron Leader, there you are!'

'Yes indeed,' Pollard muttered, 'here I am.'

M. Lebrun beamed. Did the old bugger know what had been going on?

'It would be much appreciated, Squadron Leader, if you would come downstairs. There has been what you might call a development.'

*   *   *

'Frightfully good to meet you, sir.'

The face was fresh and pink and smiling, the figure slim and garbed in an RAF flying suit.

'I'm Donaldson, sir. Flying Officer. 23 Squadron. Little Snoring.'

'Good show,' Pollard muttered. His insides felt as if they were dissolving; his fingers twitched; he had to clench his fists. Watch it! He seemed to be yelling the instruction at himself. Watch your bloody step! This is tricky!

Another figure, dark and stocky, appeared in his line of vision.

'Sir, may I present Corporal Mooney.'

The dark and stocky figure raised a casual hand.

'Hi.'

'Corporal Mooney is an American, sir,' said Donaldson, as if that explained everything.

The room seemed to be full of people: Lebrun, his wife, Jacqueline, Eisner still in his cot, two Sten gun carrying Resistance types, as well as the newcomers.

'Good show,' Pollard said again. Everyone waited for him to utter something of significance. He was the senior officer. Senior officers always had lots to say. He indicated Eisner. 'This is Sergeant . . . er.' For a ghastly moment he couldn't remember the name. Then it came back to him. 'Meade' he said, a little too loudly.

Donaldson was burbling about the trouble he had run into near Koblenz. 'I was on Mossies, sir. Night intruder stuff. It was a poor show, really. Caught up with a Ju 88. Saw him in the circuit with his wheels and flaps down. Joined him. Sneaked up behind him. Couldn't miss. One squirt and the poor beggar came to pieces in front of me. The trouble was, half the pieces hit me. I managed to get the kite up to about five thousand feet but by then things were falling off in earnest. My nav, Scotty, went first. I followed. Got down without any trouble. But couldn't find Scotty. Lord knows what's happened to him. Bumped into friend Mooney, though. So we set off together to try and reach the Allied lines. Ran into these Belgian chaps in the forest. Bit of luck, what? Now we hear the Jerries have launched a really big-scale counter-attack. What's your opinion of it, sir?'

Pollard had no opinion. But a Squadron Leader had to have opinions.

'It's localized,' he declared, remembering a BBC news broadcast about a battle at some unpronounceable place in Russia. 'I think they'll be able to contain it.'

'I'm sure you're right, sir. Didn't they do something on the same lines just before the end of the last war?'

'I believe so,' said Pollard who hadn't the faintest idea. He noticed that the American, Mooney, had sat down beside Eisner. Quickly he said, 'Better let him rest, Corporal. Poor chap did something to his back.'

'Sure,' said Mooney, not stirring. 'Goddam painful, backs.'

Donaldson said, 'I understand you've been here a couple of days already, sir.'

Pollard nodded. Don't say anything unless you bloody well have to, he instructed himself. You'll give yourself away. That bloke's a *genuine* officer, he'll see through you in ten seconds flat unless you watch your ruddy step. Be distant. Unfriendly. Remember, you outrank this pipsqueak. Be frosty. Be Woods-Bassett.

'It is great good fortune,' said M. Lebrun, 'that we chanced upon your comrades, Squadron Leader. It means, I fear, that this house will be a little bit crowded, but I am sure you will have no objection.'

Pollard swallowed. 'Of course not,' he muttered. 'The more the merrier.'

*   *   *

Donaldson was a friendly soul. And talkative. He said he came from Norwich where his father was a dentist. 'Actually,' he announced with the air of a man revealing a significant secret, 'dentistry doesn't appeal greatly. Can't stand the thought of spending one's life peering at other people's molars. Matter of fact, I've got an idea that there might be a few opportunities in the airlines after the war. Sounds a bit more like it, doesn't it, sir?'

Pollard nodded.

'But, of course,' said Donaldson, 'one has to think about the security of a job like that. It's all a bit dicey; if the eyes go, presumably you do too, what? It's the sort of thing one has to think about a bit, isn't it?'

'Yes,' said Pollard.

'Have you given any thought to the airlines, sir?'

'No.'

Undeterred, Donaldson plunged on: 'Of course, on the other hand, it would be awfully good fun to stay on in the Air Force. The trouble is, it's so frightfully difficult to know what sort of a show it's going to be when this is all over. Seems to me they're going to need only a fraction of the chaps they need at the moment. It's all a bit of a problem isn't it, sir?'

'Yes,' said Pollard.

He edged his way toward Eisner.

'Bearing up, old chap?'

Eisner nodded. His face was taut; he was a man in a trap and he could do nothing but lie still and wait to see what happened.

Pollard smiled in what he hoped was an encouraging way. 'Good show, Sergeant. Carry on.'

Corporal Mooney shook his head sympathetically. 'Back still giving you hell, uh? Tough break.' He grinned easily at the two of them. 'You guys are both English, uh?'

'I am,' Pollard replied. 'Sergeant Meade is a Canadian.'

He instantly regretted the remark.

Mooney regarded Eisner with new interest. Here at last was someone who, if not actually a countryman, was at least a close neighbour.

'Canadian, uh? What part?'

'Montreal,' Eisner grunted.

Mooney chuckled. 'Been there lots of times. Used to drive a truck up through the north-eastern States and Canada. Montreal, Toronto, Windsor – know 'em as good as I know Philly. Boy, did I love having to spend a night over in Montreal! Lot of action there, buddy! Some of those joints down on St Catharine – wow! I used to have to go down to a place near the main station there – what the hell's it called? Union Station, uh?'

Eisner stared for an eternal moment, then winced as if assaulted by new waves of pain.

The door opened. Jacqueline entered, carrying a large tray.

'Chow!' hooted Mooney.

*   *   *

'We'll be out of here by Christmas,' Donaldson declared.

'I'll buy that,' said Mooney. 'Our guys'll counter-attack pretty soon and they'll push the goddam Krauts back – farther back than where the sons of bitches started out.'

Pollard nodded. 'Possibly.'

Donaldson looked up. 'You don't sound confident, sir.'

'Confident?' Clearing of throat. 'Of course, I'm confident.'

'Yes sir, sorry sir.'

'But we have to be realistic.'

They were looking at him, waiting for more gems of military wisdom. But he had nothing more to say. His head ached; his stomach felt as if it had been tied in a reef knot. Nerves. It was downright bad for a bloke to have to exist under this sort of tension. That sod Donaldson kept on yapping about schooldays and rugger and smart places to eat in town and brother officers and the mess and stocks and shares. Was the bastard testing him? Did he suspect already? Was he saying to himself that fellow is no Squadron Leader: he's common, a nobody, no breeding, no manners. Possibly. And yet he still seemed to ooze respect; still lots of *sirs*, deference by the bagful.

'You travelled in the States much, Sarge?'

Now the bloody Yank was bleating away to Eisner. Of course he was only trying to be friendly. But why the hell couldn't he shut up and leave things well enough alone?

'Never got outside Montreal much, uh? Well, that's the way it goes. Me, I've always had a yen to see the world. So hauling a rig was a pretty good way to see it, uh?' He lit a cigarette and watched the smoke curling up toward the ceiling. 'Guess it won't be too long before we get back to good ol' North America now. I've sure as hell seen enough of Europe to last me a lifetime. Always figured Europe was real glamorous. Jesus, I'll tell you, Cleveland, Ohio is one hell of a lot more glamorous than your average European city!'

Pollard squirmed. In his own way Mooney was as much of a windbag as Donaldson.

'Listen,' the American went on, 'I'll take Montreal over London any day. That's one great town, fella. Love those stores on Delaware Avenue. Elegant! Say, I was meanin' to ask you, did you ever come across a guy by the name of Duplessis when you were back home?'

Eisner shook his head.

Mooney shrugged and puffed away on his Chesterfield. 'Thought mebbe you might have done. He was a guy I met one night when I went across the river to Hull. Lotta action there too, uh?'

Eisner nodded.

Pollard said, 'I think he's getting rather tired now, Corporal. Why don't you be a good chap and let him rest.'

'Sure thing.'

Mooney stood up, yawned and stretched himself.

'Take it easy, Sarge, uh?'

Was no sentence complete without its 'uh'? An irritating bastard, the Yank. He had a monotonous, mechanical way of talking.

Now Donaldson was yapping on about Wimbledon. And Ascot. And Brooklands.

Resolutely, Pollard kept shaking his head. Not much interested in sports. No time. Too busy.

'Have you always been on bombers, sir?'

'Yes.'

'You should really try to get your hands on a Mossie, sir.'

'I will.'

'Delightful kite. Absolutely wizard in every way! A clean one will do jolly nearly 400 mph!'

His eyes lit up; he looked like a schoolboy describing a prize conker.

It was a relief when he and Mooney moved off and began talking about something in the corner. Pollard sighed and lay back on his cot. Sod the two of them. It had been a bit of all right before they came along; things were beginning to shape up very nicely indeed. Now it was impossible to relax; his nerves were twanging like piano wires. God only knows how long he could keep on convincing them that he was a bonafide Squadron Leader . . .

He smoked one of Mooney's cigarettes. It helped. The blue smoke wreathed soothing patterns above his head. The fact of the matter was, this state of affairs could go on for weeks, even months. And in all that time he mustn't let his guard slip once. Strewth. He bit his lip, gnawed at it as he wrestled with the problem.

Eisner was no help. He shrugged with his eyebrows when Pollard glanced in his direction.

'How's the back, old man?'

'OK.'

'Good show.'

A final puff of the Chesterfield. The trouble was, when blokes were stuck together, they chatted. They wanted to find out about each other. It was only natural. And the longer they chatted, the more they found out . . .

'Excuse me, sir.'

Donaldson. Looking ill at ease. Voice low and confidential, pink tip of tongue repeatedly wetting lower lip.

'Yes?'

'Would you mind coming over here, sir?'

'What for?'

'There's something you should see, sir.'

'What is it?'

'It's just over here, sir.' One more wetting of the lip. 'Please.'

Sighing, Pollard got to his feet. Donaldson thanked him.

Mooney stood in a corner of the room, behind a packing case.

'Well?'

Donaldson said, 'Actually, sir, we want to ask you something.'

'Couldn't you ask me over there?'

'It's a bit awkward, sir.'

'And kind of important,' said Mooney.

Pollard's stomach nerves seemed to sniff danger. He cleared his throat. 'What is it?'

'It's about your flight engineer, sir,' said Donaldson.

Every nerve started twanging.

'What . . .' It was necessary to clear his throat again. 'What about him?'

'We're a bit concerned about him, sir.'

'I'm concerned about him too. Poor chap hurt his back.'

'Yes sir, but it isn't his back that concerns us.'

'It isn't?'

'Has he been on your crew for a long time, sir?'

'Long enough.'

'He's from Montreal, isn't he, sir?'

'Yes.'

'That,' said Mooney, 'is what bothers the hell outa me.'

'Why?'

'Because,' declared the American, 'when I was talking to him about Montreal, I goofed. Called the railroad station "Union Station". After I said it, I realized I was wrong. Union Station's in Toronto.'

'I see.'

Pollard felt his body go rigid with fright.

'So,' Mooney went on, 'I go outa my way to drop a couple more goofs. Talked about the elegant stores on Delaware Avenue, Montreal. Wrong. That street's in Buffalo, New York. But your buddy didn't bat an eyelid. Then I asked him about a guy named Duplessis. The name didn't seem to mean a goddam thing to him, which is strange as hell considering that Duplessis is the boss man in Quebec Province where Montreal is!'

'Clever,' breathed Pollard.

Mooney shrugged. 'I tried one more on him. Talked about going over the river to Hull. You can't do that in Montreal, buster! You do that in Ottawa! I know, 'cause I've done it. I tell you, that guy has never been in Montreal in his life!'

'And I tell you to put your hands up!'

Donaldson's mouth dropped open.

'Good God,' he said in a curiously level tone.

'Jesus,' said Mooney.

Eisner stood there. One arm pointed; the other terminated in the Luger. Pollard gaped at the thing; he had forgotten its existence.

'You will both stand over there by the wall,' said Eisner.

'You son of a bitch,' said Mooney. 'You're a goddam Kraut!'

'That is correct,' said Eisner. 'Into the corner, if you please. That is good. Your faces to the wall. Let us not have any trouble.'

Donaldson turned imploringly to Pollard. 'Sir . . . what does this mean? Is he really . . .? But you, are you in *league* with him?'

'It's a bit difficult to explain,' Pollard mumbled.

'I'll bet my ass it is,' Mooney grunted.

Eisner grabbed Pollard's arm. Curtly he nodded toward the door.

'But . . .'

Eisner shook his head. There was no time for explanations, no time for anything but running!

Before they reached the door, it opened.

Lebrun appeared. Smiling. He saw the gun. The smile faded.

'Please stand aside,' said Eisner.

'But . . . what is this?' Lebrun looked Eisner up and down, his brain apparently refusing to accept the evidence of his eyes.

'I'm sorry it was necessary to deceive you,' said Eisner. 'Now you will please get out of our way.'

'You'd better do as he says,' Pollard advised.

'He's a Kraut!' Mooney yelled from the corner.

Lebrun's brow darkened. He lunged at Eisner. The pistol cracked. The bullet hit the door beside Lebrun. He staggered back as if struck, the colour draining from his well-fed cheeks.

'Goodbye,' said Eisner. He turned to Pollard. 'Come.'

Through the doorway, along the passage, up the stone steps.

Jacqueline. Eyes bulging, mouth open.

'Sorry about this,' Pollard gasped as he hurtled past her. 'No time for explanations. Sorry!'

In a moment they were outside.

It was snowing.

15

They ran – they hurled themselves – across the snow-covered village high street. They rushed by an astonished old man who spun on his heels like a dancer and dropped the two loaves he had been carrying. A woman emerged from a shop; she stopped dead in her tracks and clapped both hands to her mouth.

'There!' Eisner yelled, pointing to a narrow passage between the houses.

Pollard tried to change direction. He slipped, skidded and nearly fell. Arms flailing, he managed to regain his precarious balance – and in so doing almost hit the woman who still stood rigid, terrified. Their eyes met for an instant.

Then Pollard was clattering along the passage in pursuit of Eisner. Heart pounding, lungs straining, every nerve trembling in anticipation of a burst of Sten gun fire. Oh, Christ, please, please. It's all a great bloody *mistake*!

But it was too late for explanations. Too late for everything except running. And hoping.

The passage led to a football field. Like forlorn skeletons, the goalposts stood amid the swirling snowflakes.

Eisner set out across the field, heading for a clump of trees a quarter of a mile away. Pollard gasped along behind, his eyes seeing only the German's feet and the explosions of snow he kicked up with every step.

Someone shouted. A man. Now a woman.

In a moment his lungs would split, his bones would snap. But keep going! Got to keep going!

They scrambled through a thorny bush. Pollard tripped. His hands plunged into the frigid snow; the stuff slid up his sleeve. He sprawled full length. Then he was on his feet again, panting, pushing, propelling himself with the instinctive desperation of the hunted animal.

The only thing in the world that mattered was running. Escaping. Forcing the legs to fight the snow and ice, making his body produce the energy. Got to keep going!

Eisner turned. Beckoned.

At last, dizzy with fatigue, they reached the trees.

They looked back. Their tracks were horribly evident: great blemishes in the smooth carpet of snow, as glaringly obvious as a highway. Point A to Point B. In a moment the Belgians would be coming, eager to reach Point B.

Without exchanging a word, the two men set off again, hurrying on through the trees. Caked with snow, their breath escaping in great silvery clouds, they made their way down a wooded slope. Now their tracks were less obvious, thank God. But then the trees thinned. They came to an open field. They peered ahead but the snow was so thick that they couldn't see beyond the field. There was nothing for it but to go on.

Bloodybarmybloodybarmybloodybarmybloodybarmy . . .

They had to kick their way through the snow, they fell, they staggered to their feet again, they scrambled, they clawed a path for themselves.

They came to more trees. A forest of some substance, a place to hide, a place to rest and recover their strength.

*　　*　　*

'Personally,' said Pollard, 'I think it was bloody silly, shooting at them.'

Eisner shrugged. 'It startled them,' he said. 'It gave us time to escape.'

'You might have hit someone.'

'I don't think so.'

'Seems to me we could have talked to them . . . '

'*Talked* to them?'

'Yes, we could have explained the situation, you know, put our cards on the table. They'd have understood. They weren't bad blokes.'

Eisner sniffed. 'You might have been able to explain your situation, but I doubt very much that I would have managed it. They were Resistance, my friend. And Resistance are not known for their tolerance as far as Germans are concerned.'

'You can't blame them for that.'

'Perhaps not. I merely pointed out a fact, an undeniable fact, one that prompted me to act as I did.'

Sod you, thought Pollard. He shivered. The chilly wind bit easily through the thin material of his battle-dress blouse. He had felt sorry for himself when he was walking about Europe in his flying togs; now he was far worse off. He came to the conclusion that he would probably freeze to death within a few hours. He'd look like one of those corpses from the Russian front; they'd pick his body up and it would be stiff and solid, a statue of one of the world's leading half-wits, ready for mounting in front of the nearest public convenience.

Eisner was studying his map.

'D'you know where we are?'

The German shook his head.

'So we could have gone round in a bloody great circle.'

'It's possible.'

Pollard sighed. Despair was a great lump in the pit of his stomach. What hope was there, with both the Germans and the Belgians after them? And cold. And hunger. It was just a matter of time until one of their many enemies did the trick. The only questions were: which enemy and when? All this running was a stupid waste of time, just prolonging the agony, postponing the inevitable a few more miserable hours – or perhaps just minutes.

'I suppose you didn't bring anything to eat with you?'

'Are you hungry already?'

Pollard shook his head. 'I just wondered,' he muttered. 'Just a passing thought, a foolish whim.'

Eisner ignored that. He folded the map and put it in his breast pocket. 'I have no idea where we are,' he announced.

'That's nice,' said Pollard.

'It is difficult to find one's location on a map when one does not know the point at which one started.'

'I'd have thought that'd be a snap for you, mate.'

'A snap?'

*　　　*　　　*

Arms clutching their shivering bodies, they trudged through the darkened forest. They didn't know where they were going, but it was too cold to stay still; they had to walk to stay alive.

It had stopped snowing but the wind still whipped between the trees, icy, merciless.

I've probably got pneumonia already, Pollard thought gloomily, but I'm too bloody cold to feel it. If I get you out of this, he promised himself, you'll never be cold again, mate. Never. You'll go and live in California or Africa or somewhere where it's always warm.

It was odd, he was talking to his body as if it was another individual. Was the cold attacking his brain, freezing the cells one by one?

Then he realized that Eisner was no longer walking beside him. He stopped and turned. The German was standing a dozen yards back, looking off to the left, map in hand.

Clasping his hands to his mouth and puffing on them, Pollard retraced his steps.

'What's up?'

'Does that look like a river to you? There. It's frozen and snow covered but it still looks like a river, doesn't it?'

'I think so.'

'I think so too. And that appears to be this road here, see?' He indicated a spot on the map. 'It runs north and south. Which makes me believe quite strongly that we are in this vicinity.' He pointed. 'I suggest we head in that direction.'

*   *   *

At first they thought the truck was slowing because the driver had spotted them. They flung themselves down, half burying themselves in the snow. Fearful, they watched the truck slowing, its rear wheels slithering on the icy road surface. The vehicle came to a halt.

It was a *Wehrmacht* truck.

The motor coughed into silence.

The door opened. The driver emerged – a short, stocky fellow wearing a soft forage cap. He stepped to the side of the road and fumbled with layers of clothing in order to relieve himself. Afterwards, he lit a cigarette, carefully cupping the flame in his hand. He puffed appreciatively.

'A bit of luck,' Eisner whispered, slipping the Luger from his belt. 'Let us go and have a little chat with that fellow.'

* * *

Eisner peered ahead along the dark road. 'We must expect to encounter an army checkpoint sooner or later. My suggestion is that when we do, I simply drive straight through. Do you agree?'

'Anything you say,' Pollard murmured sleepily. He was content – warmed by the truck's engine, filled by the driver's cheese and apples which they had found on the seat, lulled by the monotonous rumbling of the wheels. He felt sorry for the poor sod of a driver in the back, exposed to the freezing night air. But he was warmly dressed, and no doubt he had found something with which to cover himself. He was better off than the blokes who had to stagger along on Shanks' ruddy pony.

Eisner kept mumbling about being uncertain about his precise location. He would point out a bridge or a village and ask Pollard to try to identify the spot on the map. Pollard tried. But it made no sense: just a collection of lines and dots. His eyes felt heavier and heavier; it was a superhuman effort to keep them open.

'I believe we are heading north,' Eisner muttered, 'but I wish I could be sure. I don't know where we are or where we're going!'

'Right,' Pollard managed, wondering vaguely why he worried so much. Why couldn't he just sit back and enjoy the trip like any sensible bloke?

The snow began again: whirling, spinning flakes that danced for a scintilla of an instant before the windscreen and then vanished to be replaced by a few million more.

They drove past a cluster of trucks. Two soldiers stood beside them; they waved in friendly fashion. Pollard waved back. Nice chaps, he thought as his eyelids drooped and finally closed.

Trude was standing in the back of the truck, wearing that diaphanous nightgown; the wind was doing a marvellous job of blowing the thing flat against her breasts, sculpturing her whole body in lovely, slinky, sexy silk. He had a beautiful view of her through the window at the back of the cab. The trouble was, he couldn't reach her. She kept beckoning to him and he kept shrugging and throwing up his hands. How did she think he could get back there while Eisner was pounding along the road as if he was at Brooklands? That was when she clenched her fist and drove it straight at the window. It shattered.

'Duck!' Eisner yelled.

The first shot hit the windscreen; a section of the glass suddenly snapped away admitting a torrent of freezing air. Half a dozen soldiers – like lead jobs, some kneeling, some standing. All around. As the truck swept past Pollard saw a soldier aiming his rifle at him. He looked right down the barrel. The soldier fired. Something buzzed angrily past Pollard's head.

You missed, Pollard thought matter-of-factly.

Eisner fought the wheel as the truck slewed on the icy surface.

We're going to turn over, do somersaults all over the place. The thought crystallized quite slowly, as if everything was happening in slow motion. Here we go. Over on two wheels.

Thump. The truck righted itself. More shots struck the body, snapping easily through the thin metal.

'Are they following?'

'What?'

'Look, damn you! Behind you!'

'Oh . . . right.' Pollard twisted around and peered through the cab's rear window. No Trude. Just a rapidly fading glimpse of soldiers with rifles. The night closed over them. The road behind seemed to be empty.

Eisner said, 'Those soldiers we passed a kilometre back – they must have telephoned ahead. They were waiting for us . . . damn!' He hit the steering wheel with his fist.

'What's the matter?'

Eisner nodded curtly at the truck's bonnet. A plume of steam wobbled in the wind; oddly, it looked as if it was about to snap off.

'They hit the radiator.'

'That's torn it,' Pollard gulped.

Eisner pushed harder on the accelerator, determined to get as much as possible from the truck, before, inevitably, the motor seized.

They sped on for a mile, another mile, another . . .

Then it banged and heaved convulsively. Eisner braked.

The stink of burnt oil and scorching metal filled the cab as they scrambled out. Pollard threw a glance into the back.

'You can have your lorry now . . . ' he began.

But the driver couldn't reply. Half his forehead had vanished. He lay cuddled against the tailboard, his hands together; he might have been praying when the bullet hit him.

*   *   *

They hid, shivering, behind a clump of bushes. It was light now; a grey day with a cruelly insistent wind. They were exhausted; they had trudged for hours after abandoning the truck, wending their way through woods and over open fields. At one point they had seen the soldiers but, more by luck than design, they had managed to evade them.

Eisner kept studying his map.

'I think we have come east.'

Pollard stared at him. '*East?*'

'Unfortunately it seems to be some distance. I believe we were on this road.' Painstakingly he indicated the road on the map. 'Do you see it? This one. If I am right we are probably back inside Germany.'

Pollard didn't reply. He knew no words to express himself. It was a nightmare: all that bloody stupid effort, all that slogging through the snow, all that damned horrible *suffering*, all pointless. They were back, almost where they had started, back inside Germany again! It was enough – more than enough – to make a bloke weep.

'We cannot possibly stay outside dressed as we are,' Eisner said, carefully, as if he had thought out every word before speaking. 'We will freeze to death. I think we must consider our options.'

Pollard sniffed. 'How many have we got?'

'One or two. We can, of course, attempt our journey all over again, heading west, back toward Belgium, on foot.'

'Christ,' Pollard muttered, tightening his arms around himself.

'The idea does not appeal to you, I see. Well then, I suggest that you surrender to the German Army. You will, I think, be quite well treated. It will be preferable, I think, to freezing to death.'

'What about you?'

'I shall attempt to get to Wiesbaden and find Trude.'

'You're barmy. You'd never make it and you know it.'

'But I must try.'

'We could both surrender,' said Pollard. 'You could pull your back injury stunt again. It worked with the Belgians; it'll work again with your lot.'

But Eisner was shaking his head. 'Our encounter with Mooney and Donaldson and the Belgians made me realize how quickly I would be unmasked by genuine RAF questioners. Besides, this is the time, I feel, when I must strike out on my own. I have been a burden on you too long, my friend. We must be sensible and think clearly about our situation. We are in a giant trap. Even if we were able, we dare not go back into Belgium; there is nowhere here in Germany where we can rest and obtain food and the proper clothing. I think we have to accept the fact that we tried very hard but we failed. The question now is whether to try again or to give up.'

Pollard shook his head. 'No, there's got to be a way out. All we've got to do is find it. We've come a hell of a long way. Can't just give up now. Besides, it'd be a shame to break up the old team, eh?'

Eisner smiled in spite of himself. The snowflakes melted on his face; he kept wiping them away as if they were tears. 'We must accept the truth,' he said. 'We cannot survive for long.'

Pollard found himself still shaking his head, doggedly. He wasn't sure why. 'Never say die,' he muttered.

Eisner gazed at him. 'What does that mean?'

Pollard started to explain but gave up halfway.

Eisner stared into the distance, his eyes traversing the bleak snowy landscape. Then, abruptly, he turned to Pollard. 'In your own way, Sergeant, you are quite a remarkable fellow.'

Pollard frowned, wondering if he had heard the man correctly.

Eisner said, 'It is curious to think that only a few days ago I very nearly killed you. I came closer than perhaps even you realize. I was frustrated and angry. I had been hiding too long. It does things to a man, you know. It affects his sanity, his balance, his perspective.'

'You did seem a bit shirty,' Pollard agreed.

Eisner smiled, shivering. 'I sense that I frequently irritate you. Is that not so?'

'I suppose so,' Pollard shrugged. 'You're so bloody *right* all the time. But I s'pose I'm not what you'd exactly call perfect, am I?'

Eisner didn't answer. After a moment he said, 'Whatever happens, Sergeant, I want to thank you for your loyalty. You have been a splendid comrade. It would have been a simple matter for you to turn me over to the Belgians, but you didn't.'

'It wouldn't have been right,' said Pollard. 'That's all there is to it. I say we stick together.'

Eisner was counting his fingers. 'Something just occurred to me.'

'What?'

'It's Christmas Eve.'

* * *

It was still light but they were too cold to remain stationary. Bent almost double against the biting wind, they trudged across one field after another. It began to snow again. Soon they could see nothing beyond a yard or two. They stumbled on, blindly, numbly.

They walked into the fence without seeing it. Automatically, Pollard started to clamber over the wooden struts. Then he became aware that Eisner was pointing. A farm. A cluster of buildings. Shelter.

Without exchanging a word, the two men turned and walked along the fence, touching it as they went as if they were afraid of losing it.

The house stood, square and businesslike, in the foreground. Beyond it there were barns.

*　　*　　*

Pollard awoke. It took a moment to sort out where he was. Then it came back to him. The storm. The farm.

His stomach ached. Sod that swede! They had found the thing, dry and tough, in a corner of the barn. Carefully they had sliced it and had consumed it before going to sleep.

Now his stomach was complaining. Pollard apologized to it. He wanted to do better; he would have dearly loved some nice roast turkey and mashed potatoes, sprouts and sausages, all swimming in piping hot gravy . . .

No, for Christ's sake, no. He would burst out crying if he thought about food any more. He examined his toes and fingers. All present and correct, thank God. He lay back in the prickly but superbly cosy straw. Warmth wrapped itself around him, hugging him.

Eisner stirred. Vigorously he rubbed the sleep from his face. He wriggled free of the straw, brushing fragments from his clothes. 'Stay here. I shall have a little reconnaissance.'

'What's the time?'

'Nearly eight o'clock.'

'Happy Christmas.'

The German smiled. 'And to you.'

Pollard indicated their surroundings. 'All we need is the three wise men and we'd be all set.'

Eisner didn't get it. Never mind. His loss. I hope, thought Pollard, that he'll find a place that sells eggs and bacon and toast and tea . . .

Blimey, don't start that again!

It was odd, now that he was warm, he couldn't think of anything but food. Hot, steaming, cooked to perfection. He dozed and dreamt of hot crumpets oozing with butter that ran over his fingers when he picked up the tasty morsels and popped them into his mouth, one by one . . .

He woke, heart thumping. Someone was approaching the barn. Someone heavy. Authoritative.

Where was Eisner?

Christ.

He lay there, immobile, trying to breathe quietly, but fear shortened his breath. He longed to take huge gulps. Now the footsteps came nearer, crunching through the snow, pausing at the door, as if surveying the interior before entering.

Pollard felt sick. His stomach heaved; his throat contracted; his hands became clammy with sweat.

The footsteps were slower, more cautious. Another pause. A scraping as if the man was turning and looking about him. Another couple of paces. Another pause. The man's breathing was clearly audible. Now he was inside the barn.

Pollard bit his lower lip. Where the bloody hell was Eisner? The man was only a pace or two away. And suspicious as hell.

A new sound. Like something pecking.

Tap, tap, tap.

Then the gun barrel hit his leg.

'Ah!'

Triumphal bleat.

The gun barrel poked its way through the straw. Pollard found himself face to face with a squat, fleshy individual with a bushy moustache and an enormous double barrelled shotgun. About fifty-five. Tough, leathery.

He yelped something in German. The gun motioned.

Nodding, agreeing, trying to tame his wobbly limbs, Pollard tottered to his feet, gasping at the roof trusses for support.

More German jabberings.

'All right, I'm coming, I'm coming.'

Pollard scrambled down to the ground, brushing the straw from his hair and his uniform.

The farmer's ample chest swelled with pride. He was the courageous hunter who had come up with the catch of the season. His small eyes travelled up and down Pollard, pausing with interest on the rank badges and ribbons.

Now a woman appeared at the barn doorway, thin faced, apprehensive.

He yapped at her, like a sergeant-major addressing a recruit. She nodded nervously, then hurried away.

The farmer prodded Pollard's ribs with the gun barrel as if testing him for fleshiness and muscle. Pollard assured him that he concealed no weapon. He turned out his pockets to prove it.

'*So*,' muttered the farmer.

'That's right,' said Pollard. 'So.'

The farmer said something else in German. Pollard shrugged. The German spoke louder, presumably believing that with volume would come comprehension.

Pollard shrugged again; he thrust his hands in his pockets and hunched his shoulders. It was cold standing close to the open door.

The farmer raised two fingers. Pollard shook his head. The German seemed angry. Still covering Pollard, he kicked at the hay with his boots. Failing to find the second man, he motioned with the gun barrel. Pollard was to go through the door.

Pollard did so.

The farmer kept talking, spouting what Pollard took to be warnings about what would happen to him if he failed to obey every single instruction. Pollard nodded at everything the man said.

He shivered as they stepped outside into the snow. The sun was glimmering through wispy clouds.

The farmer pointed at the footprints in the snow; they were still faintly visible, still revealing the fact that two men had passed this way.

Pollard shrugged yet again. The farmer's brows darkened; his lower lip jutted aggressively. More German jabbering, more pointing at the tracks, more shrugs from Pollard.

Then Eisner appeared at the corner of the barn, Luger in one hand, finger to lip. He was directly behind the farmer. He stepped forward. Simultaneously he thrust the gun in the farmer's back and reached forward to push the shotgun barrel to one side.

'You did that very neatly,' said Pollard.

'My pleasure,' said Eisner.

Terror stamped a grey pallor on the farmer's features; his mouth kept working but no sounds emerged.

'Would you kindly relieve him of his gun?'

'Delighted,' said Pollard.

The farmer offered no resistance. His beady eyes had assumed a curiously glazed look. Pollard wondered if he was about to suffer an attack.

'Get in the house,' Eisner commanded, in English.

'*Ja, ja.*' The farmer was breathless but anxious to please.

Pollard said, 'There's a woman too. His wife, I suppose.'

'I know,' said Eisner. 'He told her to ring the police. She's probably done it already. Come on, let's find out.'

The woman met them at the door, her mouth hanging open as if her jaw was broken. She swore that she hadn't telephoned the police. She pleaded for the life of her husband. He slumped into a chair, his face pasty, his breathing husky.

Eisner said, 'She may be telling the truth. But we can't be sure. See if you can get a couple of pairs of boots and some warm clothing. And food. Lots of food.'

It took five minutes. They tied the farmer and his wife to chairs. Then they hurried outside. It was quiet. Pale sunlight was glimmering on the snow.

Eisner turned. 'West?'

Pollard shrugged. He was getting good at shrugging. 'Why not?' he said. 'If at first you don't succeed . . .'

16

The Messerschmitt 110 came low, wobbling in the wind, undercarriage and flaps extended for landing. The sun glinted on its wingtips; the whirling propellors looked like semi-transparent discs. Steadily the aircraft descended, disappearing beyond a line of trees. Pollard stood on tiptoes, but the airfield was out of sight.

Another machine was already in the circuit. It came into view, wings swaying as the pilot lined up with the runway.

'Night fighter,' Pollard commented. The Lichtenstein radar antennae protruded from the Messerschmitt's nose like antlers. He watched as the machine passed overhead. It might have been the one that shot Woods-Bassett down. A small Union Jack on the tail or on the side of the fuselage would have denoted the victory for all to see and admire.

Eisner munched his sausage as he peered through the trees.

'Anyone around?' Pollard asked him.

'Not yet.'

'You think there will be?'

'Eventually, I expect.'

You should have shot the bastard dead, Pollard thought, but didn't say. It was easier to talk about such things than to do them.

'Perhaps they're still tied up,' he said.

Eisner shrugged. 'Perhaps.'

Pollard pulled the farmer's coat tighter. It was an ugly garment, but stout and substantial. Its pockets were stuffed with ammunition for the shotgun and all the sausage and bread he could find in the kitchen. He wished there had been time to have a bath and a shave. A change of clothing would have been pleasant too. If I get out of this, he promised himself, I'll have a bath every day and I'll change my shirt and my socks and my underwear every day. In fact, he declared, if I'm going out at night, I'll change my socks and my shirt twice that day.

He nodded his head as if to signify that the promise was a solemn and important one.

The trees loomed over him, black and leafless against the winter sky.

Another aircraft engine could be heard. The boys seemed busy. Were they expecting lots of trade that night? Had they already picked up transmissions from England, indicating that a big raid was imminent?

Another Messerschmitt. It was very low. Pollard could see the markings on its fuselage, denoting the *Staffel* to which it belonged. The twin Daimler-Benz engines buzzed in their distinctive, pulsating manner. The rear gunner's face was a white dot against the canopy; he seemed to be looking down; did he have orders to look for two fugitive RAF men believed to be in the vicinity? Instinctively, Pollard shrank into the bushes.

The sun was bright now; the clouds had dispersed, leaving a clear blue sky.

They wrapped themselves in the coats and tried to snatch a little sleep. But Pollard couldn't relax. His heart thumped like a trip hammer; every muscle seemed to pulsate. You're in a bloody great cobweb, he told himself, and you don't know how to get out of it.

He opened his eyes.

And saw the soldier.

A young, keen looking bloke, carrying his rifle easily in the crook of his left arm. His right hand was on the trigger; the weapon was ready for instant use.

He walked slowly, methodically, his head turning left to right, right to left.

Twenty yards away, he stopped and gazed up into the branches above him.

Pollard whispered, 'Don't move a bloody muscle, but open your eyes.'

Beside him, Eisner tensed. Pollard heard the German's hand move beneath the coat. Would he be able to fire the

Luger before the soldier fired his rifle? And if there were shots, how long before the soldier's comrades came pounding along?

His chest seemed to vibrate with the beating, bumping of his heart.

Where was the shotgun? Was the safety catch on?

I'll surrender, he promised himself. Hands up right away. No messing about. No point trying to shoot it out with the whole bloody German Army. If Eisner wants to do battle, that's his business, nothing to do with me . . .

The soldier moved on.

Eisner relaxed but didn't move.

'There must be others,' he whispered.

'That's what I was thinking,' Pollard hissed.

They heard them a moment later. A loud voice of authority.

'He's telling them to search diligently,' said Eisner.

'Sod him,' said Pollard. 'What do we do now?'

'We wait.'

'Here?'

'I think so. We escaped detection once, therefore it must be a reasonably good hiding place, wouldn't you say?'

'Christ knows, I suppose so.'

'Our only chance of getting out of this area is to move at night. We must wait until nightfall. It should be dark in three hours.'

*   *   *

Stiff with cold, they made their cautious way out of the forest. It was a clear night, perfectly still, beautiful in a frozen, dead sort of way.

They had to cross an open field. Every step sounded like the crushing of eggshells, hundreds of them; the din was frightful. Surely it was audible a mile away. At any moment a fusillade of bullets would put an end to this nonsense once and for all.

Pollard told himself that it was bound to happen sooner or later, probably sooner. You only had so much luck; when you'd used it up, you got yours and there wasn't a ruddy thing you could do about it.

He looked back. Incredibly there seemed to be no one in

pursuit. But their footprints were as plain to see as Belisha beacons.

The roar of an aircraft engine shattered the silence of the night. A moment later another engine burst into life, then another.

'Sounds as if they're expecting some customers tonight.'

'Customers?'

'Our blokes. Bombers.'

'I see.'

'If I was a ruddy pilot,' Pollard muttered, 'we could have a go at liberating one of those kites. We'd be home in no time, then.'

Eisner looked up. 'But didn't you tell me that you had done some flying?'

Pollard nodded. 'But I just took over after Hatch had trimmed the kite. Got it all nicely balanced, you know. I wouldn't have a bloody clue how to take one of those buggers off. Impossible.'

'I suppose so,' Eisner murmured.

Cautiously they made their way along a scraggy hedge. They stopped. There was a building fifty yards further on. Crouched, they made off to the left, to give the place a wide berth. Another engine burst into life. The noise seemed to come from directly behind them. Startled, they turned. Someone shouted something. The voice was drowned in the din of the engines as they were run up.

The airfield was coming to life.

They were closer to the place than they had realized.

For a nightmarish moment, Pollard was convinced that they had blundered onto the field. He felt a thousand German eyes looking and pointing at him, a curious specimen from the other side. He shivered the image away.

The din was appalling now. It sounded as if they had a thousand aircraft blaring away at full throttle. Had they chanced upon a giant German air attack just as they had chanced upon the great land assault? Was the war lost already?

They listened as an aircraft took off, roaring along the runway then lifting off and vanishing into the night. A second machine was already on its takeoff run; a third and a fourth followed in rapid succession; more machines ran up their engines and taxied.

A dozen machines. Not quite the armada that his imagination had painted.

The air seemed to vibrate even when the noise of the engines had faded. In a few minutes the Messerschmitts would be wading into the bomber stream, blasting away at the poor overloaded Lancs and Hallybags, blowing blokes to smithereens and burning them to cinders.

Eisner was beckoning. He had crept forward a dozen yards, up a slight incline. Pollard followed, using the shotgun as a kind of walking stick.

There was the airfield, clearly visible through a break in the fence. A few shadowy figures moved about: ground staff returning to the warmth of the crew huts after getting their charges away.

'I suppose,' mused Eisner, 'that it is pointless to think about stealing an aircraft.'

''Course it is,' Pollard said, 'unless you've got someone to fly it.'

Eisner nodded thoughtfully.

Pollard said, 'Even if I *could* fly the thing, we'd never be able to steal one.'

'I suppose you're right.'

Pollard gestured. 'Bloody right I'm right. You can't just walk onto an airfield and get in a plane and fly it away. They guard those things. Anyway, it's barmy wasting time thinking about it. For a start, they'd never let us get near one of those kites; and if we did get near we wouldn't know what the hell to do with it. How would we get the sodding engines going?'

'I suppose it would be difficult,' Eisner admitted.

'Difficult? It'd be bloody impossible, mate. It's not like getting into someone else's car. Not a bit like it. Every aeroplane is different. And complicated as hell.'

'I understand,' said Eisner. 'I assure you I do understand.'

'There's nothing I'd like better than to fly home in style, but I *can't* fly one of those things. Honest. I don't know how so there's no use thinking about it.'

'I see.'

They started to walk but again they saw guards. Soldiers with rifles. They hid under a hedge, half buried in snow. Later, shivering against a tree, they watched the aircraft return and land. Then they saw the first reluctant glimmer of the new day.

They ate the remains of the food they had taken from the farmer.

Two Luftwaffe men strolled past them, talking earnestly, angrily, their hands moving to emphasize their words. It sounded important. But when the Germans had gone, Eisner said they were discussing nothing more important than the inadequate supplies of cigarettes at the canteen.

Pollard squatted down against a tree. It was cold and uncomfortable. He felt filthy; sweat and fright had formed a slimy second skin all over him.

The notion of stealing a Jerry plane was barmy, of course. Of course.

What he told Eisner was perfectly true. He hadn't a clue how to start a Messerschmitt and even if he did, by some outrageous miracle, sort out the buttons and the levers and get the thing going, he certainly wasn't capable of flying it.

The very thought sent shudders through him. Those Messerschmitts were hot as hell, fast and powerful. They were like the Mossies and Beaus. You had to be good to fly them. And if you weren't good enough, they'd kill you, in double-quick time.

Don't even think about it.

That's an order!

But it was hard to think of anything else. He had spent dozens of hours in the Lanc, helping Hatch jockey the throttles to make sure the kite stayed on the runway in a straight line, then when the rudders took over, pouring on full coal and easing the stick forward to get the tail off the ground. You had to be careful not to try and get her off too soon; some of the high performance jobs would drop a wing and then you'd be up the creek and no mistake. Hatch used to say that she would more or less fly off herself if you had her set up properly . . .

He shook his head. No. Madness. Even *thinking* about it was crazy.

Hatch was always pointing out that aeroplanes really wanted to do the right thing, it was idiotic pilots who made them do the wrong thing.

Hatch was the fount of all aeronautical knowledge. Pollard had tried so hard to emulate his skill, diligently working the ailerons and rudders to turn the Lanc, simultaneously watching the needle on the turn and bank indicator as it measured the success of his efforts: a clean, smooth change of direction, or an ugly slithering and snaking around the sky, or something in between. He had ignored the hoots of the other members of the crew deriding his efforts. To hell with them. He would get it right. He *would* change to 090 without losing altitude. But invariably the nose would sink as if drawn by a magnet. And by the time he had observed the loss of height and had tugged back on the yoke, the turn would have become uncoordinated; the turn and bank needle would have slewed to one side, glaring evidence of his incompetence. There were too many things to watch at once. Height, speed, altitude, course. A bloke only had one pair of eyes, for God's sake. And then, to get the adrenalin flowing, the kite would hit turbulence and lurch in the sky as if about to lose its balance and tumble like the enormous chunk of metal and plastic and rubber it really was.

Hatch kept saying that he was getting the hang of it. 'If I get the chop,' he told the other members of the crew, 'Polly will be able to fly the kite home.' Which produced cries of protest and simulated terror.

'Let's hope Polly gets the chop, and not you,' yelped Lucas, the mid-upper gunner, an Irishman from Dublin.

'If Polly flies the kite, I'm baling out,' was the opinion of Sloan, the navigator.

'Where do I go to resign?' Beale, the wireless op, wanted to know.

Humorists, one and all. But not any more.

'The whole point of landing,' Hatch told him, 'is to get the kite lined up with the runway, then peel off the power so that she comes down steadily, nose up a bit as if you're set for touchdown the whole way in. Then, when you're down there you must cut the rest of your power and try to keep it flying as long as you can. As soon as she starts to drop pull back a bit so that your nose comes up and your speed drops off even more. After a bit she'll settle on the tarmac as sweet as you please.'

It sounded easy, the way Hatch told it. He had a way with landings. They were always perfect three-pointers, the wheels giving little squeals of delight when they touched. No clattering, bouncing and banging with Hatch. Even when there was a cross-wind he was able to compensate in just the right way at just the right time.

Hatch had the *feel*.

You haven't got the feel, Pollard told himself. You haven't got a bloody clue. You were shooting a bloody great line of bullshit to Trude. You're no pilot, mate.

But – just supposing – if he did actually succeed in getting a Jerry kite into the air and if he managed to get the thing pointed in the right direction and – biggest of all – if he wasn't shot down by flak or fighters, was there the slightest chance that he could get the beast *down* on the ground again, in one piece?

In theory, he knew how to do it. He had read countless books on flying. He had seen Hatch land scores of times. He knew every movement in the process. But he had never actually *done* it.

It was absolutely bloody barmy even to think about it.

And yet.

And yet what a bloody marvellous *coup* to bring back a Jerry kite (fitted with God nows how many secret devices that the boffins might be thrilled to death to have) plus a Jerry colonel who had been personally involved in the world-famous plot.

He'd be famous. Interviews with the press. Gongs galore. A commission perhaps. Flying Officer Pollard, DSO.

No! Absolutely not! He mustn't think about it!

Actually it was stupid to think about it. There wasn't really any purpose in worrying about how to start the bloody thing or get it off the ground or land it, because they wouldn't even get *near* it.

And even if they did get near it, they wouldn't get into it without being seen.

And if by some fantastic bit of luck they did manage to get inside one of those kites, what good would it do?

'Honest,' he said, 'I couldn't start a Lanc in the dark, let alone one of those kites.'

Eisner nodded. Understanding as hell.

'Of course. It would be very difficult.'

'No, it wouldn't be difficult, mate, it'd be *impossible*. You'd need a bloody guide book to tell you what knob did what.'

'I see.'

He didn't, of course. Sod him.

'Christ,' Pollard flared, 'I'd try it if I thought we stood a chance. But I've never actually flown a plane by myself, never taken one off or landed one. Honest to God, you've no bloody idea how mad it is even to think about it.'

'I understand.'

'So let's forget about it.'

'Very well.'

But they remained in the vicinity of the field.

17

One of the Messerschmitt's engines was spewing smoke; it spluttered and coughed as the fighter swept overhead. Pollard could see the holes that had been punched through the wing. Cannon fire had mangled the port aileron; its trailing edge was torn and buckled. The fighter landed heavily, bouncing when it touched down. It rolled to one side of the strip, then to the other side before disappearing from view.

Pollard nodded in satisfaction. It looked as if some Flying Fort gunner had done a good day's work.

Another Me landed a minute later; it taxied hurriedly to its dispersal, the pilot evidently keen on getting parked before the Typhoons and Thunderbolts came visiting.

The Jerries had scattered their kites around the perimeter of the field, each one shielded from blast by revetments of sandbags and concrete blocks.

The runway had been patched again and again. One brick building was little more than a shell; it looked as if a giant hand had ripped off its roof and scooped out its contents. Not one of the hangars appeared to be undamaged. The place was a shambles, but it was still a going concern.

Cautiously, Pollard and Eisner made their way along the barbed wire fence. The trees were thickly clustered; it was possible to catch only glimpses of the field. Then the barbed wire ended suddenly. Had the Jerries suddenly run out of the stuff? Pollard found himself wondering about it; then he wondered why he was wondering. He was too cold to care.

'Look.'

Eisner said it quietly; he pointed through the trees.

A Messerschmitt stood there. It had just returned from action. The engine cowlings still crackled as they cooled. The ground staff were busy refuelling and re-arming, feeding in the

belts of bullets for the machine guns and shells for the 30 mm
Rheinmetall Borsig cannons.

'Crikey,' Pollard muttered.

The dispersal area had been cut out of the trees. A roof of
netting had been added, intertwined with branches and leaves.
From the air the dispersal would be almost invisible.

Work on the Messerschmitt went on for half an hour. Then
the crewmen retired to a tiny hut huddled in the trees. An hour
elapsed. The light faded. Soon after dark, a bell rang. Airmen
– aircrew and ground types – came scrambling out of the hut.
Alert! The aircrew, awkward in their bulky flying gear,
clambered aboard the Me. A mechanic stood on the wing and
assisted the pilot with his straps.

The engines burst into life, sending a windstorm raging
through the trees, scattering leaves and twigs and snow and
ice. The mechanic snapped the pilot's canopy lid in place;
inside, the pilot reached up and locked it. The mechanic
jumped down as the Me began to roll, ailerons and elevators,
flaps and rudders flapping and extending as the pilot tested
them. The fighter swung to the right; the gale subsided.

The ground crewmen watched their aircraft roll away into
the darkness then, hands thrust into pockets, ambled back to
the warmth of their crew hut.

Eisner nodded to himself as if cataloguing the things he had
seen.

He said, 'The pilot appears to have side arms, but not the
other airmen.'

Pollard pointed out that the rear gunner had a couple of
thoroughly dangerous looking machine guns in the back seat.

'True,' Eisner stroked his chin. 'Nevertheless, I think we
might manage to persuade the pilot to fly us out of here.
What do you say, my friend?'

Pollard gulped. 'I say we'd most likely get our silly heads
blown off for our trouble.'

'The idea doesn't appeal to you?'

'It scares me to death.'

'But we will have a great advantage,' Eisner pointed out.

'We will?'

'Most certainly. We will have surprise on our side. In war,

it is of paramount importance. In a mission such as this it can make all the difference.'

He was *relishing* the thought of action. You could see it in his eyes. He kept studying the dispersal area; it was as if he was watching endless rehearsals of the operation, observing how the *Luftwaffe* men reacted, how they could be covered, how the aircrew could be coerced into cooperation.

'But I don't even know how to fire this bloody gun,' Pollard complained.

'It's very simple. I will show you.' Eisner took the shotgun and indicated the safety catch and how the weapon was hinged, exposing the breech. 'The cartridges go in here, you see, then you simply snap the gun back together. There.'

Pollard shivered, imagining himself fumbling with the thing, trying to pull used shots out and push new ones in, all in the heat of battle.

'Look,' he said, 'I really don't think this is . . . my cup of tea exactly. I'm not a soldier, you know.'

'I have the greatest confidence in you,' said Eisner with a grin. The odd thing was, he sounded as if he meant it.

'What if the pilot says no?'

'I think he will be more sensible.'

'Yes, but he might not be.'

'In my experience, people usually do what you ask when you have a loaded gun in your hand.'

'But he might not.'

'True.'

'Then, will you shoot him?'

Eisner shrugged. 'It's hard to say. The moment will decide.'

*　　*　　*

The Messerschmitt taxied back to its dispersal, engines emitting impatient little spurts of noise as if they found progress on the ground too slow and tedious after hurtling through the air at twenty thousand feet. With a squeal of brakes the aircraft came to a halt. The canopy lid swung open; the pilot emerged, all smiles beneath the smooth leather of his helmet. He held up two fingers to the ground man scrambling toward him over the wing. They shook hands. Quickly the news of the victories sped to the others. They grinned and slapped each other on the back as if they had personally been involved in the action.

Pollard wanted to tell them to put a sock in it. Some pleasant blokes had undoubtedly met extremely unpleasant ends. Getting shot down in flames was no joke. He knew.

The airmen chatted until a battered Opel came and took them away. The ground types busied themselves with fuel and ammunition.

Pollard grimaced. The Me didn't have a scratch. God knows what those silly sods at the Air Ministry were thinking about. Why weren't they busy installing belly turrets on the Lancs and Halifaxes? Then the Jerries wouldn't be able to sneak in below and blast away at the fuel tanks without being seen. And why the hell didn't they put heavier gauge machine guns in the turrets so that they'd be a bit of a match for the night fighters' weapons? There was a rumour that some squadrons were beginning to receive aircraft armed with half-inch calibre machine guns, but Pollard knew of no one who had seen them with their own eyes.

The night's work appeared to be over. In an hour it would be daylight. The bombers had gone home – to bacon and eggs and nine or ten hours in the pit. Lucky buggers.

The Jerry night fighter crews were probably doing the same thing. The day crews were just waking up. The ground crewmen were still busy, readying the Me for next time – fighting the Yanks perhaps.

The minutes ticked away.

If you don't do something about it, Pollard informed himself, you're going to be in the middle of a bloody shooting gallery in a little while. Do you understand what that *means*?

Yes, he did understand. But somehow the understanding possessed no reality.

They searched through their pockets and found a few fragments of bread and sausage. It was gone in a moment. Eisner shrugged as if to say that now they had no choice; they had to get out by air. Pollard didn't respond. He kept thinking of his mother and how she used to insist that he couldn't possibly face a cold day on nothing but toast and tea; he had to have hot porridge and golden syrup. It would, she assured him, make a lining for his stomach. Stomach linings were vital.

His hands were thrust deep in his trouser pockets. His fingers were like little chunks of ice against his legs. If I have to fire the bloody gun, he thought, I won't be able to. I'll pull and nothing will happen. Typical!

God, how the hell did he ever get into this mess?

*   *   *

The sun emerged. But it might have been a picture on a box of chocolates for all the heat it provided.

There was a changeover of ground crews: a new group arrived wearing clean overalls. They marched to the dispersal like a platoon of troops. All very Teutonic and military; very un-RAF.

'Do you agree that we should order the pilot to fly west and simply land at the first airfield inside the Allied lines?'

Pollard stared at him. Christ, was it really going to happen?

'We must decide,' said Eisner.

Pollard nodded. 'Head west,' he muttered. We'll go bloody west all right, he thought.

Towards noon, a new aircrew arrived to start the Messerschmitt up. They ran the engines for a few minutes, then closed them down again. They stood in their flying clothes, chatting and looking up at the sky as every airman since the Wright Brothers has done.

The bell jangled in the crew hut. Scramble! Suddenly the dispersal looked like Paddington Station: men dashing about, scrambling aboard the aircraft, checking trolley-acc connections, giving the windscreen one final polish. The big three-bladed VDM propellers jerked into motion, spun, dissolved into shining discs as the mechanics buttoned down the canopy and removed the chocks.

Pollard and Eisner lay flat, pressed into the damp ground; the gale screamed over their heads.

*   *   *

The Messerschmitt returned a couple of hours later. No grins and back-slapping this time. The fuselage had taken several hits and the metal skin was scarred and lacerated. The ground crew clustered around the cockpit. Gently they pulled the bloody remains of the gunner from the rear seat. An ambulance arrived.

Suddenly one of the ground types broke away and ran straight for Pollard.

Icy, useless fingers fumbled at the shotgun trigger.

Eisner extended a restraining hand.

The man had run from his comrades simply to vomit.

Pollard breathed again.

The man seemed to stand there for ever, holding his stomach, muttering to himself in his discomfiture.

'For Christ's sake, get it over with,' Pollard grunted to himself. How long did it take a bloke to bring up his breakfast? The bastard was lucky to have any breakfast to bring up.

*   *   *

Maintenance officers came to inspect the Messerschmitt; bespectacled characters who looked like bank clerks in uniform. They pointed, discussed, nodded, agreed. The Me was to be patched up in time for the night's operations. In-hangar work could be postponed. Get to it. Already the light was beginning to fade. The Tommies would be along shortly.

Pollard had to clench his teeth to keep them quiet. Any relaxation produced a rattle like machine gun fire. Rigor mortis, he decided, was setting in before he was even dead. 'Honest to God,' he whispered to Eisner, 'I don't think I can stick it much longer. I'm freezing to death.'

Eisner, his eyes still roaming the dispersal, murmured, 'Try not to think about it.'

'I know. You told me that before. It doesn't work.'

'It does for me,' said Eisner.

It bloody well would, Pollard thought. Irritably he wrapped his arms around his body and tried to pull his head down inside the collar of the farmer's coat. He moved his legs. He couldn't feel them but at least they still worked. But would they still support him? Bloody marvellous assault it would be if he stood up with his gun and promptly fell over again.

No such thoughts seemed to trouble Eisner. He scanned the

dispersal again and again. Professional soldier at work. Napoleon planning Waterloo. No. Pollard mentally kicked himself. Not Waterloo, for God's sake. What battles had Napoleon *won*? He couldn't remember. Why, he wondered, did his mind persist in occupying itself with such unbelievably unimportant matters when it had a subject of life and death to consider?

Eisner sketched the dispersal in the snow, using a twig as a pencil.

'The aircraft is here in the centre. The crew hut is there. We are at this point. Now, when they start up the aircraft we have seen how they all are occupied. Some men are on the wing, helping the pilot and gunner, one is underneath the machine, two seem to be doing something to the engines. The important thing is that their attention is directed this way. Very well, then, I suggest we approach in this manner. You will proceed, here, behind these trees. But you will not show yourself until I have made my presence known to them. I shall come out of the trees at this spot. I shall walk up behind the aircraft. There will be a great deal of noise so that it will be pointless to say anything. I shall simply motion with the gun. Then you will come this way, across the dispersal area to the front of the aircraft, looking in the crew hut as you do so to ensure that no men are in there. By this time I shall be on the wing beside the pilot. We will thus have everyone well covered. We will line the ground staff up here, with their backs to us. I shall tell the gunner to get out. When he has done so and when the pilot has agreed to our suggestions, then you will jump aboard and we shall be off.'

It sounded as easy as buying a tube of toothpaste.

'What if one of them makes a run for it?'

'Then we shoot,' Eisner said with a shrug. He had the same maddening disregard for problems as Woods-Bassett. It would be done because he said it would be done. QED. Pollard sucked in air as if to inflate his flagging courage. It didn't help. His mouth tasted foul with fear. He remembered reading boys' stories in which craven characters (usually Arabs and Lascars) were despised for not having 'stomach for the fight'. Now he knew what they meant. He didn't have stomach for this one. He didn't want any part of it. The mere thought of it was enough to send his stomach reeling and his gorge rising.

He wanted to tell Eisner that much as he respected him and wished him the very best of British luck, he didn't think this was really worth the risk, considering everything and that he was hereby withdrawing his services.

Eisner grinned. 'OK, my friend?'

Pollard gulped. 'Well, I'm not sure . . . '

Eisner held up his hand. Something was happening on the dispersal. The little Opel car came bounding across the uneven grass; it squealed to a halt and disgorged three men in flying gear. The night crew. They examined the aircraft with interest, studying its scars from the daytime battle; there were various conferences with the ground staff. Was everyone quite certain that no serious damage had been done? The airmen clambered inside the cockpit to examine the damage from there. Shrugs from the NCO in charge: he had been instructed to patch the machine up for the night's operations, he was merely following orders; if the *Leutnant* didn't agree with the opinion he should, with all respect, talk to the *Hauptmann*. It was beyond a mere *Feldwebel*'s responsibility to disregard the orders of his superior officers.

Angrily the pilot pointed to something beneath the Me's nose. More shrugs and gestures of explanation from the NCO. The pilot wagged an indignant finger. The whole matter was extremely unsatisfactory and it was only his sense of duty and loyalty that was preventing him from taking further action.

It was dark now. The aircrew went into the hut and waited for the call to action. Everyone seemed convinced that Bomber Command would be visiting Germany that night. Perhaps the Luftwaffe's monitoring service, the *Horchdienst*, had already picked up signs of unusual activity from England: hundreds of wireless ops testing their radios in preparation for the night's operation. A dead give-away, as bad as sending a telegram to Hitler saying the boys would soon be on their way.

Even if we get a bloody pilot to fly us, Pollard thought, we're likely to be shot down by one of our own kites. Or flak. It was an unappealing prospect. Desperately he tried to think of some way of signifying surrender while in the air. Dangle a white flag out of a window? Put up their hands? Put down their wheels? The trouble was, everyone was so bloody trigger-happy these days. They blazed away and asked questions afterwards. Like the convoy in the channel, firing at Hatch just because he came within range. It didn't matter to those silly sods that the plane was British. It was a plane. That was reason enough.

They've most likely got a machine gun in that hut, he thought. They're smart, the Jerries. They've thought all this out. Escaped prisoners trying to steal a plane. What could be more natural? There's a bloke in there whose job it is to sit and keep his hand on the trigger of the machine gun and watch and wait.

We'll come charging out with these silly popguns, he thought, and we'll be mown down, cut to pieces . . .

I'm going to refuse. I won't go through with it. I can't. I'm no good with bloody guns. I'll bugger everything up. Look, frightfully sorry, old man, but upon sober reflection, I really do think it would be unwise of me to participate . . .

The alarm bell again.

Eisner grasped Pollard's shoulder. That grin again. Flash of white teeth. Teutonic Errol Flynn.

'Things appear to be happening.'

Pollard nodded dumbly.

'Remember. They are not expecting us. We have the advantage of surprise.'

And the disadvantage, Pollard thought, of sheer bloody funk.

'Don't forget the safety catch.'

'No . . . I won't.'

'Good fellow,' said Eisner. 'It's a little like stage fright, isn't it? One is always nervous before one goes on the stage; and a soldier is always nervous before he goes into battle. But it is all different when the moment comes.'

Worse, Pollard thought. He saw the aircrew hurrying to their aircraft, tugging their helmets over their heads, looking like something out of a Battle of Britain newsreel. They clambered aboard the Me; the ground wallahs helped to strap them in. The engines clattered and roared into life.

'I think,' said Eisner calmly, 'that this is the moment.'

It all had a curious dream-like quality. It wasn't real. It was someone else clutching the shotgun, someone else looking at those pop-eyed faces. It could have been a photograph: the instant was frozen. But then the eyes flew to Eisner who was bellowing something in German as he sprinted for the aircraft. He shoved a mechanic off the wing, then in one movement – smooth and polished as if he had practised it a thousand times – he flung open the canopy lid, pressed the Luger against the pilot's head and gestured to the other aircrew members to disembark. Rapidly.

Pollard threw a glance inside the crew hut. It was empty. No machine gun. But half a loaf of bread and some sausage in the middle of the table amid papers and magazines.

A mechanic moved. Pollard fired over his head. An enormous, shocking boom. The recoil almost knocked him off his balance. He staggered back, his chilled hands struggling to retain his grasp on the weapon.

God, he was hungry. But how, he wondered, as if with an unoccupied part of his brain, can you think about being hungry in the middle of all this? You've got a dozen Jerries at bay. The gunner and the radar man are getting out of the kite. Eisner is bellowing instructions to all and sundry. The ground wallahs are falling back, hands held high, faces sullen and confused. Everything worked according to plan.

Except for one thing. The pilot is shaking his head.

Categorical refusal.

The sod.

The gunner and the radar man have joined the others. Now, on Eisner's orders, they have formed a tight little group facing the trees. A bundle of bods. Easy to supervise. One movement and there's a bullet for you and you and you. Quickly, snap the gun open. Remove used shell. Thrust in new one. Damn! Dropped it. Fingers too bloody sodding cold. Another one. In securely.

Still the pilot's head keeps shaking. No, no, no. He will not do as Eisner demands.

Eisner's grey eyes meet Pollard's. A slight delay in the

proceedings. A minor hitch. It will be fixed up in a jiffy. Reason will prevail.

But the pilot keeps shaking his head.

Eisner places the muzzle of the Luger squarely in the middle of the pilot's forehead. Oddly, awkwardly, the man keeps shaking his head. He won't submit.

Pollard has advanced. He stands behind one wing of the fighter; the metal and oil and fright smell of all aeroplanes assails his nostrils. For some lunatic reason it makes him think again of food. He holds the gun to his shoulder and squints along the barrel, traversing the cluster of backs. Dimly, in the distance, he hears the ringing of the field telephone. No doubt someone in authority wants to know why the bloody hell fighter number so-and-so isn't taxiing across the field in preparation for taking off and engaging the enemies of the Third Reich who are at this moment swarming toward its sacred shores . . .

Eisner is beckoning. Come up here! On the wing!

Right. But keep the gun pointed; hold it with one hand, finger on trigger, while fumbling for a fingerhold with the other. Why the hell do they always make aeroplanes so bloody difficult to climb onto? Eisner's strong fingers grip his arm and hoist him on to the gale-battered wing.

'He doesn't want to fly us!'

The words register but they seem to have no significance. Just another statement in a world reeling from barrage after barrage of statements. The pilot won't do it. Dear dear. What next? Eisner will make it come out all right. He has the answers. He and Woods-Bassett. They know everything.

The shotgun is becoming heavy as hell. It wasn't designed for holding with one hand while hanging on to an aeroplane with the other.

Eisner is shrugging at the pilot as if to say that he has no alternative.

That gun, Pollard thinks numbly, will blow the poor bastard's head right off. The rather handsome features will become so much gristle and offal and it will all go flying through the air and make a bloody awful mess over in the inside of the aeroplane. He remembers the photograph in

Madame Tussaud's, of a Chinese revolutionary being executed by decapitation: his head is already in flight and blood fountains from his severed neck.

One last demand.

One last shake of the handsome head.

Discussion time over.

Jesus, Pollard thinks, Jesus, Jesus, Jesus.

Eisner suddenly moves. He brings the barrel of the gun around in a rapid, swinging motion. It catches the pilot on the side of the temple. His head bounces to one side then the other.

'You cover them!' Eisner bellows. 'I'll get him out of here!'

Pollard nods. He feels the whole aircraft shudder on its undercarriage as Eisner leaps astride the cockpit, hoisting the unconscious pilot out of his seat. The head that had been so resolutely shaken now flops limply on the man's chest. The man is draped over the windscreen. Eisner drags him off; he collapses onto the wing and slithers to the trailing edge and down to the ground. He is lucky, Pollard thinks, he didn't fall forward; he'd have been cut into bacon slices by the propellers.

His mind seems to be working at half speed.

That's all very bloody well, he thinks, glancing at the pilot lying in an untidy bundle on the ground, but what the hell are we going to do now?

Eisner indicates the empty cockpit.

'It's up to you, my friend.'

18

Pollard gaped.

'You're bloody barmy, mate!'

Eisner shrugged as if there was all the time in the world to discuss the matter and consider the pros and cons.

'There isn't much choice.'

Pollard felt as if someone had him by the throat.

'But I told you – I *can't*! I don't know *how* to!'

His voice was a panicky croak.

'The motors are already running,' Eisner pointed out.

'Yes, but . . .'

'Do you have any better ideas?'

A truck was bouncing across the grass. Full of troops? Fingers itching on triggers? Pollard felt terror within him, racing from limb to limb.

He clutched the canopy.

The cockpit looked like some monster's mouth, full of threatening knobs, switches, levers, dials. If he got in there, it would gobble him up, consume him, swallow him.

'No, honest to God, I *can't* . . .'

He caught Eisner's eyes. There was pleading there. This was it. The last chance. There was no other way out.

Pollard quailed, limbs turning rubbery. His brain tried to grapple with the enormity of the problem that faced him. He had never even been inside one of these bloody things before, let alone tried to sort out how to *fly* one . . .

But he found himself tumbling into the pilot's seat, his uncertain fingers gripping the joystick, feeling the textured surface of the grip, his feet groping for the rudder pedals. Dimly he was aware of the canopy lid thumping down over his head, a hand banging it in a curiously cheerful gesture.

He remembered seeing the pilot reach up to lock the canopy in position. There was the knob. Easy. So far.

But which knob controlled the brakes? Which the throttles? Flaps? Undercarriage? He didn't know. He was a child, helpless, unknowing. Vaguely he remembered reading that the Germans had standardized colour coding systems for their essential systems. But what use was that intelligence? It was dark; everything was grey.

Please God, get me out of this! I can't . . . I *can't* . . .

'Let's go!'

Eisner's voice. Bright and alert. The mad sod was sitting behind him in the gunner's position, fiddling with the twin guns, sorting out how they worked, presumably. Tools of the trade.

His quaking fingers found a pair of levers on the left side. He shifted them; at once the engines roared. Throttles! But where was the brake? And, Oh Christ, he had to be bloody careful not to hit the wrong knob or he'd fold the sodding undercarriage up and that would be the end of the whole crazy business . . .

Motion! He wasn't sure what he had touched but suddenly the Me was lurching forward, rocking as its wheels trundled over the uneven surface.

Eisner yelled something.

Pollard couldn't hear what. No matter. Just go. That was all that mattered. More throttle. And fright at the collosal power it produced. The fighter went careering in a semi-circle, threatening to tip over onto one wing.

The undercarriage squealed, complaining.

Any more of that and it would collapse. Straighten up. Bit of brake on that side. Ease off one of the throttles. No! Not that one. The other one! Right. Now it's straight. Past the truck. Cluster of white faces. Gone. Hands full, no time to think about those blokes.

Out, bounding, creaking, into the blackness of the airfield. Where to now?

No sign of activity. All lights off. No other machines to be seen. A man with a peaked cap, standing, watching, wondering, hands on hips. He vanished.

Now the fighter was on a hard surface. Where the hell was he? It had to be the runway! Frantically he peered ahead into the blackness. Yes, there seemed to be some shadowy lines stretching away and merging with the night.

Then, with a violent shock, he remembered that he had to attempt to fly this monster. His brain seemed to have decided to feed the awful truth to him in instalments. At first he had thought no further than getting the Me out of the dispersal and taxiing it across the field. That had been bad enough. But it wasn't enough. Not nearly enough. Now it was time to face the impossible task of getting this mechanical bucking bronco into the air.

Christ-all-bloody-mighty.

Flaps? Got to have a few degrees of flap; Hatch always had flap when he took the Lanc off. But where the hell were the switches? How could anyone *possibly* find the bloody flaps under such circumstances? There were words on several of the switches but what did they mean?

He seemed to be lined up on the runway.

All right. No time to hang around. Prop pitch? Hope for the best. Have a go! *Please!*

Throttles open.

The Me trembled with the power of her engines. Wilfully, she swung to one side. Shocked, scared, Pollard adjusted the power to the starboard engine. Still the fighter swung; one wheel ran off the solid surface onto grass.

Power down. The fighter slowed, bouncing, creaking as the wheels found the hard surface again.

Pollard ripped at his collar; he had to have air; he was suffocating in this horrible Perspex coffin. The bloody aeroplane wanted to kill him, that was the fact of the matter. It knew he was English; it knew he wanted to use it to escape his captors, and it knew he was clueless and incompetent.

Eisner was bellowing something from the rear cockpit.

'Belt up!' Pollard yelled in reply, as he fumbled with the unfamiliar controls.

A touch of throttle straightened the Me up again. Dimly he could see the runway in the darkness. Which way was the wind blowing? He couldn't remember. No time to ask. No time to do any bloody thing but shove the throttles open and try to hold this frisky bastard in a straight line. God only knows what would happen when the thing decided to take to the air. It was something that might occur in the impossibly distant future. No time to think about that now. One thing at a time. The immediate problem was to get the contraption rolling.

Oh God, don't let the bastard swing.

Straight. Right down the middle of the sodding runway. That's it! Feet bounding on rudder pedals ready to correct a change of direction; hands steadily feeding power to the twin Daimler–Benz engines.

All very expert.

Except that this wasn't the runway.

It was a taxi strip.

Eyes popping, he saw the hut approaching through the darkness. Tiny figures were scattering in every direction, hurling themselves away from the lunatic, errant fighter that was bearing down upon them.

Power off!

Brakes! Swing her to one side, off the taxi strip, onto the grass again, sending her ploughing through the melting snow, bumping, bouncing, skidding.

Someone was chasing him. The Opel perhaps. Headlights swept the field as he turned. For an instant they caught the careering Me but then they lost him again.

Got to keep going. Stop – even slow down – and you'll be stuck in the bloody snow, mate. So give her more power.

But where was the runway?

He didn't know. All he could see was blackness punctuated by vague shapes and sudden, blinding lights.

In half a mo, he thought, I'm going to drive this sod right into a hangar or a van or something. That's if the bloody undercarriage doesn't snap off first.

The entire structure squealed and cracked, trembling, shivering with every bounce.

The truck appeared out of the blackness, its headlights like two minute eyes. It came at right angles. It would, Pollard decided with a curious calm, cut the Me right in two, probably hitting the fuselage just about at the point where poor old Eisner was sitting.

But the driver saw the shape suddenly appearing in front of him.

He hit the brakes and swerved.

Pollard saw the truck skid past his nose, the front wheels angle ineffectually, then the vehicle toppled, revealing its underside.

It vanished.

Bang! Thud!

Suddenly the Me was on solid ground again. The runway! This time it had to be the runway! Please God!

The tyres shrieked their complaints as he swung the Me to one side.

OK. This looked like a runway. It might be a taxiway again but there wasn't time to stop and find out. Throttles open. No, stop your wandering, for Christ's sake. Straighten up! Obey! Please! A little more power to the right side, a wee bit less to the left. Tarmac surface unrolling before his little square window. Ahead, nothing but a great big black bag, just waiting.

A building. Was that a building? No, funky imagination playing tricks. Still gaining speed, wandering from side to side of the narrow strip. Men running, pointing, then left far behind.

Ease the stick forward. Hatch used to do that. Get the tail off the ground. Then the kite'll pick up speed more rapidly.

The thought terrified him. Any forward motion of the column would surely send the bucking, ferocious machine arse over tea kettle.

But he had to.

If he didn't the thing would just keep on barrelling along like a charabanc going to Southend and it would go smashing into whatever the hell there was behind that great big sodding wall of blackness ahead.

Right. Now.

The control column, vibrating against his hands, seemed eager to snap forward.

His mouth dropped open. The whole runway reared up in front of him. Now the machine was balanced on its main wheels, engines screaming. But she was wandering, arguing, threatening to tip over. Time stopped. Every fragment of his being was concentrated on the all-important task of keeping her going straight. A touch of rudder. Too much. She kept wandering. She wanted to swerve, to lift one wing and go cartwheeling into oblivion.

No. He wouldn't – couldn't – let her. She had to obey.

Eyes popping, he gazed at the shadowy strip, feeling the awful, terrifying power shivering through the structure around him. The thing wanted to swerve and bounce and throw him out. He had to keep it going straight. Mustn't let it have its own way. Must keep a firm grip. Stay on the tightrope, stay in balance, make the crazy, overpowered monstrosity do as he said. A nudge here, a shove there.

Then the trees burst out of the blackness.

The end of the runway.

And he was still on the ground.

'Bloody hell . . . !'

He heaved back on the stick.

He was going to hit the trees. No question about it. They were coming at him at 150 mph. He was going to be smashed into tiny pieces. In a moment he was going to look as if he'd been through a mincer.

But he couldn't do anything to prevent it.

Except wait and see.

A banging, scraping sound.

The Me lurched and swerved like a car on a bumpy road.

He stared ahead, petrified. He saw only blackness. He didn't know what to do. He was paralysed. Do *something*!

The nose – with its clumsy great antennae – was wandering.

Hatch's voice said, 'Rudder, oaf!'

Yes, right, rudder, of course. First lessons aboard the gentle Lanc in the sunny Yorkshire skies. Get her in balance. She'll do anything you want then.

Now one wing was beginning to lift.

'Aileron, nitwit!' Hatch commented.

The world tilted. Rushed at him. Disappeared.

'Speed,' yawned Hatch. 'Why aren't you looking at your airspeed indicator?'

Lose flying speed and you'll stall. And you'll be dead. Lesson number one for aspiring aviators.

The dials and gauges were incomprehensible: a nightmare of jogging needles and numbers.

Right. Stick forward a bit. Glimpse of terra firma through the windscreen.

A thousand feet or so.

Flying. Actually flying. Wings more or less level. Nose apparently heading in a straight line. In balance. An uneasy balance, but a balance nevertheless.

'There,' said Hatch. 'That's the way to do it.'

Right. Ease off the power a bit. No point in wearing out the motors.

Ground dimly visible.

Wheels still down.

Worry about the wheels later. First, sort out the altimeter, the airspeed indicator and the turn and bank indicator. The basics.

It took several moments but at last he found them.

Three dials, side by side in the middle of the instrument panel. They told him that he was travelling at 220 kilometres per hour. What the hell was that? More or less in mph? He couldn't remember. No matter. Keep it at that speed. Height not bad. Sinking a bit but only a bit.

In balance. You lucky bugger. You got her up all right. She didn't spin in.

Not yet anyway.

He wanted to glance behind him, to see Eisner, but he daren't turn. He daren't take his eyes off the shadowy, speeding ground or ease his grip on the stick. The column wanted to pull forward. The aircraft needed trimming out. Something else to worry about later.

The ground unrolled beneath him like some endless carpet.

Speed OK. Height OK. Still in balance. But the Me felt as if it would suddenly disobey this incompetent twerp at its controls and go twisting and cavorting into the ground. It was biding its time, waiting for just the right moment to strike.

'Everyone over-controls,' Hatch had instructed him a hundred years ago. 'Just a little nudge here and there; that's all she needs. Treat her gently and she'll treat you gently.'

Pollard nodded.

'See?' said Hatch. 'Told you so, didn't I?'

There was a small indicator on the left-hand side of the cockpit. It resembled the undercarriage indicator on the Lanc. So would it be logical to assume that the knob immediately beneath it might operate the undercarriage?

He licked his lips and gulped. Worth a try. Maintaining his hold on the column with his right hand he extended his left and pushed the lever.

At once there was a grinding noise beneath him.

He froze.

Oh my God. What the hell have I done . . . ?

The fighter wobbled as if wanting to shake something off itself.

Two sweating hands flew to the stick, clutching it as if it was trying to escape. Imploring the aeroplane to behave, to be kind, to understand the fearful predicament he found himself in, really through no fault of his . . .

The indicator showed the wheels had retracted into their wells beneath the engine nacelles. The speed built up now that the undercarriage had been removed from the slipstream.

He grinned, foolishly, triumphant.

A major achievement.

The gauge in the centre of the panel, at the bottom, looked as if it showed the fuel on board. All tanks full apparently. Right, so there was no worry about running out of petrol, at least not for a while.

But where the hell was he going?

The ground told him nothing: just a procession of fields and villages shrouded in darkness. Thank God it was a clear night; at least he could see which way was up.

At last he found what looked like a compass. Right. So he wanted to head west, straight for the Allied armies. So due west was . . . Think! Work it out! You've got to! All right. Three hundred and sixty all the way round the bloody thing. Right? Yes, he seemed to think that was correct. So halfway round had to be what? Half of three hundred and sixty. One hundred and eighty. Ten out of ten, mate. But that wasn't due west. That was south, surely to God, if north was zero. So west had to be halfway between south and north. Half of one hundred and eighty. Ninety. Right. Perfectly simple. But what wasn't perfectly simple was the task of turning to the new heading. He had to coax, to persuade this roaring, trembling contraption to change its direction of hurtle. Without upsetting its wobbling balance.

It's up to you, mate, he told himself. If you don't, you'll end up Christ only knows where.

He cast a hasty glance at the compass. The numbers conveyed nothing to him. Senseless symbols, joggling and trembling in the dashboard. But he had to make sense of them. They had to show him the way home.

'You've got no one to ask,' he told himself aloud. 'You've got to sort it out for yourself.'

All right. But first, try a turn.

Now what I'm going to do, he told himself, is to move the stick ever so gently over to the left, not pulling it back or pushing it forward otherwise the kite'll go up or down. All I want it to do is go to one side. And as I'm shoving the joystick over, I'll be applying a bit of left rudder, just as Hatch used to tell me.

OK. Now's as bad a time as any.

Nice, coordinated movements.

But too much! Terror gripped him as the Me lurched, threatening to tip over onto its side.

Jesus Christ! Back to normal again. Sweat flowing freely. Stick straight, rudder pedals level. Sorry, sorry as hell about that. Overdid it. Unfamiliar with the kite, you see. Not like the Lanc. Sweet disposition, the Lanc. Very different kettle of fish, a fighter. And a Jerry fighter at that.

Who the bloody hell did he think he was apologizing to? Eisner couldn't hear him and no one else cared.

All right. Try it again. Gentler this time. Just a nudge, like old Hatch told him. A tickle and she'll do anything for you. Dear old Hatch. Was he watching, laughing his head off at this pitiful, amateurish exhibition?

Another thing he'd said once: 'Flying's like swinging a wildcat at the end of a bit of string: as long as you keep your speed up it's reasonably safe.'

Right. Must keep speed up at all times.

Lose speed and you lose the whole game because you cease to be an aeroplane and become a large, ungainly chunk of metal that loses no time in seeking Mother Earth.

So if the airspeed indicator needle starts to move back, then shove the stick forward; if you don't, you'll stall. If the needle starts to move forward get the stick back otherwise she's liable to convert a simple turn into a power-on spin.

He *knew* these things. He had read the books; he had had dreams of being a famous aviator, beloved and admired by millions. He knew the theory of it all. But his hands and his sense were unskilled. They hadn't learnt to act instinctively. He had to think out his actions and reactions ahead of time. If port wing drops, stick over to the right; if starboard wing drops, stick over to the left. Stick back if speed rises, forward if speed falls. Keep her in balance; keep the string taut at all times.

The turn was better this time. The antler'd nose edged its timorous way to the left, across the bleak, wintry landscape. Slowly, agonizingly slowly, the compass began to turn. But anti-clockwise. He expected it to go the other way. Sod the damned thing! He almost abandoned the turn and started again. But then he reasoned that it would eventually get around to the direction he wanted. All he had to do was to hold the controls steady; as Hatch had said, the kite would do the rest.

She lurched in a patch of rough air. He caught his breath, his eyes staring in terror. She was getting away from him!

But no, she settled down and continued her turn.

Ninety degrees.

Centralize controls. Height up a couple of hundred whatever-they-ares: metres, presumably. Speed down a bit. Not too bad, considering the total incompetence and stupidity of the half-bloody-wit at the controls.

Quiet countryside. Like something off a Christmas card. No sign of war. Snow-covered. Everyone's gone to bed and turned all the lights out.

Then the first doubts began to intrude.

Ninety degrees?

He saw a map of Europe. England. The Continent. A line heading straight up through Glasgow. North. Another line coming off at right angles, going through Southend. *East.* Ninety degrees!

Good God almighty, he was flying to *Russia*!

Icy fingers clutched his throat; sweat beaded his forehead. He wanted to go to the lavatory. Badly.

All right mate, don't panic. Just a simple matter of turning the bloody thing all the way around again. No trouble. Good practice, in fact. Hone the old skills. Develop a spot of cunning in the fingers . . .

Shut up!

Stop babbling. Concentrate! Gentle pressure on the stick to the left; foot prodding the left rudder pedal. Anxious eye on altimeter and airspeed indicator.

Again the compass began to turn, the numbers moving like those on some ponderous gambling wheel.

Gently . . . gently . . . a wee bit too much angle and she tries to get away and start a spin; watch for the slightest indication, then back on the stick; straighten her up and start all over again.

Skidding a bit but never mind. Flat turn one hell of a lot safer than trying to bank the beast around and risking a spin . . .

Odd how the starlight seemed to change the texture of the snow. It looked like grey toothpaste. Thank God for the clear night. It helped enormously, being able to see the ground. Hell of a time to start learning instrument flying.

Eyes bouncing from compass to altimeter to airspeed indicator and back again, endlessly, afraid of what the instruments might reveal, only momentarily relieved that they indicated a more or less uneventful turn.

Just as the needle reached the two hundred and seventy mark, the shooting began.

19

It came out of the shadows: a slim, flitting shape, material-izing like some ghostly bat. Pollard hardly had time to focus on it when it opened fire.

Suddenly the air was lacerated by fiery streams that seemed to approach in an almost leisurely fashion, then accelerated with terrifying rapidity, whirling past him.

Then it was gone, flashing over his head, turning away into the darkness.

'Oh my God,' Pollard bleated. But the words were drowned in the din of his engines. He gaped, momentarily paralysed. Where had the sod gone? And when was the sod coming back? What should he do? What *could* he do? I'm going to be shot down again, he thought, quite calmly. And this time there isn't going to be any jumping out because I haven't got the bloody parachute on. I'm sitting on the pack and on all the sodding harness . . .

Then he heard a new sound. The aeroplane vibrated. He twisted in his seat and peered past the armour plating, down the long transparent canopy. Eisner had the twin machine guns in action and was blazing away into the night.

More gunfire. Something hit the canopy behind his head. Again the attacker banked away after his approach.

He saw it this time. A black, twin-engined shadow, fleet-ing, flashing, disappearing.

He shook his head, aghast. He couldn't dogfight with the Jerry. Christ, he could hardly fly the bloody thing at all. Wasn't that obvious, for God's sake?

Dive. The only hope. Get near to the ground. He might lose you. A bit of a chance. Not much. But if you stay here he'll blow you to smithereens.

Stick forward. He felt himself rise in the seat. For a heart-stopping moment he thought he would be projected into the instrument panel.

The engines whined as the speed picked up. The night-shrouded earth hurtled toward him. Blimey, was he diving too fast? Would the plane refuse to pull out? Would it go straight into the ground?

Ease back! Now!

The church appeared in his windscreen like an image suddenly flashed on a cinema screen. He had time to see a detail or two. Part of the brickwork around the foot of the spire had been knocked away but the spire itself was undamaged.

Stick hard to starboard. Earth turning on its end.

Engines screaming. Terror gripping every nerve and muscle because the bloody aeroplane was about to turn over and go straight in. He felt it – controls fighting his grasp. At last the lunatic has gone too far. Now let the inevitable happen.

Frantically he hurled the stick back to the left.

His eyes closed. Instinctively. He didn't want to see the ground rushing up to meet him, to smash him into several thousand tiny portions.

But he was still flying.

He opened his eyes. He was hurtling past a factory building. A river, partially frozen, went skidding beneath the nose. A man and a woman stood in the middle of a path, pointing. Trees, fields, a cluster of houses with snow on their roofs.

Still flying.

I didn't hit it, he thought, dazed. Christ knows how.

Was the Jerry still behind? Daren't turn around to look. Daren't do anything but keep eyes glued on the ground. Hands, sweaty and uncertain, gripping the stick, easing it forward, backward, to the left, to the right to maintain the same approximate height. Feet just resting on the pedals. Not worrying about coordinated movements. Just worrying about keeping the thing in the air.

What about Eisner? Was he dead? Don't know. Can't find out. So forget about it. Just concentrate on trying not to collide with anything.

He gulped as the field abruptly rose before him as if it had been inflated. Stick back. A hill, for God's sake. Now, down on the other side . . .

Was that Jerry just tootling along behind, getting his sights nicely lined up? A couple of well-placed bursts and it would be all over. Like Donaldson and his bloody Ju 88.

Why the hell didn't they put rear-view mirrors in these things?

Then he remembered: in normal operations the pilot didn't need a rear-view mirror; he had two crewmen to tell him what was happening in the rear. And how did they communicate with him? Through the bloody intercom, of course. It would have been nice, he thought elaborately, to have been able to discuss things with Eisner on the intercom. Being out of touch with one's back-seat driver was no help to the cause . . .

That was when the hand hit him on the shoulder.

A voice bellowed in his ear:

'Well done, my friend! He's lost us!'

Startled, Pollard twisted in his seat.

Eisner, beaming from ear to ear, was sprawled in the radar operator's compartment. Looking happy as hell.

'You're doing well, my friend!'

Pollard licked his lips. Talk about ignorance being bleeding bliss.

He eased the stick back. Obediently, the Me shot skyward. Stick forward again. Level off at about five hundred feet. Safer altitude. Better for the nerves. Open country again, rolling into the antlers, field after field, trees, like umpteen blackheads on an endless face . . .

'I told you you could do it!'

'I learn quickly,' Pollard snapped back.

Eisner laughed, as if he didn't have a care in the world. 'Fantastic!' he yelled. 'You are a fantastic pilot!'

Pollard swallowed. You couldn't deny that.

But he had acquired a modicum of skill. Already the controls had a semi-familiar feel to them. He knew how the Messerschmitt behaved when he applied pressure to the flying controls. She had given up some of her secrets. But her price was slavish attention. He couldn't afford to ignore her for an instant.

'Are we heading in the right direction?'

What? God, he hadn't given it a thought. Where was that bloody compass? What did the needle point to? He had to sort it all out again. Two hundred and seventy, wasn't it . . . or was that the wrong one? Come on, think! Line straight up through Glasgow. A second line to Southend . . .

The ground looked odd.

Eisner's hand gripped his shoulder again.

'I'm going back to be with the guns.'

Pollard nodded. OK, OK, God, he wished he could find the tailplane trim. His arm ached from the effort of holding the stick back. Why did the silly bugger of a pilot have the trim wound all the way forward?

The ground still looked odd.

He stared at it, unrolling before him.

It looked odder than ever. It took him moments to sort out why.

It wasn't ground. It was sea!

'Crikey!' He twisted in his seat. No sign of the coastline, no sign of any bloody thing except choppy waves and sky.

Eisner beamed back at him from the gunner's station. Pollard pointed over the side. Eisner looked, then nodded, still beaming. Happy as a sandboy. What, he found himself wondering, is a sandboy?

His first instinct was to turn around and seek the protection of the land he had just left. But was that such a good idea? He'd been lucky, lucky as bloody hell, to have slipped away without being shot down. Sheer beginner's luck, nothing else for it. So wouldn't it be a bit dense to go back, looking for more trouble? Wouldn't it be more sensible to try to fly to England?

It would. No question about it.

He seemed to have plenty of fuel on board – if those two gauges in the centre of the panel were indicating correctly – and were indeed tank gauges. He felt capable of keeping the machine in the air.

But how would he find England?

He was tiny, insignificant, incompetent – and stuck out in the middle of the North Sea, if it was the North Sea. What else could it be? The Baltic? No, surely to God he hadn't flown far enough east. But perhaps he didn't have to fly very far east. Perhaps he was already a hell of a long way east when he set off.

His teeth scraped his lower lip as he tried to unearth the answer. God, he didn't even know where the hell he had set off from. He could be going round in sodding great circles! In the end his fuel would simply run out and that would be the end of everything . . .

No, no, no. Mustn't panic. No lip-trembling permitted. No tears. Self-pity never solved anything, did it?

He shook his head, reluctantly admitting the truth of the statement.

All right, then, think. Got to do the intelligent thing, mate. Got to. And there's no one else who can help you. It's all up to you.

He wanted to tell the one side of his brain to belt up with the words of encouragement. He had to think. He had to sort things out.

Fly west. Didn't matter whether he was over the North Sea or the Baltic. West was the right direction. He was almost certain to find England, wasn't he? Yes, he told himself, he was as long as he didn't go too far north and go off looking for Greenland; the other possibility was that he could fly along the English Channel and go out into the South Atlantic heading for Rio de Janeiro. Very nice, but he wouldn't get there. A quick glance into the dark corners of the cockpit. No maps. Nothing to help.

Radio? *This is Sergeant Ron Pollard. I'm flying a Messerschmitt 110, carrying a senior German officer as passenger. Would it be too much trouble to give me the directions to Croydon?*

Marvellous. The only slight snag was that he couldn't see anything in the cockpit that looked like radio equipment. It was probably in the back somewhere . . .

Turn to port. You'll be going more or less parallel with the coast. Then, with a bit of luck you should be able to find England.

He wanted to throw up his hands and say he couldn't do it and it was unfair to expect him to try. That way, the end would be quick. The stick would snap forward. Nose down. Splash.

'One Of Their Aircraft Is Missing.'

According to one compass, he was heading almost due south; the other indicated north-west. All right, he said, as if bargaining with the two instruments, we'll go somewhere in between; can't be fairer than that, can you?

You're relying on your luck, aren't you? You've always been lucky, haven't you? Always pulled through, haven't you? So you think it'll work this time, don't you?

Quiet! Let a bloke think, for crissake!

If land comes into sight over there, to the left, then it's probably Germany.

But if it shows up on the right, then it's England.

What if it comes straight ahead?

It won't, it can't.

But it might.

Then I'll have to investigate.

Right. Decisions, of a sort. Plan of action. Not much, but better than nothing.

There was no sign of land. The grey, rubbery-looking water stretched away into the night, blending with the blackness to create a huge wall that encircled the tiny aeroplane.

Pollard tried to keep his jaw still. Engines vibrations affecting it. Have to synchronize one's jaw with the engines. Well-known aeronautical fact.

Lindbergh must have felt like this. Lucky Lindy. Lucky Polly. Sounded as if he was talking about a bloody parrot.

Two main tanks, 375 litres in each. Two reserve tanks, 260 litres in each. About a third gone, according to the gauges. Temperatures a bit near the red line. But don't know what to do about it, so do nothing. Engines buzzing very nicely. Good engines, the Daimler–Benz. So said someone knowledgeable. Lots of knowledgeable bods. All the answers. But they still got killed, just like everybody else.

He could hear Hatch encouraging him, telling him that he really wasn't doing too badly, considering everything, and that if he applied himself, studied like mad and worked diligently he might one day become a pilot. Would the RAF consider him pilot material now? They had turned him down when he first applied. The interviewing officer – moustache and puffy skin with spots – had almost sneered. You, with your pitiful educational qualifications and thoroughly dismal background, do you really think for one moment that His Majesty's Royal Air Force would under any circumstances seriously consider you for pilot training? No, be fair. The officer hadn't actually *said* that, but the curve of his fat lips had indicated that his thoughts were running along those lines.

If you manage to find England, you're going to have to land this thing.

He nodded, acknowledging the fact. He hadn't forgotten. He had simply not given it a great deal of thought because too many other more urgent matters had cropped up, demanding his total attention. Stage one completed, stage two in progress, stage three still to be thought about. Right. Time to think about it.

Near Manston there was a massive runway, two or three miles long someone had said, put there solely for the convenience of damaged or low-on-fuel kites which couldn't make it back to their airfields. Helpful, but at the moment he had his hands full trying to find England, let alone Manston.

But what if he did find Manston? Would he be able to land? Just fly along the runway, cut the power and let it come down? His innards squirmed at the thought. It might not be that simple. Some high-performance kites were said to have nasty habits when they got near to stalling speeds. Like the early Beaufighters. They would come in for a landing, it was said, but if the pilot let the speed drop about two mph below the correct level, the Beau would suddenly drop a wing and spin straight in, before anyone could do anything about it. Did the Messerschmitt possess bad habits? He shrugged. How the hell was he to know? Perhaps it would be safer to land wheels-up; but weren't you more likely to cartwheel that way? He tried to recall whether Hatch had said anything on the subject.

The grim truth was that he might fly this monster all the way to England and then get killed trying to put her down. Christ, even Hatch would be dubious about flying and landing this thing. How, then, could he, Ron Pollard, Flight Engineer, Sergeant, be expected to manage it? Another monstrous injustice. A complete upheaval of good sense and order. Lunacy.

But there was no one else.

* * *

More than half the fuel was gone now. And still no sign of land. At one point he had seen something solid-looking emerging from the blackness, but his eyes had deceived him. Wishful seeing. The grey sea kept sliding beneath his nose. Perhaps he had already flown too far north; perhaps he was already past the Shetlands and striking out for Iceland and Greenland and perhaps he would miss them too and be lost somewhere in the frigid waters . . .

That's enough of that, he told himself. You're not contributing to the cause by spreading alarm and despondency. So don't do it. Cease and bloody well desist. Look on the bright side: you've still got lots of fuel left, motors working well, nobody shooting at you.

All that was very nice, of course, but the fact couldn't be denied that he was lost. He didn't even know what sea he was over. He wasn't at all sure what direction he was flying in. And even if he did find his goal he stood a damned good chance of killing himself when he tried to land.

All of which tended to balance things up, he decided. Would fifty-fifty be a reasonable way of judging his chances, considering everything?

He had a feeling that fifty-fifty was leaning a bit on the optimistic side, but no matter. He would accept fifty-fifty.

He just hoped he wouldn't get burned, like that poor sod in the Lanc that broke up after landing from Berlin. The mid-upper gunner. They hacked away at the fuselage but they couldn't get him out until he was, as one callous bastard put it, 'done to a turn'. When at last they reached him it was impossible to get a grip on him; his flesh kept peeling off in layers like soft plastic. For some incredible reason he was still alive. Rumour had it that the MO put him out of his misery that night.

His hands throbbed with the effort of holding the stick back; the ache had travelled up his arms and into his shoulders.

He threw a glance back along the transparent tube. Eisner was sitting, relaxed as hell, scanning the sky.

Trust me to run into a mad sod like him, Pollard thought. Not a bad sort in his own way. Lots of guts, you had to give him that. Crusty exterior. What would happen to him in Britain, *if* he got there?

Pollard had no idea. But presumably the appropriate officers in the appropriate department would have the answers and would do the appropriate thing. Pollard shrugged helplessly. Had he done the right thing? It all depended how you looked at it. He saw a flinty-eyed interrogator – a Conrad Veidt type.

'And did you, Ron Pollard, Sergeant, knowingly give aid and comfort to the enemy in the person of Colonel von Eisner?'

'Yes, but only because he gave aid and comfort to me first – and to Squadron Leader Woods-Bassett.'

He frowned. Something was different.

The instrument, the controls, the framework of the cockpit – everything was becoming more distinct. He could read the word *Sauerstoff* on a dial at his right elbow.

Dawn!

Of course! Bloody obvious! The sun was rising! Beginning of a new day!

Marvellous! But where was the sun rising? Behind him. Yes. Eisner was pointing at it, grinning like a Cheshire cat. But it had to be thought out. Where the hell did the sun rise? East or west? Oh God, didn't he know *anything*? A Western picture – bloke on a horse twanging a guitar and mumbling something about the golden sun setting in the west. But that was over there, in America. Did that make a difference? No, surely to Christ it was clear even to him that the bloody sun rose and set in the same place all over the world.

All right. Think about it for a mo. Sun rising behind tail. In the east. Aeroplane flying in opposite direction; therefore opposite direction must be west. Which is what was wanted, wasn't it?

He nodded. The logic seemed sound. All right. So far so

good. He appeared to be heading in the right direction, more or less, give or take a few thousand miles . . .

Odd, the sea seemed darker, blacker, now that the light was beginning to touch the Messerschmitt high in the sky.

Still no sign of land.

Time to switch tanks. Good. It worked. Engines still humming along nicely. Well done, Messrs Daimler and Benz.

Was that a glimmer of light touching the sea? Yes . . . the swell, heaving, breaking into white foam. Bloody cold-looking. To be avoided at all costs.

Seeing the dawn pumped him up with a new confidence. It made all the difference in the world. He'd been groping around in the dark. Now he'd be able to *see*!

Gradually the cockpit filled with light. He looked along the broad wings. They were painted in a grey-green camouflage pattern. The port one was down a bit. A nudge on the stick brought it level. Very sensitive on the controls, the Me. A high-strung racehorse . . . 'And actually, Hatch, mate, you really can't compare it with flying a dear, gentle old thing like the Lanc – a regular carthorse, if you don't mind my saying.'

Idiotic, wasting time thinking of stupid conversations that would never take place. He told himself to concentrate. He still had plenty of problems; which was, perhaps, the understatement of the week.

The night was like a fog that had to be pushed away by the morning light. It was a laborious business; the night fell back in gigantic banks trailing across the choppy sea.

His new-found confidence dwindled. Nothing but bloody water. Where the hell was he? Out in the middle of the Atlantic? Should he turn around? Go back? South? North?

He swallowed, glumly contemplating the inevitable running out of fuel, the crashing into the ocean, the lonely death in freezing water. Christ, it was a rotten way to end up. Tears blurred his vision. He blinked them away, automatically ashamed of them. But then he wondered why he bothered. Who could see them?

They stood a chance of seeing a ship, that couldn't be denied. There were God knows how many ships floating about the ocean. Correct? He nodded to himself. Definitely. So he was almost certain to see a ship sooner or later. It stood to reason.

The clouds came with the daylight. Dismal, stringy looking layers that took up their positions directly overhead; the sea assumed a metallic tone. A few drops of rain hit the windscreen.

And then he saw land.

20

It appeared on his starboard wingtip. Dark and beautifully solid-looking. A strip of land, complete with cliffs. White cliffs.

It was England, or he'd eat his forage cap.

He felt his mouth break into a smile.

He turned the fighter, sliding across the sky to head directly for the land.

God knows just where he was. But surely it would be possible to sort things out from it. Get one's bearings. Christ, it was nice to know there *was* land out there, after all that bloody water . . .

He twisted in his seat to point the land out to Eisner.

And then the Mosquito attacked.

Guns rapped in their insistent, urgent way.

The Messerschmitt shuddered. Shivered. Shells slammed into her slender fuselage. A canopy panel vanished. A frigid gale suddenly howled through the narrow cabin.

Pollard stared open-mouthed at the British fighter.

'Go away . . . you bloody fool!'

The Mossie, all tapered wings and cigar-like body, went sliding away to the right. At once, a second machine took up the attack.

Aghast, Pollard jammed the control column forward. The sea loomed up in his windscreen. The howling of the wind through the broken panel became a scream that merged with the bellowing of the engines to create a lunatic cacophony.

Dimly, through it all, Pollard heard more gunfire. He felt the fighter stagger, twisting, it seemed, as if instinctively trying to escape the hail of shells.

He heaved the Me out of its dive.

The sea raced along just a few feet below. Hungry waves snapped at him, foam dancing in the air.

The cliffs were only a little way away. A few miles.

But the Mosquitoes weren't to be denied.

They came hurtling down at him, blazing away, their shells bursting in the water, smashing through the fragile skin of his wings, tearing the aircraft apart around him.

He acted mechanically.

He wasn't frightened. He was a spectator, watching, waiting for the inevitable to take place, observing with professional interest how long the torn trembling structure could hold together, how long before the screeching shells found him and blew the life out of him.

Moments. It could only take moments. Fragments of a lifetime. Long enough for someone in Kilburn to sneeze or light a cigarette.

Water spattered the windscreen. Too low. Ease back. Keep trying. Wings level. Full power.

The cliffs were still there, dead ahead, waves breaking.

Then the world became fire.

Both wings streamed flame. And suddenly, deliberately it seemed, the Me began to break up. Chunks of wings snapped away. A cowling panel disappeared. Part of the canopy vanished. Freezing air battered him.

The rudder pedals were slack, lifeless.

Numbed, he felt only a curiously mild disappointment. He had failed. He accepted the fact.

He twisted. He saw Eisner. The side of his head streamed blood. Grey eyes: lit by the streaking, biting flames.

Eisner smiled. He said something. His lips formed words. His hand reached forward as if to touch Pollard.

But it was too late. Everything was too late.

He heard the impact rather than felt it. The Me seemed to bounce on the water like a flat stone a-spinning. Arms in front of face. Futile gesture. Hopeless. Pointless. Water swamped him. He was turning over and over – *spinning*. Struggling. Reaching. Then it was silly to do anything. None of it mattered now. All ancient history. Hardly worth the effort to think about it. Thinking a great big bore. Turning gently and smoothly the only thing that made the slightest sense. Funny, water quite warm. Soothing. Full of soap suds like the tin bath in front of the fire on Saturday nights. But no eye-sting-ing with these soap suds. Nothing stings now; everything soft and sweet and warm and wet and dark and utterly, superbly peaceful. No need to try any more. No need to worry or try to hold the plane in balance or sort out directions or identify seas. Farewell all tensions and stresses. Soft, silky blues and purples enveloping him, weaving patterns around him, mobile kaleidoscopes going about their lawfully appointed business . . .

But now something jarred the peacefulness. Something hard, unyielding. Prodding, pushing.

No, no, go away. He resisted the thing. He didn't want it. It was ruining everything. It was frightening away the colours, the patterns, the warmth, the sweetness . . .

Strong fingers gripped his shoulders. He heard his uniform rip.

'Come on, Fritz, let's 'ave you.'

No, go away, please go away . . .

Cold, merciless cold invaded him, sweeping away the last fragments of tranquillity.

He felt himself slump onto something hard. One leg seemed to have crossed over the other. He wondered whether he should try to move it. No, it was too much of an effort.

'Is he breathing?'

'Think so.'

The voices had an odd echo effect.

'Christ almighty.'

'What?'

'He's not a Jerry. Look at 'im. RAF pilot's wings!'

'Crikey, a Squadron Leader!'

The light hurt his eyes. His head felt as if it was in several badly-connected pieces.

'Are you all right, sir?'

'What . . . Where . . . ?'

'Lie still, sir.'

'No.' He pushed himself up on one elbow. His vision wob-bled. Oilskin-clad figures clustered around him like doctors around a patient.

'There's another man. I was with another man in that plane. Where is he? Did you pick him up?'

The oilskin head nodded.

'We got him aboard, sir. But . . . '

'Where is he?'

Pollard struggled to his feet. The deck swayed beneath his feet. A launch. Air-Sea Rescue.

Someone took his arm.

'Here, sir.'

They led him into a cabin. Eisner lay on a tiny bunk, wrapped in blankets.

His face was so pale that it looked transparent.

But he managed a smile.

'You did well, my friend.'

His voice was thin and wavering; he sounded like an old, sick man.

Pollard muttered something about having to practise his landings.

Eisner's fingers touched his hand. 'One day – when it is possible – please find Trude and tell her.'

'You'll do that yourself, chum.'

Another ghost of a smile.

'Good fellow, good comrade.'

The fingers tried to grip. But there was no strength in them.

A man pushed past Pollard and bent over the prostrate German.

'I think he's gone, sir,' said someone.

'What?'

'Have a seat, sir.'

Pollard shook his head. It was irritating; he couldn't see Eisner; there wasn't room in this cubby hole of a cabin.

'He's dead.'

'Damned sorry about it, sir.'

Pollard turned away. He wanted to kick something, vent his frustration at the bloody pointlessness of it all.

An officer wearing a duffel coat said, 'Sir, may I ask what you, a Squadron Leader, were doing flying that Jerry plane?'

The waves slapped against the boat's side.

'I'm not a Squadron Leader. I'm a Sergeant.'

'I don't think I quite understand.'

Pollard shrugged. He was immeasurably tired. 'It doesn't matter now,' he said. 'And you probably wouldn't believe me even if I told you.'

Hank Searls
Jaws 2 80p

It's two years since the Long Island resort of Amity was terrorized by the monster killer shark . . . the nightmare story that thrilled the world as *Jaws*. Out in the deep water there is a new and even more terrible predator . . . the pregnant mate of the great shark who is even larger – and deadlier than the male.

Ernest Lehman
The French Atlantic Affair 95p

170 people with nothing to lose and everything to gain from the biggest hijack ever attempted. Their target – the *Marseilles*, their ultimatum – the liner, its passengers and crew will be destroyed in forty-eight hours unless the demand is met. Just thirty-five million dollars and a safe getaway . . .

'A first-class ticket to a voyage of suspense . . . Ernest Lehman is a superb writer' SIDNEY SHELDON